THE REGENCY LORDS & LADIES COLLECTION

**Glittering Regency Love Affairs
from your favourite historical authors.**

THE REGENCY LORDS & LADIES COLLECTION

Available from the
Regency Lords & Ladies Large Print Collection

The Larkswood Legacy by Nicola Cornick
My Lady's Prisoner by Elizabeth Ann Cree
Lady Clairval's Marriage by Paula Marshall
A Scandalous Lady by Francesca Shaw
A Poor Relation by Joanna Maitland
Mistress or Marriage? by Elizabeth Rolls
Rosalyn and the Scoundrel by Anne Herries
Prudence by Elizabeth Bailey
Nell by Elizabeth Bailey
Miss Verey's Proposal by Nicola Cornick
Kitty by Elizabeth Bailey
An Honourable Thief by Anne Gracie
Jewel of the Night by Helen Dickson
The Wedding Gamble by Julia Justiss
Ten Guineas on Love by Claire Thornton
Honour's Bride by Gayle Wilson
One Night with a Rake by Louise Allen
A Matter of Honour by Anne Herries
Tavern Wench by Anne Ashley
The Sweet Cheat by Meg Alexander
The Rebellious Bride by Francesca Shaw
Carnival of Love by Helen Dickson
The Reluctant Marchioness by Anne Ashley
Miranda's Masquerade by Meg Alexander
Dear Deceiver by Mary Nichols
Lady Sarah's Son by Gayle Wilson
One Night of Scandal by Nicola Cornick
The Rake's Mistress by Nicola Cornick
Lady Knightley's Secret by Anne Ashley
Lady Jane's Physician by Anne Ashley

A MATTER OF HONOUR

Anne Herries

First published in Great Britain 2000
Large Print Edition 2009
Harlequin Mills & Boon Limited,
Eton House, 18-24 Paradise Road, Richmond, Surrey TW9 1SR

© Anne Herries 2000

ISBN: 978 0 263 21046 0

Set in Times Roman 15½ on 17 pt.
083-0909-86691

Harlequin Mills & Boon policy is to use papers that are natural, renewable and recyclable products and made from wood grown in sustainable forests. The logging and manufacturing process conform to the legal environmental regulations of the country of origin.

Printed and bound in Great Britain
by CPI Antony Rowe, Chippenham, Wiltshire

Chapter One

'Marry the Thornton gel!' The Dowager Lady Longbourne almost sat up, and she would have, had it not been positively too warm for any such exertion. She lay amongst silken cushions on her elegant daybed and waved a languid hand at her visitors. 'Carlton, you really shouldn't make such tasteless jokes. I confess I am surprised at you.'

'It was not meant as a jest, Mama.' Lord Vincent Carlton's lazy smile flickered over his mouth. He was exceptionally good looking and far too wealthy for his own good; though generous to anyone he cared for, he was considered by some others to be stand-offish and rather too high in the instep. 'That is why I have come to see you this afternoon. If you will be so kind, I want you to invite Cassandra to stay here so that we can get to know one another properly before I propose.'

'Ask the Thornton chit to stay *here*?' Lady

Longbourne's limpid blue eyes took on an expression of dismay. 'You surely cannot mean that, Carlton? You are not seriously considering a mésalliance?'

'He has to,' the second of her visitors said. 'It is a matter of honour, Mama. Vinnie has to marry her.'

One satin-shod foot touched the ground, followed closely by the second. Lady Longbourne sat up! An expression of shock mixed liberally with disbelief on a face that still retained some measure of the outstanding beauty which had been hers in youth. She stared at Sir Harry Longbourne, her younger son and her favourite, being the precious fruit of her second marriage, which had been happier than the first.

'What are you talking about, Harry? Why should Carlton be obliged to marry this gel?' she demanded. Her cheeks turned pale as she looked at her eldest son incredulously. 'Carlton! Surely, you…haven't dishonoured the girl, have you?'

The smile left Vincent's eyes. He was deeply offended by the suggestion that he would stoop so low as to dishonour any woman—especially a lady of quality! However, he was too fond of his mother (despite knowing only too well that she had always favoured his brother) and too much a gentleman to let his anger show.

'Of course he hasn't!' Harry jumped in before he could think of a suitable reply. 'What a hummer! You ought to know Vinnie better than that, Mama.

It was a promise we all made to Jack Thornton just before he was killed at Waterloo.'

'Promise? What promise?' his mama asked, irritated at having her peace disturbed on such a warm day. 'What has a promise to Cassandra's brother have to do with Carlton offering for her?'

'Jack had just heard the news of his father's death,' Harry went on patiently, while Carlton rose to his feet and wandered over to the windows of the small back parlour Lady Longbourne favoured at Carlton House. He stood gazing out at the neatly manicured lawns and rosebeds as Harry elaborated for their mother's benefit. Behind him, an enamelled French clock ticked relentlessly on the rather fine mantelpiece designed by Mr Adam. 'Naturally, he was shocked—'

'As anyone would be,' interjected Lady Longbourne. 'To throw most of one's fortune away at the gambling tables while one's son and heir is fighting for King and country. And then to…' She gave a shudder of distaste. 'It must have been terrible for Cassandra to find her father dead by his own hand…'

'Exactly, Mama.' Carlton turned to take up the story, his expression carefully controlled and giving no sign of the horror any decent person must feel. 'Jack was distraught. Out of his mind with grief and shock. He implored us to take care of his sister, begging all of us to promise that one of us would marry her if he died…'

'But why must it be you?' inquired his mama. 'You could make a much more prestigious match, Carlton.'

'You mean I should marry an heiress—or the daughter of a duke, perhaps? To restore the family fortunes…'

He was a tall man, lean, but wiry and with the bearing of a soldier. His dark hair was cut short in one of the new styles that were just now fashionable amongst the *ton*, and his clothes bore all the hallmarks of the very best tailors; his boots were a work of art. He looked what he was, a gentleman in possession of a large fortune with the liberty (since his return from France after Napoleon's defeat) to do exactly as he pleased.

'Well…' She saw the mocking look in his eyes and pulled a face at him. 'No, I do not, Vincent! I know well enough that you have taken good care of the estate since you came into it—and that we have all benefited from your good sense. But the daughter of a mere baronet…you should think of your own consequence and the family pride.'

The dark eyebrows rose, a challenge in Vincent's quizzing gaze which brought a flush to her cheeks. Because, of course, little as she liked to be reminded of it, his late father had also been a reckless gambler and, had he not died suddenly, might have brought them all to ruin.

'Yes, I know it was only an accident that saved us

from your father suffering a similar fate to Sir Edward Thornton—but that isn't the point.'

'The point is, Mama,' Lord Carlton reminded her gently, 'that you have been saying for an age that you wished I would marry to provide an heir for the Carlton family and—'

'Well, how could I not?' she spoke indignantly. 'With your uncle Septimus forever telling me it is time you did your duty—and as for that odious wife of his, preening over her abominable brat as if she could already see him in your place. I vow I hardly knew how to hold my tongue the last time they stayed here. She was examining the curtains as if she saw herself moving in at any moment. You may be past the first flush of youth, Carlton, but you ain't about to drop down dead! And since you returned safely from the war, I have every hope of your living for some years yet.'

'Thank you for your confidence, Mama. I am heartily relieved to hear it.'

'Oh, you!' She gave him a fulminating stare. 'You will always have your joke—not that I find them at all funny. You have a very odd notion of humour, Vincent!'

'Forgive me, Mama.' There was a gleam in Lord Carlton's grey eyes. 'I am very sorry you do not appreciate my jokes.'

'What I do not appreciate is this absurd idea that

you must marry the Thornton gel,' Lady Longbourne said on a sigh. 'If Jack Thornton asked all of you to look out for his sister, which was not so unreasonable after all, in the circumstances of our having been neighbours while my dear Bertie was alive…' she dabbed at the corner of her eyes with a wisp of filmy lace kerchief '…and still would be, I dare say, if you had not been generous enough to allow me to return here to Carlton, which I much prefer to Longbourne, being much less draughty in the winters—why must you be the one to marry her?'

Having had years of practice of unravelling his mama's often tangled speeches, Lord Carlton understood immediately what was on her mind.

'It was less generous than you imagine,' he replied, smiling at her reassuringly. 'I do not care for this house. I prefer my own house in London—and do not forget I have Grandfather Hamilton's estate in Surrey, which would make a very pleasant country home if I had it refurbished in a more modern style.'

'Well, with your wealth I suppose you may do as you please,' Lady Longbourne said, sinking back against her piles of silken cushions with relief. 'I dare say you could afford to buy a dozen houses. I always thought it was a little unjust of my father to leave the lion's share of his fortune to you.'

'No, no, Mama,' Harry rushed in as always, a

flush in his cheeks. He had often benefited from his half-brother's generosity after a night's ill luck at the gaming tables, and was embarrassed at the suggestion that he should have been left part of the Hamilton estate. 'I have Papa's estate, which, though not as large as Vinnie's, was flourishing when it was passed down to me. Vinnie had hard work of it to bring the Carlton estate about after he inherited the title, you know.'

'Yes, well, I suppose that is true enough,' Lady Longbourne admitted. 'I know Papa thought Vincent had an excellent head on him and said as much to me just before he passed away…' Again she sighed and dabbed at the corners of her eyes. 'And we've all felt Carlton's generosity…but what I still don't understand is why he has to marry the gel.'

'Jack's body was never brought in,' Vincent said, a haunted look in his eyes. 'He was my friend, Mama. His body lies in an unmarked grave somewhere in France. I owe him this at the very least.'

Lady Longbourne was temporarily silenced. Her son's passionate words and the pain in his eyes had surprised her. It was unlike Carlton to show his feelings so plainly.

'There were five of us,' Harry said before his brother could stop him. 'We drew straws for it and—'

'I won,' Vincent said, glaring at Harry. 'I remember Cassandra as being a little thin and plain, but she was only twelve or so at the time so I imagine she must have changed somewhat by now. Besides, a promise given on the field of battle to a comrade is a matter of honour, Mama—and I intend to keep it.'

'Supposing she won't take you?' Harry asked, wrinkling his smooth brow. He was four and twenty, fair of skin and hair, blue-eyed and possessed of a sunny nature which won him friends easily. He was seven years younger than the brother he admired more than he would ever dare show—because if there was one thing Vinnie couldn't stand, it was people fawning over him! 'What shall we do then?'

'I won the first shot at courting her,' Vincent said. 'If she turns me down, it will be up to the rest of you.'

'Turn you down?' Lady Longbourne's eyebrows rose incredulously. 'Whatever else Cassandra Thornton may be, I do not think her a fool. She will snatch at such an offer, Carlton. In her circumstances, you must appear to be a gift from the gods…and she may have changed, but plain is plain and there's no way she could ever be a beauty.'

'I do not expect her to be a beauty, nor do I particularly wish for beauty in the woman I marry,' replied a man who was famed for the remarkable looks of the various mistresses he had kept since reaching his majority. 'I find the young ladies described in London's drawing rooms as "Fair Beauty" and "Goddess" rarely have natures to match their faces; they are usually spoilt and often vain. No, no, Mama, I am not to be put off by your cavilling.' He smiled at her to ease the sting of his words. 'Now, my very dear Mama—will you oblige me by inviting Cassandra to stay here as your guest?'

'Of course. You had no need to ask, Carlton. You are my son, and the only desire left to me in life is to serve my dearest ones. Much as I fear for your happiness married to such a girl—as plain a gel as could be, she was!—I shall naturally do all in my power to promote the match, if you wish it. If you will be guided by me, you will give up the notion at once…but invite her here by all means. I am completely at your command.'

Which meant, of course, that she considered the visit an inconvenience, but felt obliged to do as he asked because of past favours.

Lord Carlton sighed inwardly. Lady Longbourne had for some time considered herself to be delicate and spent many hours lying indoors when she might have been employed in some more rewarding activity. Her indolence had been brought about through a genuine illness following the unhappy demise of her beloved husband (a chill had turned to a malevolent fever and carried Harry's father off in a matter of days) and it saddened Vincent to see his mother this way. He remembered her as the glowing bride of Sir Bertram Longbourne, and wished he could see her as happy again.

He acknowledged privately that there was justice in her words. Cassandra Thornton had indeed been a plain, often quiet, child, but she had also had a bright smile and plenty of spirit when it was aroused. It was Vincent's hope that, in taking temporary charge of a girl who had been left with no relatives to care for her, his mother might recover her own spirits.

'You are very good, Mama,' he said and bent to kiss her cheek. 'Will you write to Cassandra this afternoon?'

'Before dinner,' she said, half smothering a sigh. 'You must know that I would do anything to oblige you, Carlton…' She reached up and patted his cheek. 'I do love you, you know.'

'I know that,' he replied, smiling at her. 'I have never doubted it.'

'You are a comfort to me in my autumn years,' Lady Longbourne said, then looked at Harry mistily. 'I am very fortunate to have two such devoted sons. Some sons hardly ever visit their mother—they prefer to racket about London, enjoying the pleasures of town without a thought for those unable to do so…'

'Mama…' Harry looked uncomfortable, as though he wished to escape. 'If you will excuse me…I think I shall go for a walk before dinner.'

'We are both devoted to you,' Vincent said as his brother made a hasty exit. 'But I think I should warn you, Mama—Harry is unlikely to stay here long, unless you can persuade him. He has lost his heart to a lady…but pray do not look so alarmed. I do not imagine my revered brother has marriage in mind. *She* is at least ten years his senior and of dubious reputation. Harry is not so lost to reason that he cannot see the drawbacks of such a connection; he will no doubt make her his mistress for as long as it suits him—but I thought it best to tell you something you might otherwise have heard from a less well-informed source. I have been instructed to tell you that Uncle Septimus intends to visit you very soon.'

'Oh, no!' cried Lady Longbourne, sensibly dismayed more by the impending visit than her son's intention of taking a mistress. 'Pray do not say so. I hope he means to come alone, for if he brings Felicity and Archie with him I shall be pressed beyond bearing.'

'Since he does not come for another few weeks, you may have Cassandra with you. I am persuaded that, together, she and I may protect you from submitting to too many of my uncle's lectures.'

'I hope you do not mean to desert me until after your uncle has gone?'

'I shall stay until Cassandra has either accepted or refused me. After that, we shall have to see…'

* * *

Vincent was thoughtful as he strolled around his estate later that evening, noting various details which must be brought to the attention of his bailiff. It *was* time he married and provided the family with an heir. Since he had never yet encountered a woman he felt in the least inclined to make his wife, the obvious answer was to make a marriage of convenience to a woman who would not demand too much of him.

When Jack had first suggested he marry Cassandra, Vincent had been reluctant. Had he given his word that first time, that nonsense with the straws would never have been necessary. After Jack's death, he had known it was his duty to marry Cassandra. He was honour-bound to it!

Why, then, had he delayed all this time? It was almost eleven months since Napoleon had been defeated and banished to the island of St. Helena, and nine since Vincent had come home. His own wounds had long healed, but still he had done nothing about redeeming his promise to Jack Thornton, though of course he had written to Cassandra from France.

He had his reasons for not going to see her. Against all hope, he *had* hoped—but that was nonsense. The fact that all his efforts to trace Jack's body had been futile did not mean that he was still alive. He had seen his friend fall, knew that the shot must have been fatal. Many soldiers had been buried where they lay, some too badly mutilated by the French cannon to be recognised even by their friends.

'God damn it, Jack!' Vincent cursed aloud as he stood alone, watching the sun go down. 'I never wanted you to die. Why won't you let me be at peace?'

But he would never be at peace, unless he atoned in some way for letting Jack down. And the only thing Jack had ever asked of him was to take care of his sister.

'She ain't pretty,' Jack had said to him once as they sat talking over a dying fire. 'But she will make someone a damned good wife. She needs a decent man, Vinnie. I can't stand to think of anyone hurting her. I've always thought you and Cassie might suit.'

Vincent had denied him then, but days later, after the news of Sir Edward's terrible suicide, he had given his word with the others.

'All right, Jack,' he said now, glaring up at the night sky. 'You win, damn you! I'll marry her—if she'll have me.'

It was two days later and Miss Cassandra Thornton was in the bedchamber of her home, staring at the array of gowns spread over her bed. They gave her some considerable pleasure. She had never owned so many new clothes before in her life, and though she knew they would not carry her through the London season that she had been planning since the news of her rather startling inheritance had arrived, she could not help but feel some satisfaction.

'They are lovely,' her companion said, stroking a particularly pretty green cloth walking gown. 'You are so lucky, Cassie. I've never seen anything so fine.'

'Do you like that one?' Cassie asked, picking up the gown and holding it against the younger girl. 'Yes, the colour is just right for you. It brings out the gold lights in your hair, and the green of your eyes. You must have it, Sarah.'

'Oh, I couldn't possibly,' cried Miss Sarah Walker. The fifth daughter of a country parson, she had been unable to repress a little stab of envy on seeing the clothes, since her parents, though kind and generous within their means, would never be able to afford a season for her. 'You haven't even worn it yet. I was only admiring it. I did not expect you to give it to me.'

'I know that, silly!' Cassie laughed, her brown eyes as warm as melted chocolate as she pushed the dress into her friend's hands. 'I shall still have as many gowns as I need until I go up to London.'

'When do you leave?' Sarah asked, looking at the gown with undisguised longing, yet still hesitating. 'Are you sure you don't want this, Cassie?'

'Quite sure. It will suit you far better than it would

me. I was misguided in my choice of style in that gown. I shall do better in future. In fact, I believe the brown velvet and the blue muslin would look well on you. I think you should have them all.'

'Cassie! You are too generous. You cannot possibly afford to give me all these clothes.'

'Yes, I can,' Cassie said, snatching up a paisley shawl and two rather fetching bonnets, and adding them to the growing pile. 'Aunt Gwendoline was so very, very rich, Sarah. I am sure I nearly died when that lawyer came all the way up from Cornwall to tell me she had left me everything. She was Mama's elder sister, of course, and I vaguely remember seeing her once when Mama took me to stay…it was a few months before she died.'

Tears hovered on her thick, dark lashes but she blinked them away.

'Dearest Cassie,' her friend said. 'You still miss her, don't you?'

'I know it was a long time ago. I was only fourteen when she fell ill, but I loved her very much,' Cassie said. 'Yet I had Father and Jack. To lose them both so suddenly…' She smothered a sob. 'But losing Jack was the worst of all. We were always such good friends. I miss him so much, Sarah.'

'I know…' The two girls embraced affectionately. 'And it was awful when the lawyers told you you had only months to find somewhere else to live. I think it is so unfair when an estate is entailed to some distant cousin or other.'

'There wasn't much left after the debts were paid. Just the house and a few bits and pieces—but it was still upsetting to be told I must go. Particularly when Father's cousin Kendal is so odious,' Cassie said. 'I could not wait to leave…and yet I had nowhere to go.'

'You could have come to us,' Sarah reminded her. 'I should have been glad to have you. Papa told you you could share my room, and stay with us for as long as you wished.'

'Your father is so kind,' Cassie said, 'but I did not want to be a burden to him. No, I had almost made up my mind to hire myself out as a governess or a companion…and then poor Aunt Gwendoline left me her fortune. I wish I had written to her more often now—but she did not encourage it.'

'Was she not almost a recluse in her last years?'

'So I have been told. She did not particularly welcome us when Mama took me to visit—but she *has* left me her whole fortune.'

'And now you are off to London to find yourself a handsome beau!'

'Oh, at least a dozen of them,' Cassie said, her dark eyes alive with mischief. 'I mean to be the toast of London…despite not being a beauty. Money, you know, makes up for many faults in a lady's appearance.'

'You are not plain,' said Sarah loyally. 'Papa says you are a handsome woman—and, you must know, that's a compliment from him.'

'Yes, indeed!' Cassie laughed deep inside her. She was not what most people would describe as beautiful; she did not have the fair, delicate looks she knew to be all the rage—but neither was she plain. Or not so plain that it would discourage gentlemen from offering for her once they discovered she possessed a considerable fortune. 'I know it to be so. And I am gratified.'

'So when do you leave?'

'When Mrs Simmons sees fit to answer my letter. She was recommended to me by Lady Fitzpatrick as a chaperon—and, as you know, I cannot go to London without a respected chaperon to lend me consequence or I shall never do more than flutter at the edges of society.'

'She will surely write soon,' Sarah said, slightly wistful. 'I shall miss you, Cassie.'

'Well, you need not,' Cassie said, making up her mind to something that had just occurred to her. 'Why do you not come with me? It would not be fitting for us to visit alone, because you are only nineteen—and though I am one and twenty, it would not be considered proper for us to go unchaperoned. But I should be much happier if you accompanied Mrs Simmons and me…'

Sarah stared at her, in disbelief. 'You cannot mean it? No, no, Papa could never afford to let me go.'

'You will not need to trouble your father for money,' Cassie said. 'The clothes I've already given you will do for a while, and when we go to London I shall buy more for us both. It will be my present to you for all the kindness you and your family showed me after my father…died.'

Cassie's eyes reflected the grief and hurt she had felt at the shocking circumstance of her father's suicide. Although the elderly Lady Fitzpatrick had continued to welcome her to her house at the other side of the little Hampshire village, many of the neighbours who had been to dine with her father had shunned her. Had it not been for the Reverend Walker and his family, Cassie might have given way to the despair that had been so very overwhelming.

She had, in fact, struggled bravely against a series of misfortunes—the worst by far her discovery of her father's lifeless body in his library. His death had not caused her as much grief as her beloved brother's, but it had given her a horror of guns and led to nightmares. For some weeks she had been unable to sleep without waking with tears on her cheeks, and though the bad dreams had finally ceased, the memory still lingered at the back of her mind.

Only a girl of strong resolution could have put such a terrible time behind her, retaining both her sanity and her determination not to be crushed. There *had* been moments when Cassie had felt there was no reason for her to go on living, but some months had passed since her world fell apart. She had slowly come to terms with her loss, making up her mind to rebuild her life, and the news of her inheritance had aroused her fighting spirit once more.

Until the double tragedy that had almost destroyed her, Cassie had always been able to live well within herself. Her parents had always treated her fairly, but they had both idolised Jack. He was the son and heir both had wanted: a laughing, confident young man who must make any parent proud. As a young child, Cassie had not blamed her parents for putting Jack first. She had adored him herself, and he had always been her champion.

From the very beginning, they had been close. Cassie still ached for the loss of him. She was sure she would never be as close to anyone again. Perhaps because of that, she had made up her mind not to look for love in her choice of a husband. Love was too painful: she had no wish to be hurt again. She had money; what she needed now was a man of some consequence. Someone who could give her a place in society.

Cassie had spent long enough being looked down at by her neighbours. She wanted neither pity nor condescension, but a respect that was hers by right. As the daughter of a gambler who had taken his own life, she could only achieve her heart's desire by marrying a man of good family— a leader of the *ton*!

'Oh, do not look like that, dearest,' Sarah begged, recalling her thoughts to the present with a touch of her hand. 'I cannot bear to see you so unhappy.'

Cassie shook her head. 'I am not precisely unhappy, Sarah. I was thinking of Jack. I shall always miss him, but it is getting better. I am determined to put it all behind me. And you can help me by agreeing to come to London with me.' The sparkle of mischief was back in her eyes. 'In fact, I shall not go without you. I shall persuade your father to agree.'

'I am sure he will if *you* ask him,' Sarah said, excitement dawning in her eyes. 'But only if we are properly chaperoned, of course.'

'Lady Fitzpatrick promised…' Cassie began, pausing as there was a knock at the door. Then a maid entered. 'Yes, Ellie, what is it? Do you have something for me?'

'You asked me to bring any letters to you, miss.'

'Has it come at last?' Cassie eagerly took the letters she was offered, breaking the seal of one which had come from London. 'This is from Mrs Simmons…' She scanned the first few lines. 'She will join me as a companion…oh!' Her disappointment was sharp. 'But not until the end of next month.'

'Next month?' Sarah looked at her. 'That is not so bad, is it?'

'It will be August by the time we are in London,' Cassie replied. 'The season will be as good as over. Perhaps we should go to Brighton instead?'

'Brighton is fashionable in the summer…'

'But it is not London,' Cassie said, frowning. 'Oh, well, I suppose it will have to do…' She was opening the second letter and, as she began to read it, gasped in surprise. 'Good gracious!'

'Is something the matter?'

'No…' Cassie gave her an odd look. 'It is from Lady Longbourne. Do you remember Sir Bertram? When he died, his widow moved to Lord Carlton's house. The Longbournes' house, which belongs to Sir Bertram's heir, of course, has been let to tenants for some years.'

'I do just remember the family,' Sarah said. 'I never knew them well, but Papa visited after Sir Bertram died—it must have been eight years ago. I went with him, but I stayed in the garden with Sir Bertram's son…I think his name was Harry.'

'That's right. Lady Longbourne has two sons, Harry and his half-brother Vincent.' Cassie blushed. 'I mean Lord Carlton, of course.'

'Did you know them well?'

'Quite well. My mother often had tea with Lady Longbourne. I remember once…' She hesitated, then shook her head. 'It doesn't matter. I was only a child.'

'Oh, do tell,' Sarah pleaded. 'It must have been something particular or it would not have stayed in your mind.'

Cassie laughed, her cheeks still a little pink. 'I had been given a kitten as a present from Jack. It was for my birthday. I was twelve.'

'What happened?'

'My kitten climbed a tall tree. I called and called, but she would not come to me. She was mewing so pitifully and I couldn't bear to hear her. Jack was out riding with Father—so I climbed up the tree to rescue her and got hopelessly stuck.'

'Cassie!' Sarah stared at her, halfway between amusement and dismay. 'Whatever did you do?'

'I sat on a branch and waited for Jack to come home—but Vincent Carlton came first. He had called to see Jack, of course: they were such good friends.' A strange, reminiscent expression had crept into Cassie's eyes. 'I shouted to him and he climbed the tree after me. I made him take Kitty first and then come back for me. He was wearing a pair of pale cream riding breeches—and he tore them in a very revealing place.' She laughed, looking a little embarrassed. 'They were new, too, as he informed me in no uncertain manner.'

'Was he angry?'

'No—just embarrassed, I think. He went off at once without stopping to see Jack. I never saw him to speak to again. He went away to London, and a year or so after that Sir Bertram died. I haven't heard from Lady Longbourne in years, though Lord Carlton wrote to me from France and begged me to send to his own lawyers in London if I was in any sort of difficulty. It was a very kind letter…'

'He must have forgiven you, after all.'

'Or he felt it his duty. His friendship with Jack had continued out there. My brother often mentioned him when he wrote…'

Again, Cassie's eyes clouded with sadness. However, she was not a girl to feel sorry for herself, and she had made up her mind that the time for grief had passed. Jack would not have wanted her to go on breaking her heart for him. He had thought too much of her for that!

'Do you care to go riding?' she asked Sarah. 'You can have my mare and I'll ride Jack's bay. We used to ride him together sometimes. So he will allow me to exercise him, though he can be restive and difficult to manage.'

'What will you do with the horses when you leave here?'

'I shall take them both with me. I told Kendal

Saracen was my brother's personal property, his to do with as he pleased—and Jack's own will left his possessions to me. I've had everything else of Jack's packed into large trunks and sent them to Nanny Robinson's cottage. I refuse to let Kendal get his hands on anything that belonged to my brother!'

'Is he so very awful, Cassie?'

'Detestable!' Cassie replied and shuddered. 'He visited me not three weeks after Jack was killed and used his title! Then he dared to—to offer me the chance of becoming his wife. It was so very obvious that he could not wait to get his hands on what little was left of Papa's estate—or Jack's as it was by then. And that he imagined he was doing me a very great favour by offering for me!'

'That was most insensitive of him. How fortunate that you refused him. Now that you have so much money of your own, you may choose where you will.'

'No doubt he would have tried to get his hands on that had he known.' Cassie's eyes sparked. 'He implied that he had a right to guardianship over me, because he is Father's cousin—though the relationship between him and my father was never friendly. To be plain, they hated each other. After meeting Kendal once, I can understand why he was never invited to stay here.'

'What did you say to him?'

'I told him I was old enough to do without his help—and that I had a lawyer to look after my affairs. He was not best pleased with me, and went off in a huff.'

'Do you suppose he could have known of your aunt's intention to leave you her money?'

'How could he? There had never been the slightest hint of it. I'm sure he could not have known about her fortune.'

'No, I suppose not,' Sarah said, still frowning. 'Perhaps he was only doing what he felt to be his duty?'

'I dare say we shall never know. For he was in such a way when he left—and it was after that I was given notice to quit.' Cassie shook her head. 'I am sure I've seen the last of Kendal, for he is not likely to repeat his offer again.'

Privately, Sarah thought it was extremely likely that the odious Sir Kendal Thornton would make his presence felt once he had heard of Cassie's inheritance. She was thankful that her friend had at least one influential acquaintance.

'And what did Lady Longbourne's letter say?' she prompted after a short silence. 'You did not tell me.'

'Did I not?' Cassie laughed. 'We were diverted by other topics.'

'Lord Carlton's unmentionables!'

Cassie nodded, her eyes carrying secret thoughts

that seemed to please her. 'She was so kind as to ask me to go and stay at once.'

'Oh, that is nice of her.'

'Yes, so I thought.'

'And shall you?'

'Only if you will come with me. You have been my constant companion these past months, Sarah. I do not know how I should have managed alone. I cannot bear to part from you now. I shall write and tell Lady Longbourne to expect us next week. I am sure she will be happy to have us both, since she says she is in need of companionship.'

'If only Papa will permit it!'

'He can surely have no objection. He must remember Lady Longbourne.' Cassie smiled at her, sensing her dawning excitement. 'We shall walk down to the vicarage and beg his indulgence,' she said. 'I shall take Janet, of course. She has guarded me well since Father…and she will be glad to look after us both.'

Janet had been Lady Thornton's personal maid from the moment she was a bride and, though she was now nearing sixty, a thin, no-nonsense lady who never hesitated to correct her young mistress's behaviour if she thought it necessary, she was devoted to Cassie.

'Papa thinks well of your Janet.' Sarah's eyes glowed. 'Let us go and speak to him at once!'

* * *

It was not until much, much later that evening, when Cassie was alone, preparing for bed, that she had a chance to reflect on the day's events.

The Reverend Mr Walker had agreed to the visit after only a moment or two of reflection, professing himself pleased with the idea of his daughter accompanying her, both to Lady Longbourne's, and to Brighton. The younger son of an impoverished baronet, who had had no choice but to take up the church for his living, he was still worldly enough to know that a better chance for his daughter to mix in good society was never likely to present itself, and while he would not have dreamed of saying it, he had every hope that his charming and pretty daughter might find herself a husband whilst staying with her friend.

Cassie had been sure Sarah's dear papa would see the advantage of a visit to Lord Carlton's estate, as she did herself. Nothing could be more fortunate. Indeed, it would be much better if she could have made her come out in London under Lady Longbourne's patronage, but she did not expect that: yet it would do her no harm if it were generally known that she had visited with the family, and no doubt she could trust Mrs Simmons to publish the fact once they were settled in Brighton later that summer.

Now, Cassie sat brushing her long, rich brown

hair, staring vaguely at her reflection in the dressing mirror without truly seeing herself. A little smile played about her full, generous mouth as she let herself remember that long-ago incident in the garden of her home.

'Come down, Cassandra,' Vincent had commanded with all the force of his superior years. 'I'll get the kitten later.'

'You must take her first,' she had insisted, defying his efforts to rescue her. 'She's more frightened than I am and, if you try to take us both, she may struggle and fall.'

Her eyes danced with laughter as she recalled the very improper expressions he had uttered when, on the return journey, he had snagged his breeches on a branch, revealing the fact that he was wearing nothing underneath the tight-fitting garment.

She had laughed then, too, and he had looked furious, but apart from that first startled oath, had said nothing out of place. She recalled that he had always had perfect manners—and a truly amazing smile.

The young Cassie had dreamt about her rescuer for some nights afterwards, but the memory had faded after he went away and she had eventually forgotten her knight—until his kind letter from France, which had brought her to tears.

There had been other letters from Jack's friends,

but only Lord Carlton's had made any real impression on her. It had seemed he really cared how Cassie felt, while the rest merely conveyed sympathy in a conventional way.

It would be pleasant to meet Lord Carlton again, if only to thank him for the consideration he had shown her. She wondered if the invitation from Lady Longbourne had been at his instigation, and the thought made her oddly restless.

She rose from her dressing table and went to gaze out of her bedroom window. There was a pale round moon in the sky, throwing its silver light over the garden and arousing a wistful longing in her—a longing for what?

She did not know what she wanted, or at least, she did know—but to hope for something that could never be was futile.

'Oh, Jack my dearest,' she sighed. 'If only you were here to share Aunt Gwendoline's legacy— what fun we could have had spending it together.'

For one moment Cassie's skin tingled as she caught sight of something moving amongst the shrubbery. Was there someone down there? She put up the sash window and leaned out, straining to see, but a cloud had passed across the moon and she could not be sure that anything had been there in the first place.

Of course there was no one there! Cassie closed

her window and turned away. She was imagining things…but just for a moment she had thought there was a man out there watching the house.

Chapter Two

The next few days were extremely busy for Cassie as she, Sarah and Janet packed their trunks and sorted through their closets for forgotten scarves, shawls and bonnets. With a little industry, the scarves could be freshened, the bonnets refurbished with ribbons and made to look almost new.

Cassie was pleased that she had given Sarah some new gowns, because at least they could both arrive looking presentable. She wished she had had time to order more for them both, but there was not a moment to be lost, for she wanted to make the most of the summer season.

'We might just persuade Lady Longbourne to take us to London for a few days,' she confided to Sarah, as they were packing trifles they could not possibly manage to live without into one of the large trunks. 'I do not count upon it, for it is kind enough of her to ask us to stay—but it would be nice to have our clothes ready for when we go to Brighton later. Even if she does not wish to trouble herself, she may know a reliable seamstress who could be trusted to work from our measurements.'

'I am sure I never expected to own anything so fine as this,' Sarah replied, stroking the material of the green walking dress Cassie had given her. 'I shall wear it to travel in, for the journey is no more than three or four hours, so Papa says, and it will not be creased.'

'It does look well on you,' replied Cassie. 'With your honey-blonde hair and green eyes...' She glanced at her own dark hair, which was thick and glossy enough, but unremarkable beside her friend's. 'You are so pretty, Sarah. I do not doubt that you will have all the dashing young men running after you when we get to Brighton.'

'Only if they are not in need of a fortune,' Sarah said, laughing at her enthusiasm. She was a practical girl and knew that it would probably take more than a pretty face to secure the kind of marriage Cassie was hoping for. 'Poor Papa cannot give me more than a hundred pounds when I marry and an allowance of fifty pounds a year, just as he does now.'

Cassie said nothing, but made up her mind to write to the lawyers in London and see if it would be possible to settle a small sum of money on her friend. She did not yet quite understand the terms of her aunt's will, but she knew she had a great deal of money in her possession, though there were some restrictions on the disposal of capital—at least until she married.

She said nothing to her friend, who she knew would protest, nor would she until it was all settled but, being a generous girl, she tucked the idea away in her mind for future reference.

At last it was time for the girls to set out on their travels. As the Reverend Mr Walker had said, it was a journey that should take them no more than four hours at most.

The carriage was brought round at ten that morning, and after some discussion as to whether all their boxes had been safely stowed on the baggage coach, the carriage went off at a good pace.

Cassie turned round to look back at her home for one last time. The remainder of her personal things were to be sent to Nanny Robinson for safekeeping, and a groom was to walk her precious horses over to Lady Fitzgerald's stables that very morning. She might, had she wished, have lingered at the house for another month but, although torn by memories, both happy and sad, she was relieved to be leaving early.

She had always loved the old house where she had been born, but she would not want to live there without her family. No, it was for the best, she thought, relaxing back against the cushions of the very comfortable carriage Lady Longbourne had sent over the previous night to fetch her.

Cassie could afford to set up her own carriage now if she wished, and she would probably do so when she had her own establishment—but although she was a reasonable judge of horses, she could not buy them for herself. She needed a male representative, someone who could be trusted not to saddle her with bone setters or old nags: she wanted a bang-up pair, and fashionable equipage to show them off.

It was all so very exciting, so much to look forward to that she found no trouble in keeping up a flow of chatter with her friend, and it was not until they had been travelling for nearly two hours that she heard a shout from the coachman, and glanced out of the window. The horses were slowing to walking pace, and when Cassie saw what was going on just ahead of them, she pulled the cord to let her driver know that she wished to stop.

'What is it?' Sarah asked. 'Why are we stopping?'

'Someone is ill,' Cassie replied. 'She has fallen on the ground. I think…yes, I am sure she is in some trouble.'

Sarah looked out of the window and gasped. Although a kindly girl, she was the product of a strict upbringing and what she saw shocked her. 'But—but she is—'

'Yes, exactly,' Cassie said, and, as the carriage stopped, jumped out without waiting for assistance. 'You stay there, Sarah...I shall see what needs to be done.'

Janet had been snoozing quietly in her corner, oblivious to what was happening. She woke up and looked about her in a daze.

'Are we there?'

'No...' Sarah nodded unhappily towards the open door. 'It's Cassie...she insisted on stopping.'

Janet glanced out of the window, snorting in disgust over the impetuous behaviour of her mistress. She got out of the carriage with the assistance of the groom, who had jumped down from the box and was watching his mistress warily. Having assessed the situation, she then went to where Cassie had knelt on the grass verge. She was bending over a woman who was clearly in pain—a rather dirty-looking creature wearing what Janet would most certainly describe as rags.

'Now, what are you at, miss?' she asked in a voice heavy with resignation.

Years of coping with stray animals, wounded birds and ragamuffins brought home by Miss Cassandra to be fed in the kitchen had prepared Janet for the inevitable. And she was not in the least surprised when her young mistress suggested that they must take the vagabond into the carriage with them.

'Now that would not be wise,' she began, but a flash from Cassie's eyes silenced her. 'Might I suggest that the proper place for her is in the baggage—'

'No, you may not,' Cassie said firmly. 'If you and Sarah are not prepared to ride with this poor woman, you may both ride in the coach.'

'Now, there's no need to take on,' Janet said, accepting her fate. 'Give the poor lass to me. She shall sit next to me and I'll attend her if…well, let's hope it does not come to that!'

'I knew you would see it my way,' Cassie said, smiling in a way that would have charmed the sourest temper. 'I want to be with her, Janet. Just to make sure that she does not suffer…'

'Aye,' the long-suffering Janet replied with a wry grimace, 'of course you would.'

Lord Carlton was in the salon with his mama at Carlton House, awaiting the arrival of Miss Cassandra Thornton and her friend Miss Sarah Walker. It was well past three in the afternoon and they had begun to wonder where their guests could have got to, as they had been expecting them any time this past hour or more.

Lady Longbourne was looking exceptionally fine that day in her simple but elegant pale grey gown with a Norwich silk shawl draped negligently over her shoulders and her hair dressed with a lace cap of such fetching ingenuity that her son was moved to remark on it.

'That cap becomes you very well, Mama. I like it exceedingly.'

'Well, I am glad that you do, for you paid for it together with several more and various other items you insisted I should order for my birthday, besides giving me those sapphires, which were far too extravagant for a woman of my age.'

'But became you very well…'

'You had no business to be wasting your money on a woman of my wretched health,' his mama replied, suffering an irritation of the nerves. Really, it was so inconsiderate of Carlton to expect her to entertain two young and probably very silly gels! The afternoon was warm and it was well past the time for her nap. 'I dare say I shall never have the occasion to wear them.'

'I see no reason why you should not,' her unfeeling son replied. 'We must give some dinners for our guests, Mama—and perhaps a little dance if Cassandra agrees to be my wife.'

'You surely do not expect—' Whatever Lady Longbourne had been about to say was lost as the butler opened the door and announced, in hushed and important tones, the arrival of their guests.

'Miss Cassandra Thornton and Miss Sarah Walker.'

Lady Longbourne raised her quizzing glass as

two young ladies walked in. They were both wearing dresses of good quality material, but made in a way which her ladyship's experienced eye knew at once for the work of a provincial seamstress: the latest fashions had been faithfully copied, but would not do for the lady who was to become Carlton's wife. She must obviously take Cassandra's wardrobe in hand!

But which of them was Miss Thornton? She could not remember the girl, who had usually preferred to play in the garden rather than venture into the salon, when she and Lady Thornton had been taking tea.

'Cassandra, my dear!' she said and stared directly at Sarah, who looked younger and slightly less modish than her companion. 'And Miss Walker…'

'Forgive me, Mama,' Vincent said, 'I believe this young lady is Cassandra.' His grey eyes held a hint of amusement as he walked towards them and held out his hand to her. 'It is some years since we met, but the circumstances were such as to have somehow imprinted your features into my mind. Am I right, are you indeed Miss Thornton?'

'Yes, I'm afraid I am, sir.' Cassie laughed as she gave him her hand, her cheeks a little pink, yet managing to meet his teasing gaze. 'Though I would as lief not be reminded of that incident. I fear you must have been quite cross with me that day, though you did not allow it to show.'

Vincent raised her hand to his lips, placing a chaste salute on the back. 'I felt a little foolish, I admit—but hope I should never be churlish enough to subject you to bad temper.' Then, turning from her to Sarah, he kissed her hand in the same manner and welcomed her to Carlton House. 'For any friend of Miss Thornton's must always be welcome here— must she not, Mama?'

Vincent was pleasantly surprised by Cassandra's looks. He, too, recognized that style was sadly lacking in her dress, but she had an attractive, open, healthy look about her, as if she spent her days outside as often as possible, and he liked the laughter in her eyes. He had feared her troubles might have changed her, but now he could see that her spirit had not been crushed.

Lady Longbourne had come forward and was smiling. 'You are both very welcome, my dears,' she said and kissed each of them in turn on the cheek. 'You have no idea how dull it can be for a widow alone in the country, especially when one's health does not favour one—it is a pleasure for me to have such delightful company.'

As she spoke, she realized that it might after all be quite a refreshing change to have two young ladies staying with her—and the matter of

Cassandra's wardrobe was something she intended to oversee personally. It struck her then that she would have to accompany the gel to London, and she was horrified at the thought—and yet her duty was to see Carlton's fiancée safely established in society. Naturally, she would do whatever was necessary, even though it would be very troublesome and might put her own health at risk.

Cassandra had seen at once the rather languid manner of her hostess, noticing the droop of her mouth and a certain pallor, which she thought might have been caused by lack of exercise and fresh air.

'I am truly sorry to hear you have been unwell, ma'am,' she said. 'It was kind of you to invite us, and I hope we shall not be too much trouble for you.'

'No, no, I am sure you could not be the slightest trouble to me. I have often wished for a daughter—and now for a time I may pretend that I have not one but two.'

'Prettily said, Mama,' Vincent said, a wry smile in his eyes. 'Let me assure you, Miss Thornton, we have been eagerly awaiting you…'

'You must forgive us if we are late,' Cassie said. 'We were delayed for an hour or more—were we not, Sarah?'

'It was so awful,' Sarah said, shedding her reserve as the thoughts uppermost in her mind burst forth. 'We came upon a band of travelling folk on the road, and one of the women was near fainting. Cassie insisted on stopping the carriage and we took her up with us—'

'You took a gypsy woman up with you?' Lady Longbourne stared at Cassandra in horror. 'But she could have had fleas or an infectious disease…or anything!'

'Pray do not disturb yourself, ma'am,' Cassie replied. 'She was big with child and clearly near her time. She was trying to reach a camp where the wise women of the band could care for her and…'

Lady Longbourne gasped. Had it not been so clearly her duty to instruct this ridiculous child her son was determined to marry, she would have fainted and retired to her bed at once.

'Cassandra,' she said in hushed tones that conveyed her very real sense of horror, 'you must not…you *really* must not speak of such things so openly. Especially when gentlemen are present. You will be thought of as fast…or worse.'

'Oh, dear, shall I?' Cassie smiled inwardly. 'I am so sorry if I have upset you, ma'am. Please do sit down. You look quite faint. You must forgive me for my execrable manners. I fear am not used to the rules of society. My only thought was that I could not leave the poor woman to…lie there on the ground and…' She subsided with a blush as she noticed that Lord Carlton was, far from being shocked, hard put to contain his laughter. 'But it was very wrong of me. I promise you she was not infectious—and I do not think we have taken harm from the encounter. But I just could not abandon her.'

'No, that would indeed have been very unkind in you,' Vincent said, managing to look grave notwithstanding his desire to laugh. 'You could not leave a fellow creature in such extremity. Despite the discomfort it must have incurred for you—to say nothing of your travelling companions!—I am persuaded you were refreshed by the satisfaction of having done a good deed.'

'Vincent!' Lady Longbourne gave her son a quelling look. 'I beg your pardon, Miss Thornton. I dare say you might not realize it, having not come across my son's very odd notion of humour before which is hardly surprising, for I'm sure no one else could possibly imagine such remarks to be funny— but I can assure you in all good faith that he *was* teasing you.'

Cassie's startled eyes flew to Carlton's face. She had never doubted that he was making fun of her and, as she saw the expression of indulgence on his face as he looked at his mother, she was hard pressed not to laugh out loud. What a wicked sense of humour he had, very much like that she and Jack had shared!

'I am indebted to you for telling me,' she replied

in a deceivingly flat tone. 'But Lord Carlton is very good to remind me that I have inconvenienced poor Sarah, and I dare say she is itching to tidy herself— just in case the poor woman did have fleas.'

At this, Vincent was betrayed into a laugh—a laugh so deep and husky that Cassandra found it difficult not to join in. However, Lady Longbourne was clearly affronted by her son's amusement. She turned her back on him and smiled on Sarah, reassuring her she would find clean water waiting in her room.

'I shall ring for Mrs Midge to take you up at once,' she said. 'For I should not like to be subjected to such an encounter myself, and understand perfectly how you feel. If I were you, I should let one of the maids take your gown and give it a good shake, my dear, and then you may feel better. You may both come down as soon as you feel ready, and we shall have tea—for you must both be starving, having missed your lunch.'

'Oh, we were well prepared,' Cassie said blithely. 'Janet never travels without a basket of food, since, as she says, one never knows what one may encounter on the road.'

'I dare say she has travelled with you before, Miss Thornton?'

Lord Carlton's quip was neither helpful nor deserving of a reply, so Cassie wisely ignored it.

She went on unheedingly, 'And despite giving

most of Janet's food to the companions of the poor woman we helped, we ate a piece of pie and a biscuit each, did we not, Sarah?'

'Yes…but I confess I am still a little hungry, Cassie.'

The housekeeper had arrived by this time and, having been asked by Lady Longbourne to show the young ladies to their rooms, obliged immediately. Sarah was only too anxious to go, and Cassie followed, pausing briefly at the door to glance back. Her eyes encountered Lord Carlton's and, meeting his thoughtful gaze, she felt an odd flutter of her heart.

How very handsome he was! Far more so than she had remembered. She thought perhaps this visit might be even more useful than she had first thought. It was a happy chance that he was staying with his mother, when he might so easily have been in town with his friends. And a gentleman of Lord Carlton's standing would naturally have a great many friends. If he were to show his approval of her publicly, Cassie would be invited everywhere. If only she could somehow get to London before the season was over.

Vincent toyed with his wineglass as the butler was serving the second course at dinner that evening. It was a very decent dinner by country standards, consisting of pigeons in red wine, a roasted cockerel and a leg of pork removed with a dish of creamed sweetbreads, some green peas, a dish of buttered asparagus and tiny sautéed potatoes, together with a curd junket and some crab tartlets. Not quite up to the standards of the French chef he employed in London perhaps, but not so badly presented as to give offence. Yet Vincent had discovered he had no appetite.

He noticed that Cassandra ate a little of the cockerel and the side dishes, but touched neither the pork nor the pigeons. However, when the sweet course was served, she did justice to the various jellies and trifles. She was clearly a healthy girl, with a lively, intelligent manner. Very suitable for the mother of the children he must provide in order for the family line to remain unbroken.

He had wondered if he would be able to go through with his promise to Jack, but, observing her now from beneath his long, dark lashes, he thought perhaps the task need not be so very burdensome after all. She was not pretty—his mother had been right about that—but not so very plain as to be without charm.

He knew that it was fashionable amongst the married men of his acquaintance to take mistresses, and perhaps Cassie would be content with that, since she had made it clear she did not want a love match. Yet Vincent knew that it was not what he really wanted.

What then? A wry smile touched his mouth. Was he truly such a fool as to believe in the perfect love? If only one were fortunate enough to find it…

Cassie was acutely aware of Lord Carlton watching her during dinner. He seemed not to be interested in his meal, and she had seen a brooding expression in his eyes that was so at odds with his usual manner that it intrigued her. However, when he joined the ladies in the drawing room after dinner, he was his normal charming self.

'Would you care to see over the house, Miss Thornton?' he asked. 'It is not of any great age, and therefore I can promise you no ghosts or fascinating antiquities. But we do have an extensive library, which has a rather splendid ceiling.'

'Cassandra will not want to see that,' said his mama. 'You should show her the orangery, that is far more suitable.'

'I should very much like to see the house, sir,' Cassie said.

'And you, Miss Walker?' Vincent looked smilingly towards Sarah, who begged to be excused on the grounds that Lady Longbourne had just asked her to play the pianoforte for her.

Cassie stood up, then accompanied her host out into the hall and through a large open parlour, which had several rather hard, uncomfortable-looking sofas ranged against the walls but no other furniture.

'This is where we have sometimes held little dances,' Vincent informed her. 'Not grand enough for an important ball, of course. I have thought about building an extension, but my grandfather's house in Surrey is much larger. I believe, when I settle to country life, it is there I shall make my home.'

'I dare say you have not wished particularly to hold many balls before this,' Cassie said politely. 'And I am sure you could set up at least twenty couples here if you wished.'

'Yes, perhaps.' Vincent's mouth curved in a lazy smile. 'As you say, I have not felt the need to hold a ball—but I may well do so in future.'

'When you marry, your wife may wish to entertain frequently,' Cassie said wisely. 'Some ladies are more fond of company than others. I suppose your mama does not entertain as often as your wife might wish?'

'Exactly so. When I marry, things will undoubtedly change.'

'I should imagine they must.' Cassie's eyes met his candidly. 'I suppose you have been much accustomed to coming and going as you please, without a word to anyone. I have often thought gentlemen fortunate to have so much freedom. But I suppose there are compensations to being a lady.'

She sounded so doubtful that Vincent's attention was caught.

'I suppose there must be.' His eyes danced with a wicked amusement. 'What can they be? Do tell me, Miss Thornton, for I am not certain that I know. And I would venture to suggest that you have given some thought to the subject.'

'One of them is to take refuge in dignity and refuse to answer when one knows a certain gentleman is being excessively provoking.' Cassie gave him a sparkling look. 'I am eager to see the ceiling in your library, sir—if I may?'

'Just through here,' Vincent invited. 'It was designed and executed by an obscure but talented Italian artist my father brought here at some expense. I do hope you approve.'

Cassie followed him into what was obviously a magnificent apartment. The walls were lined with tasteful, restrained bookcases of rich dark mahogany with a fine stringing of a lighter wood. Two large tables dominated the central run of the room, and three leather-covered matching sofas, which looked enticingly comfortable, were set to catch the light from the long windows.

However, it was undoubtedly the magnificent ceiling which drew the immediate attention of anyone entering the room. At either end there were large semi-circles which had been painted with a delicate duck-egg-blue background. Against this was drawn a scene of half-naked nymphs partly covered by flimsy drapes, and what appeared to be a satyr. The remainder of the ceiling was garlanded with swags of grapes, vine leaves and cherubs.

'Oh,' Cassie said, a little surprised by the lascivious expression in the satyr's eyes. 'It is very unusual. Beautiful, of course, but not quite what one might expect.'

'It is exactly what one might have expected of my father,' Vincent said, a chuckle escaping him as he realized she had taken it completely in her stride. 'Mama detests it, of course. She would have me paint it over—but whatever one's personal feelings, it is a work of art. Would you not say so?'

'Oh, yes,' Cassie agreed without hesitation. 'I do not believe you should cover it over, sir. After all, one is not forced to look unless one wishes.'

'No,' Vincent replied, giving her an appreciative look. 'One does not have to look.'

Cassie was exploring the room a little further, picking up pieces of sculpture and discovering that the theme of the ceiling had been repeated in the marbles and porcelain. Noticing a door at the far end, she moved towards it. 'And what is through here, sir? Is one permitted to see?'

'The billiard room. Not of interest to a lady, I dare say?'

Cassie turned her dark, melting gaze on him, her brows arched. 'This particular lady would like to see it,' she said. 'May I?'

'Be my guest,' Vincent invited, that lazy smile she had remarked earlier playing about his mouth.

He followed Cassie in, watching from beneath thick black lashes as she stroked her hand reverently over the velvet-smooth surface of the huge table that dominated the room. She hesitated, then with seeming care selected a cue from the racks, chalked the tip and eyed the balls which had been left carelessly on the table.

'May I?' she asked.

He nodded, his gaze narrowing keenly as she lined up the balls and proceeded to pot three of them one after the other with pleasing precision. He applauded, which brought a flush to her cheeks. She replaced her cue, looking conscious as he continued to stare at her.

'So you play,' he said. 'I suppose Jack taught you?'

'We spent hours practising trick shots,' Cassie said, a little shy now. 'I suppose it is an unusual pastime for a lady—but I always preferred to be with Jack if he would have me. Mama scolded me, of course, but I fear I am sometimes inclined to be wilful and I did not always heed her as much as I ought.'

'Yes, I see.' Vincent's eyes quizzed her. 'It *is* a fault,

Miss Thornton. Undoubtedly, you would raise eyebrows in some houses if you admitted to such a terrible vice—but I promise not to hold it against you.'

'Oh, I should not dream of admitting it in mixed company,' Cassie said, an answering gleam in her eyes. 'But somehow I do not think you would betray a lady's confidence.'

Vincent made her a little bow. 'Now I am on my mettle, am I not? You make it a matter of honour that not one word of this conversation shall ever pass my lips.'

Cassie laughed, a deep husky sound from a well inside her—a sound that was wholly enchanting to the man who listened. 'I believe that must be one of those compensations we spoke of earlier, sir— do you not think so?'

It was a hit. Vincent acknowledged it with a smile, but made no comment.

'I believe we should return to the others now, Miss Thornton. I have enjoyed our little tête-à-tête. It has been most enlightening.'

Cassie blushed at the look in his eyes. Had she said too much? His teasing humour had led her into thinking she might be open with him, but now she wondered if he might think her fast.

She hoped not. It mattered what Lord Carlton thought of her, because he and his mama could open the doors of London society for her.

* * *

Alone in her bedchamber an hour or so later, Cassie brushed her long hair as she sat before the dressing mirror. In the candleglow it was a rich chestnut, the red highlights picked up by the play of the flickering flame. She had sent Janet to bed after she had unhooked her gown, because she was not yet ready to retire herself.

It had been an interesting evening. Lady Longbourne was a thoughtful hostess, but more than that, she had a charm about her that was impossible to resist. She might have little airs about her, imagining herself an invalid when she was perhaps in much better health than she allowed, but she could be lively when she chose, and Cassie had not enjoyed herself as much in an age.

Lord Carlton was much more difficult to gauge. She liked what she knew of him, but felt he kept his own feelings carefully hidden behind a mask of affability. Could he really be as pleasant as he appeared?

Blowing out her candle, Cassie went to the windows and drew back the curtains. It was dark outside, the moon obscured by clouds, and she could see nothing. She sighed, feeling unaccountably restless, and wishing that she had thought to beg a book from Lord Carlton's library before she came up.

A little smile touched her lips as she recalled his air of expectation when she first saw the ceiling.

Had he thought she would blush and turn away in embarrassment? He had looked at her with approval after that, and she had the feeling she had passed some sort of test.

And yet why Lord Carlton should be pleased that she was not a missish creature, she could not imagine.

Cassie laughed at herself. Perhaps she was letting her thoughts run away with her, as she had been accused of in the past.

'You're always arranging things the way you want them in your head,' Jack had told her once. 'Life isn't like that, Cassie. If you're not careful, little sister, you're going to be hurt one day. And I shouldn't like that. I shouldn't like that at all.'

Cassie smiled to herself at the memory. She had known what it was to be truly loved, if only as a sister. Only a fool would expect to find such real devotion a second time.

Alone in the garden, Vincent stared at Cassie's window. Her room was in darkness and he supposed she was sleeping. A smile touched his mouth as he thought of her, of the way she had countered his mockery earlier that evening. His memories of Jack's sister had not played him false. She was an exceptional woman, just as Jack had always insisted.

Vincent's thoughts returned to the last time he

had seen Jack alive and the pain twisted inside him. God damn it! Would he never be free of this torture?

'I did what I thought was right,' he muttered. 'I did not mean you to die, Jack. Forgive me…I did not mean you to die…'

It had become clear to him how much Cassie had cared for her brother, and that made his situation even more difficult…made his guilt even heavier to bear.

Would he ever be able to tell her the truth…and if he did, would she forgive him?

Chapter Three

'And where,' said La Valentina, addressing Sir Harry Longbourne with a glint of temper in her magnificent eyes, 'is Carlton? I have not seen him this past week.'

La Valentina was an opera singer, admired as much for her dark, exotic beauty as her wonderful voice. Her company was avidly sought by a bevy of eager gentlemen, but only the wealthiest amongst them could have afforded her extravagant tastes. It was said that her greed for the good things of life matched her temper—which was formidable—but that she could also be generous when she chose.

She had been Lord Carlton's mistress for six months, or so it was rumoured, and some disappointed gentlemen were beginning to hint that wedding bells were in the air. No one actually believed such nonsense, of course—Carlton marry an opera singer? Never! He was far too conscious of his duty to his family, and his pride would in any case forbid it. All the same, it was deliciously amusing to speculate on such a scandalous outcome and the busy tongues could not resist such a juicy morsel.

'Well?' La Valentina threw the shakes into Harry with a flash of her eyes. 'Have you an answer for me, sir—or have your wits gone begging?'

'The thing is…' began Harry and then hesitated. He was not one of the lady's many admirers, and having heard the malicious gossip circulating the gentlemen's clubs decided to nip it in the bud. 'The thing is, madam, Vinnie has gone down to the country. His intended bride is coming to stay with Mama and…' He quailed as those Valkyric eyes darted flaming arrows at him.

'Am I to understand that Carlton is to be married?' The shock and anger in La Valentina's face revealed that she might have allowed herself to hope that there was some truth behind the rumours of an impending proposal. Uneasy, but determined to stand his ground, Harry bore up bravely.

'Oh, lord, yes,' he replied carelessly, lying through his teeth. 'It has been understood since Cassandra was in leading strings. Not publicly known, of course, but the families were all aware of it.'

'Indeed!' La Valentina seemed at a loss for words. She nodded to Harry and sailed away, the picture of outraged dignity as she disappeared into the crowded reception room of Rochester House, mingling with duchesses, dukes, earls, and making straight for the regent, who had just arrived and was one of her greatest admirers.

Harry felt a flicker of apprehension as he wondered what his half-brother would say if news of this got out, as it was bound to do, of course. Vinnie would give him a facer if nothing more. And since Vinnie, when he was first on the town, was one of the Corinthians who had been privileged to go a few rounds with Gentleman Jackson—acquitting himself so well that he was allowed to pop one in on the champion—it was useless for Harry to imagine that he could defend himself. Vinnie would give him a bloody nose—and he deserved it. He could not imagine what had driven him to lie so wildly!

As the evening wore on, however, and the calming effect of Lord Rochester's excellent champagne began to work in him, he saw that it was all for the best and worth being milled down by his brother. It was far better for everyone to think the match had been arranged years ago, than for the truth to be generally known—and so he would tell Vinnie after he had taken his punishment, which he would, of course. He began to think it had been very clever of him to have come up with such a tale, and when friends came to congratulate him and sent their felicitations to his brother, he was able to respond with a smile and a nod.

Vinnie would probably thank him for it—after he'd knocked him down, naturally. Besides, by the time Vinnie came back to town, it would all have been settled. Cassandra would gratefully accept Carlton's offer, and once the engagement had been announced the gossips would have nothing to say.

Harry left his club feeling a little woozy and rather pleased with himself as he sauntered home. What a very clever fellow he was to be sure!

Happily unaware of his half-brother's meddling in his private affairs, Vincent was the next morning engaged in providing his guests with suitable mounts.

'I know you are a great horsewoman,' he told Cassandra. 'Jack often talked with admiration of your style over the fences.' He had spoken naturally of his friend but, as he saw the flicker of shadows in her eyes, cursed himself for a fool. 'Forgive me. I did not mean to upset you.'

'No, no, you did not,' Cassie replied, banishing the shadows. 'For a long time I could hardly bear to think of Jack, the sense of loss was too over-whelming, but...' She hesitated, unable to explain her feelings. 'I do not know why it should have happened, but just recently Jack has come back to me. He had gone—but now I feel him near me somehow.' She blushed as Vincent looked at her oddly. 'You will say my grief has turned my mind?'

'I shall say no such thing. You were very close, as close as two people can be. At first your grief was too great to be borne, but now you are beginning to remember the happy times.'

Cassie nodded but did not reply. He was right, of course, but it was more than that. To voice her thoughts too plainly might drive Jack away from her. She knew any sensible person must doubt it, but she had the strangest notion that her brother was trying to communicate with her by the power of thought. Impossible, of course! Yet so often as a child she had known when Jack wanted something of her without his saying it out loud…but he had been alive then!

Finding her unwilling to converse further on the subject, Vincent turned to Sarah, who was walking quietly at his other hand. 'And you, Miss Walker, do you ride as well as Miss Thornton?'

'Oh, no!' Sarah disclaimed. 'Cassie has a way with horses. I am a mere novice compared with her. I do not often have the chance to ride, unless Cassie lends me her mare.'

'Then I shall find a gentle mount for you,' Vincent said, smiling at her. 'I bought such a mare for Mama's use, but she will not be bothered to ride these days.'

'That is a shame,' Cassie said, joining the conversation. 'Will her health not permit her to exercise more?'

Vincent hesitated, brows wrinkling in thought. 'There is no real reason why Mama should be an invalid, but she seems to lack the desire to venture out into the fresh air. She was very ill after Sir Bertram died, but now…'

'She has gone into a decline,' Sarah said. 'I had an aunt who was much the same.'

'Might it not be boredom?' Cassie wondered aloud. 'If she has been often alone…with both you and Sir Harry away?'

Vincent frowned and for a moment she felt she had offended him, but then he gave what she took to be a nod of agreement. 'I have often felt Mama might find happiness again, if she could be persuaded to mix more in society, as she once did—instead of confining herself to receiving the vicar and a few old friends.'

'Is that why you persuaded Lady Longbourne to invite me here?'

Cassie's clear gaze made Vincent vaguely uneasy. She was an intelligent woman, spirited and more independent than he had expected. When he, Harry, Richard Cross, Freddie Bracknell and Major Saunders had drawn straws to determine who should honour the promise they had all made, with varying degrees of enthusiasm, Vincent had made certain he drew the short straw. Jack's fate had lain heavy on his mind, and he had felt very keenly that it was his duty to take care of Cassandra. And although he had had doubts afterwards, which caused him to delay making his proposal, he still felt he was honour-bound to at least ask her to be his wife.

'Partly,' he said. 'I knew you to be in awkward circumstances, and I hoped to be of service to you. You had my letter?' She nodded. 'But you have never taken advantage of my lawyers.'

'No,' Cassie said, and hesitated. She was not sure why, but she was disinclined to tell him that she was a considerable heiress. 'I was in difficulty for a while, but I am not now. My mother's sister left me some money—'

'I was not aware you had any relatives—apart from a cousin of Sir Edward's?' Vincent's brows arched. 'And I understood that he was rather an unpleasant fellow? Jack did not care for him, at all events.' He had begged Vincent to save her from falling into Kendal's hands!

'He is quite odious!' Cassie cried. 'I dislike him very much. He had the effrontery to offer me marriage out of a mistaken sense of duty! As if I should marry for such a cause. I may not be beautiful, but I believe I am not hopeless.'

'No, not hopeless at all!' His eyes appreciated her, a smile quivering at the edges of his sensuous mouth.

'It is my intention to visit London if I can—or Brighton,' Cassie went on, blithely unaware that she had given him a facer. 'Mrs Simmons has promised to chaperon me at the end of next month. With some stylish clothes and a few introductions to the right people, I do not think it impossible I shall find someone, a *gentleman*, of course, with whom I might be comfortable—do you?'

'Is comfort your main requirement in a husband?' Vincent studied her profile with interest. He was fascinated by this show of confidence. Did she disregard him totally as a suitor—or was this a ploy to arouse his hunting instincts? No, no, he did not think her so calculating. She must consider him too old, as perhaps he was, being almost eleven years her senior.

'I believe comfort—the ability to be easy with one's chosen partner—to be of the first importance.' She turned her innocent but beguiling gaze on him. 'Do you not think so, sir?'

Vincent was much amused at her idea of marriage, but held his smile inside. Her frank way of speaking was revealing a young lady of character and he was enjoying himself immensely.

He supposed he ought to have known, for Jack had often told amusing stories of his sister's escapades, but Vincent had seen them as childish pranks—like the incident of the kitten in the tree— never suspecting there was so much depth to a girl he had met only a few times.

It had been his intention to wait a few days and then make his offer, leaving her in his mother's care, while he went off to town until the wedding—but now he thought there might be far more to gain by delaying for a while.

'Oh, paramount,' he agreed in answer to her question. 'To be forever at odds with one's partner, not to be thought of. But what a charming notion, Miss Thornton! A novel way of describing marriage. A partnership. Indeed, yes. I like that idea.'

'Do you not think marriage should be for the mutual benefit of both husband and wife?'

'Oh, yes, indubitably!'

Vincent mentally reviewed the marital arrangements of his friends and acquaintances. Most had been entered into as a contract, for the protection of land and fortunes. A few *were* love matches, but even in these he had found the distribution of power lay with one or the other: whichever was the less besotted of the two usually held the bridle, however gently.

'Do you suppose the ideal is obtainable?' he asked.

'If you mean, do I expect perfect happiness—then my answer must of course be no,' Cassie replied seriously. 'Yet I believe it must be possible to live in harmony if one is prepared to give and take.'

'Ah, I see.' His mouth quivered but he controlled

his desire to laugh. 'And have you considered love, Miss Thornton?'

'Love?' Cassie hesitated, then shook her head. 'I do not think being in love would be at all comfortable. I shall not allow such a consideration to cloud my judgement.'

'Will you not?' Vincent said softly. 'What a truly sensible young lady you are.' He directed a very odd look at her as they reached the stables. 'I see my groom has our horses ready. I believe we must continue our conversation another day…'

'Augusta Simmons!' Lady Longbourne's face assumed an expression of loathing. 'No, Carlton, I cannot allow it. Why, the woman is both a fool and—and a toad eater. She is not the proper person to present your future bride to the *ton*. No, indeed! I have never liked her: she is too puffed up in her own conceit. I wonder you could think of it!'

'Forgive me, Mama,' Vincent corrected calmly. 'It was not my notion, but Miss Thorton's own. It seems she has had some money bequeathed to her, and means to spend it on a season if she can but contrive to get herself presented.'

'That is my task,' his mother replied, getting to her feet in some agitation. 'I had already decided on it. I shall suggest to Cassandra that we all go up to town next week. We shall give a dinner the following week, after we have had time to refurbish our wardrobes and send out invitations.'

'Are you sure it will not be too much for you, dear Mama?'

'I am not quite in my dotage yet,' snapped Lady Longbourne. 'I have been feeling a little better these past two days. Besides, nothing, no considerations of self, shall stand between me and duty in this matter. Your wife must have every attention due her position in society,' she said. 'My health is nothing to the point. You know I have always put the best interests of my sons first, Carlton.'

'Then, if you are sure it will not be too much for you, I should think it best to put the idea to Miss Thornton, so that she can write to Mrs Simmons. And, Mama…thank you for your kindness, but please remember Cassandra has not yet consented to become my wife.'

'Do you intend to propose before we go up to town, or later?'

'I think we must give her time to get to know us, don't you?'

'Just as you wish.' Her ladyship frowned. 'You know I did not wish for this alliance, Vincent, but having Cassandra here with us has made me think again. She has a tendency to speak more frankly than she ought, but apart from that she has pretty manners—and breeding. From her mother, I make sure! All in all, I think her a nice gel. Not a beauty, of course, but presentable—and thoughtful. I believe she will do very well for you, Carlton. Indeed, I am persuaded you could not do better.'

'Are you indeed, Mama?' Vincent smiled inwardly. 'For myself, I do not dislike her open way of speaking, I think it engaging—but whether or not we shall suit is something we shall decide in good time.'

'I thought it was a matter of honour with you?'

'Yes, so did I,' Vincent replied, smiled oddly at his mother and kissed her hand. 'But I find that is not after all the case.'

'What do you mean?' Lady Longbourne glared at him. 'Do you intend to make the girl an offer or not?'

He smiled mysteriously, leaving her standing as he went out of the French windows and into the garden.

'Well!' she exclaimed. 'Of all the tiresome creatures…'

It was really most provoking of him. Only duty would have persuaded her to give up her peaceful seclusion in the country and now… For a moment she gave in to righteous indignation, but gradually the realisation dawned on her that she did not wish to give up her plans for Cassandra. She had indeed felt much more lively since the arrival of the two young ladies, and she was looking forward to taking them both in hand.

Even though Sarah had no expectations, she did

not despair of contriving a suitable match for her. And as for Cassandra, well, if Vincent did not make up his mind, there would surely be others who would. Especially if she had a little money.

She would make a push to discover the gel's fortune. It could not be much, of course, but even a thousand or two would help Cassie to find a husband. Yet it would be rather pleasant to have the gel as her own daughter-in-law.

'Take us both to London next week?' A look of delight dawned in Cassie's eyes. 'Oh, dearest Lady Longbourne! How good you are to me. But are you sure it will not be too tiring for you?'

She looked at her hostess anxiously. The inquiry must be made but, oh, she did hope nothing would happen to prevent them going to London!

Lady Longbourne gazed up at her with an expression nicely balanced between self-sacrifice and affection.

'It will be no trouble at all, my dear child. Your mother was my closest friend. Had it not been for my precarious health I must have taken you under my wing long ago, but I am feeling much recovered of late—and I am determined not to think of myself. Whatever happens, I shall not permit that odious Augusta Simmons to present you; that shall be my pleasure.'

'I do not know how to thank you,' Cassie said, truly grateful. She was well aware that to appear in London with a paid companion could not give her a quarter of the credit that a visit with a lady of her hostess's consequence would naturally bestow on her.

'Come, sit with me for a few minutes,' Lady Longbourne said, patting the sofa seat beside her and smiling fondly. 'I think we must discuss the very urgent matter of your clothes, for what you are wearing now is very pretty, but it will not do for town, my love.'

'Oh, I know. I must buy lots of new clothes.'

'You will need a considerable wardrobe.'

'And so will Sarah,' Cassie said. 'I have promised her some new clothes as a present for all her family's kindness. And I know her papa is hoping she may find herself a husband.'

'Is he of good family?'

'Oh, yes—but there is no money, of course.'

'Well, she is very pretty so there is no telling what may happen. Are you sure you can afford to provide sufficient clothes for both of you? Because, if not, I should enjoy helping you, Cassie.'

'You are very kind, ma'am, but I believe my funds will be sufficient.'

Lady Longbourne nodded, her curiosity aroused. 'Who was your aunt, my dear?'

'Mama's eldest sister. Aunt Gwendoline. She

married a gentleman from Truro, and we visited her only once that I recall.'

'Indeed?' Lady Longbourne's eyes widened. 'Who was her husband?'

'A Mr Belham,' Cassie replied. 'I never met him—and they had no children.'

'That was a source of sadness to them, I dare say?'

'I suppose it must have been,' Cassie said. 'I hardly knew her.'

'Well, well, it does not matter.' Lady Longbourne patted her hand. 'At least she thought of you, my dear. A little money is always useful.'

'Yes…' Cassie felt guilty at concealing the truth from her generous hostess. 'It is quite a lot of money. I do not precisely know the amount, but I think it could make the matter of my marriage easier to accomplish.'

'Yes…' Lady Longbourne nodded thoughtfully. 'I imagine it would…even a few thousand is a great persuader.'

'Yes.' Cassie flushed and dropped her gaze. 'I think, rather…I have been told…I can expect to be quite an heiress.'

'An heiress?' Her hostess looked startled. 'What good fortune you came to me, Cassie! Had you fallen into the clutches of that odious creature Augusta Simmons, you might have been prey for fortune-hunters and ruthless gamblers.'

Cassie smiled at her, relieved the truth was out. 'I did not like to say before, but I am persuaded that you have my best interests at heart, ma'am.'

'Oh, yes, indeed,' her ladyship said, smiling to herself. 'This alters the case, Cassie dear. I had hoped for a modest success—but now I am determined that you shall be the toast of the season. Oh, yes, this changes everything…'

Cassie and Sarah were walking in the formal gardens, having left Lady Longbourne lying comfortably on her daybed in the small front parlour, a book lying unread beside her and a glass of cordial on the table near to hand.

'This is such a beautiful house,' Sarah said as they came upon a little Greek temple. 'We are so lucky to have been invited here. And now we are to go to London next week. Could anything have been so fortunate? I wonder why Lady Longbourne has agreed to take us?'

'Yes, so do I,' mused Cassie, looking thoughtful. 'It is exceedingly kind of her, but I had thought her health too fragile to allow it.'

'Perhaps she felt it her duty to help you?' Sarah suggested. 'Since she and your mama were such friends.'

'Yes, perhaps she did,' Cassie agreed. 'But I suspect the suggestion came from Lord Carlton— though I cannot think why he was kind enough to persuade his mama for our sakes. Unless he has fallen in love with you, Sarah? You are so pretty that it is possible he might.'

Sarah blushed and shook her head at her. She knew that Lord Carlton was only being a good host when he smiled and inquired after her well-being, but she had her own ideas as to his reasons for making sure they had a season in London.

'I think perhaps—' she began, then stopped as she saw Lord Carlton coming towards them. 'Oh, here he is…'

'Ladies…' Vincent tipped his hat to them. 'I was persuaded I should find you here. It is a very pleasant afternoon, is it not?'

'Very pleasant,' Cassie said. 'Lady Longbourne felt it too warm for walking, and we left her resting. But perhaps we should return now. I should not like her to feel that we have neglected her.'

'Mama is perfectly happy,' he assured them. 'When I left her a moment ago she was wishing to have a little sleep. I came after you, because I thought it a perfect afternoon to take a rowing boat on the lake—if that would please you?'

'Oh, yes,' Sarah responded at once. 'I should like that of all things—if you would, Cassie?'

'It would be nice and cool on the lake,' Cassie said, shading her eyes as she looked towards the expanse of glistening water. 'You were very thoughtful to come after us, sir.'

'Mama told me I am to remind you that we have company for dinner this evening, but if you think it would not be too tiring to be rowed out to the island…?'

Both ladies agreed that they would find it relaxing and so the party walked down a sloping, grassy bank to the jetty where a rowing boat had been tied ready for their jaunt. Vincent handed Sarah in first, then Cassie, taking up the oars himself.

Cassie put down her sunshade, but Sarah kept hers up to protect her fair skin from the sun.

'You are not afraid of freckles, Miss Thornton?' Vincent asked.

'My skin does not freckle,' Cassie said. 'It just gets a little darker. You may have remarked that I do not have Sarah's delicate complexion?'

'No, you do not,' he said. 'I believe the sun likes you more than it does Miss Walker.'

'Oh, I never burn,' Cassie said carelessly. 'Jack and I were forever in and out of boats on the river. And sometimes we lay on the banks in the sun—as children, you know. I loved to make daisy chains…'

She blushed as she saw his gaze narrow, turning her head aside to look at the beauty of her surroundings. The banks of the lake were deeply wooded, and in the middle there was a tiny island with a summerhouse and wrought iron seats.

'This looks a pretty place for a picnic,' she remarked.

'Yes. I should have thought to bring one,' Vincent said, and his smile had disappeared. 'But perhaps another time…'

Cassie glanced at him, but his expression made her heart catch. Just what was he thinking? Had she said something to make him angry?

In fact, Vincent had been remembering another visit to the island, when he, Jack and other friends had taken a picnic there. It was just after they had all decided to join the army, and Jack had been telling them a story about his sister.

It had been the first of many, for Jack was an excellent teller of stories, and, according to her brother, Cassie had spent the best part of her life in some scrape or other.

Once again, Vincent felt the pain twist inside him as he watched her laughing in the sunshine. He wished with all his heart that Jack could have been here with them…that he was not lying in an unmarked grave somewhere in France.

There were six persons besides themselves who sat down to dinner that evening. Cassie had been introduced to the Reverend Mr Simpson, his sister, who kept house for him, a gentleman of advancing years who was placed next to her, and seemed a little deaf, and three elderly ladies who lived together.

It was not particularly scintillating company, and

Cassie was amused as she saw that Lord Carlton was struggling to hide his yawns. He would have been distressed to let his guests see his boredom, of course, for he had excellent manners, but it was obvious to her that he was finding the evening exceedingly tiresome.

He very soon followed the ladies into the drawing room, having summarily dispensed with the custom of the port, and came to sit by Cassie's side on a sofa near the window.

'Forgive us for such a tedious evening,' he said, 'but these ladies are Mama's nearest neighbours and it would have been unforgivable had they not been invited to meet you. However, I do assure you that tomorrow the company will be more lively. I have invited some of my own acquaintances, and there will be cards and music.'

'You are very kind,' Cassie said, 'but *I* am not bored. Your mama's friends may be old, sir, but I find them interesting enough. They have many stories to tell if one is prepared to listen.'

'Yes, but *I* have heard them so many times before,' Vincent murmured with a wicked look that almost overset her. 'This is your first time, Miss Thornton—so you are unkind to judge me so harshly. I dare say you may find them a little less entertaining after you have heard them fifty times.'

'Indeed, you may be right, sir,' Cassie replied

demurely. 'But ladies, you know, are more accustomed to listening—even if they are not always interested.'

'Not one of the privileges?'

Cassie smiled but would not answer, and after a moment Vincent left her to go and talk to the Vicar's sister.

Cassie noticed that he was perfectly attentive. Indeed, she could not fault his manners. Yet she was not in the least surprised when he excused himself after the tea tray had been brought in, suspecting that, if she had been another man, he might have invited her to join him in his billiard room.

However, it would have been quite shocking had she followed him there, and so she was obliged to remain and listen to more of the stories she had not quite truthfully assured Lord Carlton she found so very interesting.

Being a caring girl, she did not let her mind stray more than once or twice to what his lordship might be doing, and she certainly did not allow a sigh to escape her even when her companion began to tell her the same story she had heard not twenty minutes earlier.

'I dare say you'll be glad to be off for some gallivanting in town,' Miss Simpson said to her. 'Well, you will be in good hands, Miss Thornton. Lady Longbourne knows what she's about—and as for that son of hers, handsome fellow, ain't he? And quite charming…'

'Oh, yes,' Cassie said. 'A perfect gentleman.'

'Well, as to that, there's more to young Vincent than meets the eye,' the wise old spinster said. 'But he has a good heart…yes, you can rely on that. He always had a good heart, no matter what larks he got up to.'

Now this was more like it! Cassie turned her opportunity to good advantage, listening with genuine interest to stories of her host when he was a lad.

'Of course, my brother wouldn't have it that Vincent was the one who put a pair of ladies' corsets on the spire, but I saw the look in those wicked eyes of his, and I knew. His stepfather would have had to thrash him had he known, so of course I never said a word to anyone.'

Cassie met her eyes and smiled. 'How very, very interesting,' she said. 'Thank you so much for telling me.'

'I thought you'd want to know,' the elderly lady said and gave a cackle of delight. 'Never know when you might want to take him down a point or two!'

'No,' Cassie said, much amused. 'No, one never knows…'

Chapter Four

Cassie had been walking within the grounds of Carlton Park for almost an hour when she first heard the whimpering sound. It was another very warm day, and Sarah had declined to accompany her, protesting that she would prefer to stay in the cool of the house with a book. Feeling a little restless, Cassie had decided to go alone, her walk leading her through shaded, tree-lined avenues, by a charming stream, which rushed and bubbled over large boulders and into this wood.

Despite having just recently wondered once or twice if there was someone behind her, she had dismissed it as sheer imagination and was neither fatigued nor oppressed by the heat. Her frown of concentration was for her thoughts, which were a little disordered and concerned Lord Carlton. She could not quite place its origin, but she knew there had been a subtle change in his manner towards her of late…not exactly a withdrawal, but a distance which troubled her.

Could she have done something to offend him? She had not thought so, but found it worrying just the same.

However, the whimpering noise broke through her thoughts and she was instantly alert. What could it be? Someone or some animal was in pain. She stopped walking, listening intently to the pitiful cry. It was a child! She was sure it was a child.

Forgetting any idea she might have had of being followed, Cassie was immediately alert to another's plight. Turning to her right, she followed the sounds of distress along a twisting path, then stood still as she suddenly saw the huddled creature lying on the ground. A child…a small girl of perhaps ten years was curled up into a ball, arms hugging her knees and making the kind of sounds one might expect from an injured cat.

'Oh, you poor child,' Cassie murmured and went over to her. 'What is wrong? Have you hurt yourself?'

The girl lifted her head as Cassie approached, alarm in her rather dirty, thin face. She attempted to rise, the instinct to flee showing in her pale blue eyes, but her efforts to stand were hopeless and she fell back to the ground with a cry of despair as her ankle gave way.

'Please, do not be frightened,' Cassie said. 'I do not mean you harm. I should like to help you, if I may?'

Now that she was closer, Cassie could see that the girl was older than she had first guessed, but pale and undernourished. She knelt down on the dry grass and looked at the ankle which was obviously causing the child pain.

'Have you hurt yourself? Your ankle looks swollen. Did you fall and twist it?' The girl nodded, her eyes still wary, frightened. 'May I look? Just to be sure you have not broken any bones.'

'It ain't broke,' the girl said, catching back a sob. She wiped her nose on her sleeve, which was already less than clean. 'I was running and my foot caught in some tree roots what had lifted out of the ground. It was the wrench what hurt.'

Cassie moved her fingers carefully over the injured ankle. The girl flinched once or twice but made no sound.

'It seems not to be broken,' she agreed, feeling thankful that the injury was no worse. 'But a nasty sprain can be very painful. I am not surprised you were crying.'

'I weren't crying for this,' the girl said, encouraged by Cassie's tone. 'It were 'cos he'll come after me and take me back. Then he'll beat me and set me to work again.'

'Oh, you poor thing,' Cassie said. 'He sounds a cruel master.'

'Ain't me master,' the girl replied, smothering a

sob of fear. 'Leastways, he don't pay me nuffing. He was me muvver's fancy man. When she up and snuffed it, he made me work for me keep—runs an inn in the village, he does, makes me scrub and clean, and serve in the taproom. But I don't mind that so much, nor that he's a mean ole skinflint. It were the other thing…'

'The other thing?' Cassie was puzzled until she saw the girl flush and look ashamed. A shudder of disgust went through her. 'You don't mean that he…but you're only a child!'

'I'm nearly thirteen,' the girl said. 'He says it's time I started me proper work. He says me ma were a whore and I ought to fetch a few guineas being as it's me first…but I don't want to lie with that rotten Morgan, so I ran away.'

'Is Morgan the name of your—your employer?' Cassie supplied for want of a better word. Having been sheltered and protected for most of her life, she was shocked and horrified that a young girl should be subjected to such wickedness!

'No, Morgan's the one old Carter wants to sell me to. But I ain't gonna let him. I was gonna walk to London to make me fortune, but now I've hurt meself and he'll find me and take me back.'

'Well, he shan't do that,' Cassie said. 'For you shall come back with me and—' She remembered all at once that she was not in her own home, but a guest

in the house of Lady Longbourne. 'I shall help you.
I shall bind your ankle, then give you money for
your coach fare to London.' She finished on a flash
of inspiration. 'In London you may find work for a
good master, who *will* pay you, will not beat you—
and certainly will not expect you to—to do *that*.'

'Why should you help the likes of me?' The girl
looked at her suspiciously. 'You're a lady, and it's
true what old Carter says, me ma wasn't no better
than she ought ter be.'

'Because I want to help,' Cassie replied. 'I am
Cassandra, but my friends call me Cassie. You need
not be afraid of me. I am your friend, and always
shall be. Do you believe me?' The girl gazed up at
her, then nodded. 'Will you tell me your name now?'

'Tara,' she said, looking at Cassie with a touch of
awe. 'Will you really pay me fare, miss?'

'Yes, certainly,' Cassie answered with a smile.
'But first I must get you to the house so that I can
look after you. If I help you to stand, do you think
you can hold on to me and hop? Otherwise I must
leave you here and go for help.'

'Don't go!' Tara looked fearfully behind her. 'Old
Carter will fetch me back if he finds me 'ere.'

'I doubt he will come here in search of you,' said
Cassie, a half-smile on her lips. 'This is Lord
Carlton's land and he would be trespassing—he
could be arrested for that.'

This did not seem to reassure Tara. She looked nervously at Cassie. 'Will I be sent to prison, miss? I didn't know this wood was private property. And I know some of old Carter's friends come 'ere poaching game; they bring pigeons and suchlike to the inn sometimes.'

'Indeed? I think Lord Carlton would be interested to know that.'

'Shall you tell him, miss? Will he be cross with me for being 'ere?'

'Lord Carlton is my friend,' Cassie said. 'He is a very kind man and would not dream of harming you, but I dare say he would deal very differently with your master—especially if we tell him what he has done to you.' She smiled at the girl. 'And now, if I help you, I think you should try to walk.'

It took some minutes of trial and error before Tara was able to get the right balance, but with Cassie's arm supporting her, and her hand on Cassie's shoulder, she managed to hop a few steps before having to rest. Their progress would obviously be slow, and it was almost time for tea. Lady Longbourne would worry if Cassie was late, but there was no help for it. She could not and would not abandon a girl who was little more than a child to a fate that was, in her opinion, worse than death. So they would just have to do their best and hope that one of Lord Carlton's servants chanced to see them and came to aid them.

* * *

Help arrived at last in the person of Lord Carlton himself some three-quarters of an hour later, when they were within sight of the formal gardens. Vincent had in fact been sent by an anxious Lady Longbourne in search of their errant guest.

'For you never know if some unscrupulous adventurer may have tried to snatch her from our care,' she told her son. 'An heiress with no family to protect her! She is vulnerable, Carlton. It is our duty to guard her vigilantly.'

'I doubt if anyone knows of her inheritance as yet,' he replied, hiding his smile at the idea of some fortune-hunter venturing to kidnap his guest in the grounds of his own estate. 'Miss Thornton was reluctant to tell even us, it seems. Why should that be, do you think, Mama?' He raised his mobile eyebrows.

'Because she is a properly brought up young gel and does not boast of her good fortune,' said his mama promptly. 'Do not waste time in asking foolish questions, Carlton. You are sometimes so unperceptive, I despair of you. Go and find her!'

'You are certain she is not in the house?'

'Quite certain.'

Vincent set off obediently, more to placate his anxious parent than for any fear of harm having come to Cassie, but as soon as he saw her he hurried to offer his assistance.

'We were worried about you,' he said. 'What has happened here?'

'Tara fell and hurt her ankle,' Cassie replied, pausing to catch her breath. The girl was by no means heavy, but it had been a long, exhausting walk. 'I could not leave her, so…'

'No, of course not. Please allow me, Miss Thornton. And, Tara, I must carry you. Do not fear, I shall not hurt you.'

'You're *him*, ain't you?' Tara said, looking at him in awe. 'His lordship what owns the land. Miss Cassie said you're kind. She says you'll likely throw old Carter in the clink or give him a bloody nose.'

Vincent's eyes betrayed him, though he controlled his very great desire to laugh. 'Did she, indeed? I think I am indebted to her, though I am not sure. May I know who old Carter is?'

Carried safely in his lordship's arms, Tara repeated her story, adding details she had not disclosed to Cassie. As Vincent heard of beatings and threats to make her submit to her master's vile plans for her, his mouth hardened and the smile faded, his eyes becoming the colour of wet slate.

'You ain't angry, are you?' Tara asked, sensing the suppressed fury in him. 'It were Miss Cassie's idea to bring me here.'

'And a very good one!' He glanced down at her. 'I *am* very angry, but not with you or Miss Cassie.

In fact, I am indebted to you for telling me, Tara. Mr Carter is my tenant. I own the Hare and Hounds and, I can assure you, you will not be returning there. Indeed, Mr Carter will not be there much longer himself.'

They had reached the front of the house. Cassie hesitated as she looked at him. 'I was wondering...where to take Tara?'

Vincent smiled as he read her thoughts. 'Not to Mama's parlour, certainly. I believe you should present yourself at once to calm her fears. She was worried in case you might have been carried off by some scoundrel or other. As for Tara, you may safely leave her to my care. If she is agreeable?'

'Best take me to the kitchens,' Tara said, looking hopeful. 'Mebbe they'll give me something to eat.'

'Janet will treat her ankle and find her something clean to wear,' Cassie said. 'She always did when...' She faltered under his quizzing gaze. 'At home, you know.'

'Ah, yes, the redoubtable Janet.' He could not prevent a chuckle escaping. 'I shall take Tara to the kitchens and send for Janet at once!'

Cassie smiled, acknowledging a hit, but did not answer as she went into the house. She paused before one of the tall pier mirrors in the hall to tidy herself before entering the parlour. Her hair was a little windblown and the hem of her dress was dirty where she had knelt on the ground. She brushed away the debris before making her way to the parlour.

Between them, Tara and Lord Carlton had solved her immediate dilemma, for she did not care to imagine her hostess's shock and dismay had she presented her with the runaway. Which, of course, she must have done for politeness' sake had Lord Carlton not arrived at the eleventh hour! Thinking about it, Cassie decided it might be for the best if she did not mention the incident at all.

'Ah, there you are!' Lady Longbourne exclaimed, jumping up as she saw Cassie and coming to greet her as she entered the parlour. 'It is nearly time for you to change for dinner. You have missed tea—though I will send for a tray should you wish it?' Cassie declined with a shake of her head. 'Wherever have you been, my love? I have been imagining you lost this past hour.'

'I fear it was my own fault,' Cassie apologised. 'Please forgive me, dearest Lady Longbourne. I did not realise it would take so long to…walk home.'

'Since you are safe, there is nothing to forgive.' She gave a little sigh. 'My only worry now is that you have tired yourself. You have not forgotten that we leave for town tomorrow? Travelling is so excessively tedious, is it not?'

'I never seem to find it so,' Cassie confessed. 'There is so much to see—and all the excitement of what lies at the journey's end. I am so looking forward to this visit, ma'am. And so is Sarah! We are so fortunate to have you as our hostess. You have such style, such lovely clothes. I cannot wait to be guided by you in the matter of our wardrobes. If only it will not make too much trouble for you?'

Well pleased with Cassie's genuine concern and pretty manners, her ladyship assured her that she could never be a trouble to her.

'When Carlton first suggested your visit to me, I was doubtful that my health would stand it—but to be quite truthful, my love, you have done me good. It is so pleasant to hear young voices in the house again. I am looking forward to introducing you into society—and I do not mean the old tabbies and bores you have met here, who are all kindly folk and mean well, but not lively enough for a young gel. You will much prefer the company we shall entertain in town, Cassie.'

At this Cassie kissed her cheek, told her that she had enjoyed her stay at her home excessively, then begged pardon because if she did not hurry away she would be late for dinner. However, Lady Longbourne kept her talking a while longer, and it was almost twenty minutes later when she reached her own room.

Janet was waiting for her, her frown one of exasperation mixed with affectionate understanding.

'Oh, do not scold me,' Cassie cried, knowing that particular look of old. 'I know it was wrong of me to burden Lord Carlton and Lady Longbourne as I did—well, not Lady Longbourne precisely, because she does not know of Tara's predicament, and I dare say his lordship will think it best not tell her—but she was in such distress, poor child. I could not leave her there to be captured by her cruel master, could I?'

'No, Miss Cassandra, *you* could not. But it is as well his lordship is so understanding. It is not exactly the proper behaviour expected of a guest, to be bringing dubious kitchen girls into your hostess's home. You have only Tara's word that she wasn't running from the law. She might be a thief—or worse.'

Cassie considered, wrinkling her brow. 'Oh, no, I do not think that likely, Janet. Poor Tara is only a child.'

'So was that dirty little vagabond you found crying outside the gate and brought in to be washed and fed only last Easter. He stole a pie and one of the butler's best bottles of brandy before he absconded in the middle of the night.'

'Well, that was very bad of him,' Cassie agreed, 'but he could have stolen something far more valuable if he had tried, so I do not think him so very bad after all.'

Janet made a clucking sound in her throat, giving her mistress a dark look and shaking her head. 'One of these days you'll come unstuck, my girl. And I don't mind telling you!'

'I am sure you *will* tell me, Janet dear,' Cassie said with a wicked smile. 'Please, will you fasten this hook at my neck? I must not keep everyone waiting for dinner—that would be very bad of me.'

Janet continued to scold as she fastened the back of Cassie's very pretty, yellow silk gown, but knowing it meant nothing, Cassie let her mind wander. Lord Carlton had indeed stepped into the breach with admirable aplomb, taking the care and disposal of Tara out of her hands. She could not but be grateful for his understanding, because Janet was right and the situation might have been difficult.

She had never forgotten the incident with her kitten, but Lord Carlton had been younger then, not quite as self-possessed as he now was, and she had not known what to expect from him as a man of maturity. Over the past few days, she had discovered that he was both kind and generous—with a sense of humour that matched her own. He was, she thought, the kind of gentleman she had hoped to meet. No one could help being comfortable with someone of his temperament, which seemed almost perfect to her. Unfortunately, he did not show any signs of feeling anything more than friendship towards her.

Dismissing the very pleasant idea which had just

occurred to her, she turned her thoughts to the coming trip to town. In London she was sure to find other gentlemen who would find her—or her fortune—attractive.

When Lady Longbourne set out on journey she did not do things by halves. Besides her own, very comfortable carriage, there was a smaller one in which travelled her personal maid, Margaret, her dresser Anne, Janet and, as yet unbeknown to her, Tara: behind them came the baggage coach, filled to the point of collapse with her ladyship's indispensable possessions crammed into so many trunks and band-boxes that some of the young ladies' boxes had had to be strapped on to the second carriage.

Lord Carlton shook his head over the sight, but allowed no hint of his amusement to show. He kept clothes at all his homes, preferring to travel light. Refusing Sarah's offer to sit beside her in the carriage, he smiled and assured her that he intended to ride on ahead of them, but would always be within call if it should be necessary.

'Not that I anticipate any trouble,' he assured his mama as she shot him an anxious look. 'There have been no reports of highwaymen for months on this road, but I shall be near—so you need not look so worried, dearest one. I promise you are all quite safe.'

'And so I should hope,' Lady Longbourne said. 'For we may perfectly well take another groom or two with us if need be, Carlton.'

As each coach had beside the driver a groom to assist him, and another riding behind—just in case of accidents—Vincent did not think it necessary to make any last-minute adjustments to his arrangements. He merely smiled at his mother, tipped his hat to the young ladies, and prepared to mount his horse. It was a particularly fine-looking black stallion, which was already restive from the delay and pulled at the bit as soon as it felt its master on its back.

'Steady, Hermes. I know you are ready to speed like the wind, good fellow, but we must think of others today. No, no, do not show off. Remember your manners, sir!'

Calmed by the soft voice, which hid the strength beneath, like iron covered by a velvet sheath, the thoroughbred ceased to fret, controlling the wild, fierce urge to take off on one of the mad gallops he often enjoyed with his master.

And so the cavalcade set off at last, proceeding down the long drive and out on to the country road which would lead in time to the high road. Because of the recent dry weather, there were not so many ruts as there might have been and the carriage swayed gently behind the team of four, perfectly matched greys, personally chosen for his mother by Lord Carlton.

A Matter of Honour

'And so now we may be comfortable,' Lady Longbourne said. 'Dear me! Have I forgotten my vinaigrette?' She began to look about her for her reticule, but Cassie felt beneath her skirt on the seat and found it for her. 'Oh, thank you, my love. I should not have liked to ask coachman to stop so soon.'

'No, indeed, ma'am,' Cassie said, smiling at her. 'Nor indeed Lord Carlton. Gentleman do not seem to understand that one must have certain things with one, do they?'

'You are very right,' her hostess replied approvingly. 'Not that Vincent ever shows he is impatient. His father was very difficult. He often refused to travel with me…' A sigh escaped her. 'My dear Bertie was so very different. Nothing was ever too much trouble for him. I do not think I could ever find his like again.'

'Is that why you have not thought of remarrying?' Cassie asked, then blushed as Lady Longbourne stared at her. 'Forgive me, that was impertinent—but surely you are still young enough to enjoy the companionship of a gentleman?'

'Yes, I suppose I am,' Lady Longbourne said, looking thoughtful. 'Carlton is one and thirty—but I was a mere child when I married his father, not more than seventeen. I am not yet…well, not old enough to think myself a greybones just yet.'

'Indeed you are not!' Sarah and Cassie exclaimed in unison.

'It was my health, you see,' explained Lady Longbourne. 'After Bertie died, I…did not wish to live. We were so in love.' She blushed like a young girl. 'Of course, it was not fashionable to care so much for one's husband. As a gel, I was always told that love did not matter, that one man was very much as another—but I must tell you, my dear, that is simply not so! If you have a choice, choose a man who can make your life happy. Considerations of fortune and consequence are nothing beside it.' She laughed. 'There! I have been indiscreet. You will not hear such advice from others, believe me. Yet I would not see either of you made miserable by an unwise marriage.'

Cassie leaned towards her, kissing her cheek. 'How lucky we are to have found you, ma'am,' she said. 'I do not know how it is, but I have come to be so very fond of you in such a short time.'

Sarah agreed to it, and they began to converse very comfortably about all the delights that awaited them in town. Fields and trees gave way to villages, and towns, then countryside once more. They passed the time by little games of guessing, telling stories and making up new and very silly words, much as country folk often did when they had nothing else to amuse them.

'"So," Squire Come'ereanddoasyou'retold said to his wife, Lady Ishan'tunlessIwant, "you are nothing

but a ditheryfeatheryhalfwit." And said she, "You
are a numbskulldiggerynincompoop!"' Cassie
finished on a whoop of triumph. 'Twenty-five! I
think that is one more letter than yours, Sarah. I win.'

'Indeed, you are both quite mad,' cried Lady
Longbourne, laughing until the tears ran down her
cheeks. 'No, no, do not expect me to top that,
Cassie. You are much cleverer than me at this game.
I can do no better than hithercomescatterbrain.'

'I think I have one,' Sarah said and was just about
to pronounce her almost unpronounceable word
when all three ladies were startled by the sound of
a pistol shot, closely followed by two more.

'Mercy me!' Lady Longbourne cried, her hand
going to her heart. 'What on earth was that?'

The carriage had come to an abrupt halt. Cassie
pulled the sash and put her head out of the window,
to see Lord Carlton riding up to them at some speed.
He reined in tightly as he came near, and, catching
a glimpse of his face, she saw he was frowning.

'What happened, sir? We thought we heard shots?'

'There is nothing to worry about,' Vincent said
roughly. 'I have scared the rogue off. He thought to
take me by surprise, but I had been aware of him
skulking in the bushes for some time.' He dismounted
and opened the carriage door, looking anxiously at
Lady Longbourne, who was fanning herself and
looking as if she might faint. 'Forgive me, Mama. I

would not have frightened you for the world, but I thought it best to scare the rogue off by firing at him before he attempted anything untoward.'

'My…my vinaigrette,' Lady Longbourne said faintly. She moaned a little as Sarah waved the little silver box under her nose, but the restorative effects of the vinegar soon brought her round. 'I thought you assured me there were no highwaymen on this road, Carlton?' Her tone was accusing, as if she held her son personally responsible for the outrage.

'Forgive me, Mama, I was not aware of any attacks. Nor am I sure the rogue meant us any harm—but when I knew we were being followed, I thought it best to put a fright into him.'

'You have made me feel quite odd,' his mama said with a frown, but as she was sitting up by this time and had recovered her colour, he was not too anxious. 'But there, it is all the same. Your father never thought of my feelings either.'

Cassie saw the slight shadow of pain in Vincent's eyes and was a little cross with Lady Longbourne for having put it there. He had acted swiftly and with no thought for his own safety, for had the rogue been intent on harm he might well have fired back. She was not sure why the thought of Lord Carlton lying wounded—or dead!—in the road was so very distressing to her, but could not prevent a gasp of dismay. She flushed as his eyes were instantly directed at her.

'How very careless I have been,' he apologized at once. 'I was too impulsive and fear I have upset you, Miss Thornton—and Miss Walker, too.'

'No, not at all,' Cassie said, rallying immediately. 'I was a little startled, that's all—but I am sure you acted with the best intentions, sir. It would indeed have been very shocking if the wretched creature had shot you in the back and then attacked our carriage—especially as the other coaches are still some distance behind us. We might have been quite at his mercy…whoever he was. I think we must thank you for your prompt action.'

'As to that…' Vincent frowned. 'I am not so sure he did mean harm, for he was trying to conceal himself and rode off at some speed the moment I fired.'

'Indeed, yes, quite shocking,' agreed Lady Longbourne, recovering her composure. 'Well, well, I forgive you, Carlton, for I dare say you did not mean to give me palpitations.'

'I am truly sorry,' Lord Carlton replied with a look of affection for her. 'I think you may be easy, ladies, for I do not imagine the rogue will trouble us again.'

A groom had come down from the driving box and closed the door of the carriage as his lordship indicated that they should set out once more.

'We shall stop for some refreshment at an inn a few miles further down this road,' Vincent said, tipping his hat to them. 'Once again, my apologies for any disturbance I have caused you, ladies.'

Cassie leaned out of the window to watch as he rode off once more. What a fine figure of a man he was! She thought that he had behaved with great restraint, and wondered if he had ever lost his temper with anyone. Perhaps he was not a man who felt things deeply? And yet at times she had seen something in his eyes that told a very different story.

Had Cassie been privileged to see Mr Carter being summarily thrown out of the Hare and Hounds by his enraged landlord the previous evening, she would have been very surprised to discover that he was a man of violent passions and some considerable skill in the art of the pugilist. However, since Lord Carlton was a gentleman of the first water, who still held to his somewhat old-fashioned notions that ladies were to be protected and never subjected to the least unpleasantness if it could be avoided, she was not likely to learn that the brute who had so mistreated Tara had been well punished for his sins.

It was to Vincent's credit, however, that he always behaved well in the face of his mama's undoubted provocation, and, with a little flutter of her heart, Cassie had suddenly discovered that she had begun to like his lordship very much indeed.

It would be interesting to get to know him a little better.

* * *

'I do hope you have recovered from your fright, Miss Thornton?' asked Lord Carlton as they walked towards the inn. Lady Longbourne was just ahead of them, leaning on Sarah's arm and seeming none the worse for their adventure. He looked at her anxiously, having remembered the unfortunate circumstance of her father's suicide. 'It was most unfortunate that I should be forced to shoot my pistols.'

'I do have a dislike of guns,' Cassie admitted, and for one brief moment her face reflected a deep sadness as she recalled a certain afternoon she had tried very hard to forget. 'But I was only startled for a second. Once I looked out and saw you, I knew there was no reason to be afraid.'

Vincent was gratified by the compliment she had made him, for it was said so openly and unthinkingly, that he knew her to be speaking from the heart.

'Believe me, I would never let harm come to you if it were in my power to prevent it.'

'I know that, sir, and I am sure Lady Longbourne must also. She was just so—so shocked that she spoke thoughtlessly.'

Vincent's smile almost took away Cassie's power to breathe. For some unaccountable reason her heart suddenly raced violently, and she wondered what could be wrong with her.

'You need not be upset for my sake, Miss

Thornton,' he said gently. 'Mama has been used to blaming me when she is suffering from a fit of the blues, or feeling out of curl. I do not defend myself, because I know myself to be in part responsible for her unhappiness.'

'Why, whatever can you mean?'

Cassie's eyes widened as she stared at him.

'Sir Bertram was fishing with me the day he caught the chill that led to his developing a virulent fever,' Vincent explained. 'We had gone out early, thinking it would be a dry day. Unfortunately, there was a sudden storm. We were both soaked to the skin. I took no harm, but he…became ill and died soon after.'

'But that was not your fault!'

'No,' he acknowledged. 'But it was my suggestion that we spend a day fishing. I teased him into the trip, believing he spent too much time indoors. Mama warned me he was not robust, but I did not believe her. I thought the fresh air would do him good. Alas, I was quite wrong. I have regretted what followed a thousand times or more.'

'But your intention was good,' Cassie said. 'I cannot find that you are to blame, sir. Had he been a child in your care…but even then such things are often beyond our control.'

'You would absolve me of all sin, Miss Thornton.' Vincent's eyes reflected the warm, deep laughter he felt, but his expression did not falter. 'I am indebted to you.'

'A fig for that!' cried Cassie. His teasing made her heart do curious things. 'You cannot flimflam me, sir. I am awake on all counts.'

'Yes, I rather thought you were.'

Cassie laughed. 'Why have you brought Tara with us? I gave her money for her fare on the Mail Coach, and something to see her by until she found work. I cannot think that Lady Longbourne would be pleased to have the girl included in her household.'

'No, nor I,' Vincent said, his mouth quivering. 'Indeed, Tara told me about the money, and offered to return it.' The laughter left his eyes as he became serious. 'But I cannot believe that having rescued her from one evil master, you would want her to fall into the clutches of another?' He smiled as she shook her head. 'No, I did not think so. She was determined to go to London, so I suggested she should try working in my kitchens there. Apparently, she likes to cook given the chance, and I thought of making her Monsieur Marcel's assistant.'

'Is he your cook?' Cassie asked innocently.

For a moment Vincent relished the thought of Monsieur Marcel's reaction to being called a cook, but dismissed the tantalising vision with a suppressed laugh.

'I myself would not dare to call him that,' Vincent

murmured, his eyes dancing with mischief. 'He is French, you know, and a little temperamental. He is more used to being called an artist, or a miracle of culinary genius.'

'Ah, yes, I recall Jack telling me once that you were fortunate in having an excellent chef.'

'Fortunate? Perhaps. Though I sometimes wonder if life might not be easier—more peaceful—if I were to employ a cook.'

'You cannot have tasted Mrs Horton's milk puddings,' Cassie said, her eyes brimming with wickedness. 'Or what she mistakenly calls porridge. It would serve any master builder well as plaster, I promise you!'

'Indeed, I have been fortunate to escape that fate. I collect Mrs Horton is your own cook?'

'She was, but I have bequeathed her to Kendal with my very best wishes.'

Vincent nodded. 'That will just serve him right, will it not? For being so presumptuous as to imagine you were an object of pity.'

Cassie blushed. 'Perhaps I was too forceful when we spoke of this matter before, Lord Carlton. I dare say Kendal may have meant well, but it was the way he proposed to me…so full of his own importance. So sure that I had no choice in the matter.' Her eyes flashed. 'And Jack was hardly cold in his grave.'

'That was both tactless and unfortunate,' Vincent

said, and for a moment his eyes held a very peculiar expression that puzzled her. What could he be thinking?

'It was painful,' Cassie replied. She blinked hard as the tears stung behind her eyes, then looked up at him, determined to change the subject. 'Tell me, sir, do you think Monsieur Marcel will be pleased with Tara as his assistant?'

'I have every hope of it,' Vincent lied. 'One must assume he has a heart—and of course she will be only one of many under his command.'

Cassie suspected him of ulterior motives. Perhaps he wished to prick Monsieur Marcel's pretensions a little, but it was undoubtedly kind of him to take Tara into his own household. She was not sure it was quite wise to foist the girl on his chef, but if it suited his humour, it was not for her to question his decision.

'Then perhaps if there are so many he will not notice,' she suggested.

Vincent hoped she was right, but thought it a vain hope. Little did she know that he was running the risk of losing the services of one of the most sought-after chefs in London, and would find it difficult to replace him. However, he thought it worth the gamble and kept his own counsel. 'No, perhaps not.'

'Well, you can always find her something else to do,' Cassie replied blithely. 'She might become a parlour maid or some such thing, you know—or a lady's dresser.'

Carlton faced this thought without blanching. 'Yes, indeed she might. I wonder why I had not thought of it?'

Lady Longbourne turned to look back at them. 'Carlton! Why do you linger? Sarah and I are ready for our dinner.'

'I think we must join the others,' he said to Cassie. 'I shall of course let you know how Tara goes on, Miss Thornton.'

'I shall be very pleased to hear well of her.' She gazed up at him a little uncertainly. 'Do you not think that… when we are private together…do you not think you might call me Cassie?'

'Oh, I think I might,' he murmured. 'If you will return the compliment. My closest friends call me Vinnie.'

'Yes, I know. Jack always did in his letters to me. He was very proud of his friendship with you.' She took a deep breath. 'I have not thanked you for your letter to me. It—it was a comfort to me. To know that Jack and you were together just before he died…'

'You are kind to say so.'

Was that pain or guilt in his eyes? Cassie could not be sure. She did know that he had been deeply affected by her words, but there was no time to discuss the matter further even had she wished.

They had caught up with Lady Longbourne, and his attention was claimed by others.

Cassie was thoughtful as she followed behind, glancing about her with interest. It was a good clean hostelry, the yard swept and tidy, and inside it smelt sweet. The landlord, who had obviously been expecting them, ushered the party reverently into a private parlour, which was well furnished in polished oak. His manner was respectful, a little anxious as he assured Lord Carlton that everything was in readiness.

It was clear to Cassie that Lord Carlton had thought of everything for their comfort. Lady Longbourne still found cause for complaint, but that was her way and her son seemed not to notice. He was unfailingly polite and considerate to all of them. And yet, beneath the surface, Cassie was becoming increasingly aware of a private grief.

Just now and then, when he thought himself unobserved, she caught a strange look in his eyes: a look she thought could best have been described as haunted, and somehow that touched her deeply. She longed in those moments to reach out to him, to comfort him, understanding what it was to feel so alone—to carry a grief that no one else could share.

Cassie suspected another very different man behind the careless, polite, laughing face Carlton showed to the world.

And it made her wonder what was the secret sorrow he held in his heart.

It also made her remember the young man who had rescued her kitten, and the memories made her wistful. She had been a young girl then, untouched by grief…and not afraid to love.

Sometimes she thought that her feelings for Lord Carlton might be more than friendship, but when that happened she fought them, not wanting to admit that she was beginning to like him too much.

His lordship had been very kind to her, but she could not convince herself that he cared for her more than any other pretty young girl his mother might invite to stay with them. It was possible that when this visit was over she would not see him again for a long time.

If Cassie allowed herself to become too fond of Lord Carlton, it could cause her pain. She had lost too many people she loved, and she did not want to be hurt again.

Chapter Five

Lord Carlton's London residence was a very large spacious house in a pleasant garden square. As she was ushered in, to be waited on by the housekeeper, Mrs Dorkins, Cassie saw at once that everything was of the first elegance. The furnishings were in what she imagined to be the latest vogue, and with a French influence: chairs and cabinets of gilt and ebony in the Empire style were just some of the items that caught her eye as she was conducted to her own apartment.

'I hope you will be comfortable here, miss,' the housekeeper said. 'His lordship had it specially refurbished on his return from France.'

'Oh…' Cassie was surprised by the look in the woman's eyes. Almost as if there was some special meaning for her in what she had just said. 'It is very elegant. Rose and cream…quite charming. And I particularly like the embroidery round the curtains—it is a pattern of daisies, I believe.'

'Yes, miss. His lordship's apartments were done over at the same time, in crimson and gold.'

'Really? How suitable.'

'I thought you would like to know…'

'Thank you. I'm sure I shall be happy here, Mrs Dorkins.'

After the housekeeper had left, Cassie explored a little further. Besides the pretty bedroom, there was a sitting room in shades of green and yellow. One door, which she thought might have led to a dressing room, was securely locked. She tried the handle, then turned away, walking over to the window to look down at the small but colourful garden. Then, hearing a knock followed by a clicking sound behind her, she looked round with a little start to see Lord Carlton enter through the door which had previously been locked. The surprise showed in her face, making her frown.

'Forgive me if I startled you,' he said. 'I discovered the key to the dressing room had been mistakenly left my side. These rooms were of course meant to connect, but in the circumstances it is more fitting that the key remains this side. I must apologize for disturbing you. You need have no fear that I shall enter your room that way again; I did so only to give you this.'

He seemed oddly ill at ease as he laid the key on a chest of drawers and turned to leave.

'Am I to understand that these rooms would normally be occupied by Lady Carlton?'

'Were I married, yes. Forgive me, Miss Thornton. My orders were misunderstood. I asked for the best guest rooms to be prepared and…' He shrugged, clearly embarrassed. 'As you see, Mrs Dorkin's assumed I meant these rooms. If it makes you uncomfortable to be so near…'

'Not at all,' Cassie replied, her cheeks warm. 'You have given me the key. Besides, I know you to be a gentleman, sir.'

'I could have another room prepared at once.'

'I see no reason for it. These are lovely rooms and I feel privileged to use them.'

'Then I shall leave you to make yourself comfortable. Please, lock the door after me and place the key somewhere for safe keeping.'

He still seemed slightly awkward over the mistake and withdrew at once. Cassie locked the door and placed the key on the dressing chest, which was a very handsome piece of marquetry furniture.

At that moment a maid knocked, and, having been invited to enter, asked if she might unpack Miss Thornton's things. Cassie naturally gave permission, taking time to change her gown for a fresh one before going downstairs for tea. By which time any awkwardness she might have felt over being given the wrong rooms had been forgotten.

It was odd that the housekeeper should have made such a mistake, since most young, unmarried females would naturally be placed in rooms away from the gentlemen's, yet there was no real harm in it. Lord Carlton had acted exactly as one would expect on discovering the key his side of the door, and the door remained locked. As it would from now on, of course.

Over the next few days, Cassie had no occasion to regret her decision to remain in her pleasant room. She heard nothing of her host, nor did he attempt to enter her room. Indeed, she would have been surprised and not a little shocked if he had.

Now that they had returned to town, Lord Carlton was not often at home. He dined with them twice during the first week, but left afterwards to visit one of his clubs. And though he always made a point of speaking to Cassie at least once a day, asking her if she was comfortable and had all she needed, his manner unfailingly polite, she thought him more distant than ever. She was a little sad that this should be the case, for on the journey to town, they had seemed to be becoming friends.

Surely he could not still be feeling awkward because of a mistake over the rooms? Cassie had accepted the situation without a second thought. She could have insisted on being moved, but it would have occasioned gossip amongst the servants, and she saw no need for it. Indeed, she thought it would have been an insult to her host. She was in no moral or physical danger. Lord Carlton was hardly likely to creep into her room at the dead of night and seduce her!

Lady Longbourne was in any case occupying the rooms which had been intended for Cassie, and would not have liked to be moved. And if any of the servants sought to read anything improper in the rather unusual arrangements, they would soon be put to rights by Mrs Dorkins, who had seen the key amongst Cassie's things and apologized abjectly for her blunder.

'I am sure I do not know how I misunderstood his lordship, miss.'

'It is of no importance,' Cassie assured her. 'And as these are the very finest rooms in the house, there is nothing to apologize for, Mrs Dorkins.'

Slightly worried by Lord Carlton's withdrawal, Cassie found herself thinking about him more and more. It could not possibly be the rooms that made him look at her so particularly from time to time? No, no, surely there must be more behind Lord Carlton's very odd manner? Perhaps some personal problem of his own?

Had Cassie been a fly on the wall at a very heated exchange between Lord Carlton and Sir Harry—

which had not ended with Vincent giving his half-brother a facer, but a truly awesome set down!—she would have understood immediately. However, she was to remain in blissful ignorance of the situation for a while longer.

'Damn you for a gabblemongering fool!' Vincent had said, encountering his half-brother at White's after having been congratulated for the fifth time on his forthcoming nuptials. 'What on earth did you imagine you were about?'

All Harry's champagne-induced notions of a smiling, grateful Vinnie vanished like a summer mist. He stood silent and ashamed, wishing his half-brother would knock him down rather than look at him so accusingly.

'I spoke without thinking. I am most awfully sorry. But surely, it won't matter what people say or think once your engagement is announced?'

'And what makes you so sure it will be? Cassandra may not wish to marry me—or you. Or any of Jack's friends. She is an heiress and has come to town to look for a suitable match. This Banbury tale has scotched her chances before she has begun. Everyone believes she is about to become engaged to me. If she rejects me now they will call her a jilt—and what do you suppose they will call me if I do not ask her to marry me? *And* if I do, come to that! I shall be branded either as a rogue or a fortune-hunter.'

Harry wished fervently the ground would open and let him through, but, as usual in these situations, nothing of the kind happened and he was left to face his half-brother's anger.

'Were you foxed?' Vincent demanded furiously.

'No, not at the time.' Harry cringed beneath Vincent's contemptuous look. He had never seen his half-brother in such a temper. 'It was La Valentina. She asked where you were…and people were gossiping, laying bets about the possibility of your marrying her. As if you would! I decided to end the rumour—'

'And started another!' Vincent frowned as his anger began to cool, and he saw that in other circumstances it might have been amusing. 'You are an idiot, Harry. You've put me in an impossible situation.'

Far worse than Harry could ever have imagined. He was not privy to his half-brother's thoughts, but would not have learned much if he had been able to read them at this precise moment. Vincent's mind was in some considerable turmoil, torn as he was between making a clean breast of the whole thing to Cassie, and risking a scandal—or far worse, some hurt to her!—if the truth came out.

Quite unaware of the storm brewing, Cassie was enjoying all the visits to the dressmakers, milliners, glovemakers, and other shops where she purchased the various bits and pieces that were essential for a successful come out.

Several days passed before she had had time to catch her breath, and it was not until the day of her very first evening party that something happened which was to turn her world upside down.

'I have never had so much fun in my life,' Cassie said, twirling before the mirror in her room wearing one of the many new gowns which had been delivered that very afternoon. 'This is such a lovely evening dress, ma'am. It makes me look elegant. Not pretty, of course, but passable, I think.'

'You are more than that,' said Lady Longbourne, looking at her thoughtfully. Over the past few days, her feelings for the girl had grown ever more fond. It was true that Cassie was not pretty. She would never be that, but there was something rather special about her—an inner loveliness that might not be appreciated by all, but was plain to those who really looked. 'You are a handsome gel, Cassie. Any gentleman of sense will see that. I do not fear that you will be a wallflower this evening, my dear.'

'I hope not!' Cassie laughed and pulled a face at her in the mirror. 'I mean to be a success, ma'am.'

'And so you deserve,' replied her hostess with a smile.

It was to be Cassie's first venture into the critical

world of London society, which was very different from dining with friends in the country. She had, of course, already met some old friends of Lady Longbourne's, who had been delighted to discover she was in town and called to present their cards, take tea or issue invitations. Most of the ladies had brought their daughters to meet Cassie; they had all been amazingly kind and friendly, though as yet none of them had been accompanied by the gentlemen of their family. Which was, when one thought about it, a little strange, Cassie thought. But perhaps the news of her fortune had not yet gone round. She was a little disappointed, for it would have been pleasant to get to know a few gentlemen before she attended her first dance, but at least she was on nodding acquaintance with some rather important ladies.

'As I was saying—' Lady Longbourne was interrupted by a knock at the door of Cassie's sitting room. 'Come in!'

The housekeeper entered. 'Lord Carlton asks if Miss Thornton will do him the honour of speaking to him in his study, ma'am.'

'I shall come down directly,' Cassie said at once and thanked her.

'I wonder what Carlton can want?' Lady Longbourne said, frowning as Mrs Dorkins departed. 'You had best go down as you are, Cassie. I dare say he will not keep you more than a few moments. It is most inconvenient. We had not yet decided on your gown for this evening.'

'I believe I have decided,' Cassie replied, 'but if Lord Carlton wishes to see me, I must not keep him waiting.'

She ran from the room with a smile on her lips. Having seen very little of her host for the past several days, she had discovered that she missed him. It was the most ridiculous thing, but the very mention of his wanting to see her had set her foolish heart racing.

She paused outside the door of his study, momentarily disconcerted. Why had he sent for her? She could surely not have done anything to displease him? Unless Tara was in trouble?

Knocking once, Cassie heard his voice requesting her to enter and did so, peeping uncertainly round the door.

'You wished to see me, sir?'

'Yes, Cassie. Please come in.' He smiled at her as she did so. 'Thank you for coming so promptly.'

She was surprised at his use of her name, because although she had given him permission to address her as Cassie, he had not—until now. His own reserve had made her too shy to use his name, in case he thought her presumptuous.

She advanced slowly into the room, which was panelled in light oak and had many pictures of horses and dogs on the walls. There was a very large desk, its leather top spread with papers and various trinkets, two matching bookcases and several sofas and chairs. Obviously a gentleman's room, it yet had a light, airy atmosphere that Cassie immediately liked.

'Is something wrong, sir?'

'You promised you would return the compliment,' he reminded her gently. 'My name is Vincent—or Vinnie, if you prefer.'

A pale rose colour crept into her cheeks. 'Yes, of course I did—but I thought you might have changed your mind.'

'Because I have been distant these past few days?'

His directness startled her. 'Well…yes. I did wonder if I had offended you in some way.'

'You? How could you?'

Vincent was standing by the fire grate, which was laid with logs but not lit because of the warm weather. Now he moved towards her, and the expression in his eyes made Cassie's heart jerk. Why did he look so serious? Her heart raced and she felt oddly breathless. What was it about him that could make her feel so very peculiar sometimes?

'I must tell you that I have been wrestling with my conscience,' he declared with the air of a man who had come to a decision. 'It has been in my mind to ask you to do me the honour of becoming my wife, Cassie.' He heard her gasp of surprise, but ploughed on bravely. 'I have been distant these past days, because I felt it would be unfair to speak before you had had a chance to have your season. However, I find I cannot wait any longer…I must speak out now or forever be damned.'

There was no doubt in Cassie's mind that he was labouring under a heavy burden of emotion—and passion! Usually so calm, there was evidence of real torment in his eyes. His voice held a tremor and he could hardly bear to look at her.

Was he so much in love with her that he could not countenance the risk of losing her to another if he did not speak now? Cassie was shaken to the core by this revelation of a man she had only suspected might exist beneath the surface. To be regarded with such passion was more than she had ever dared contemplate—and it overwhelmed her.

Her voice was steadier than her heart as she said, 'Am I to understand you are making me an offer of marriage?'

'Yes, of course. Did I not make myself clear? How foolish of me.' He smiled oddly, then took her hand in his before going down on one knee before her. 'I have the highest regard for you, Cassie, and if you would consent to be my wife, I should count myself the most fortunate of men.'

'Yes. Yes, I will marry you.' The words flew out of Cassie's mouth before she'd had time to consider them. 'I had not expected to find great passion. I am not a beauty, sir. No, no, do not deny it. If indeed you have formed a *tendre* for me, my lord, it is not for my face. However, I do not question your regard, for I too have come to—to like you very well. And I think I could be comfortable as your wife.'

Vincent kissed her hand and stood up. 'I think we shall suit,' he said, a faint smile in his eyes. 'I am indebted to you for looking kindly on me, Cassie— and I hope you will always be pleased with your choice.' He took a ring from his waistcoat pocket. It was shaped like a daisy and set with beautiful diamonds. 'This is merely to seal our bargain. I shall send at once for the Carlton jewels, and you will no doubt find something you like amongst them.'

'I am quite content with this,' Cassie said. The ring fitted her hand perfectly and had a sweet simplicity about it that pleased her. 'This could almost have been made for me.'

It had indeed been made for her for several months, but Vincent did not mention this fact. One day he hoped to tell his wife the whole truth, but to do so now would only raise doubts in her mind, and that was something he wished to avoid. He kissed her gently on the cheek and smiled.

'You look very well in that gown,' he said. 'That particular shade of yellow becomes you, Cassie. Were you trying it on for this evening?'

'Yes.' She laughed up at him, perfectly at ease. His proposal had surprised her, but she was beginning to feel extremely pleased at the idea of becoming his wife. She did not know why, but it seemed right, as if everything had somehow fallen into its proper place. 'I'm glad you approve, sir...I mean Vincent.'

'I approve of everything you do,' he assured her. His eyes suddenly leapt with mischief. 'Ah, yes, now I think of it—I have been meaning to tell you about Tara...'

'Oh, dear,' Cassie said, pulling a face. 'Was Monsieur Marcel terribly displeased?'

'Only when she allowed some tartlets to spoil in the oven,' Vincent replied. 'He was, in fact, very appreciative of the trust I had placed in him. At least, I am reliably informed that he said that he would move heaven and earth to please me and that it would not be his fault if she went straight to—' He stopped short, recollecting that he was talking to a lady, though funnily enough it did not seem wrong to tell Cassie things he would never have repeated to his mother. 'Well, it was somewhere rather warm, but we need not go into that, I think.'

Cassie's laughter rang out. Vincent was struck by her looks at that moment, realising that there was a new sparkle about her. His surprise turned swiftly to admiration. Her beauty was not conventional, but it *was* there, inside her. At times she could, and did, appear almost plain. Yet now she was so vibrant that desire surged within him and he knew an urgent longing to sweep her up in his arms and make love to her.

'When shall we be married?' he asked, his voice husky with suppressed passion. 'It is very bad of me, Cassie, but I find myself impatient to have you to myself.'

Cassie blushed and looked down, her heart beating so fast she could scarcely breathe. 'We could announce our engagement this evening—and marry as soon as you could arrange it.'

'Thank you.' He bent to kiss her cheek once more. 'I shall tell Mama at once—and we shall have champagne. Yes, this must be a celebration. I will let you go and change your gown, Cassie, or it will be too crushed for you to wear this evening.'

She smiled and left him. Walking upstairs, she felt slightly dazed. It had all happened so quickly. Just over two weeks ago, Lord Carlton had been only a hazy memory. Now they were to marry, and Cassie could feel the beginnings of a very real, sharp joy spreading through her.

Vincent's proposal had left her in no doubt that his feelings for her ran deep. He had been very moved when he confessed his need to propose to her at once, that could not be doubted—even though it was hard for her to believe he could love her so much. He could have found a much prettier woman! And he had no need of her fortune.

For her part, Cassie had liked him at their first meeting, no, the second! At the first she had thought him a hero! For a few days she had in fact believed she was madly in love with him, but that was a girl's foolishness, of course.

Her feelings for Carlton now were very confused. She was aware of her own inexperience where gentlemen were concerned, and did not know what to make out of what was happening to her. Cassie had never had a love affair, nor yet a mild flirtation. As a young girl she had adored her brother and, apart from the incident when Carlton had rescued her kitten, had never met anyone who came close to touching that private inner core of her.

But now her sleeping heart had begun to respond to a man's teasing smile, to a wicked sense of humour and kindness. She had not looked to find real love in her marriage, yet now she could see how very pleasant a loving relationship might be. She remembered the look in Carlton's eyes when he had asked her how soon they could be married and was shocked at the immodesty of her own thoughts. Properly brought up young ladies were not supposed to think about things of that nature—at least until they were married. But she could not help imagining what it would be like to be kissed on the lips by her fiancé and…other things that made her blush and tingle all over.

Was it possible that she was falling in love with him? Cassie considered the idea. It was true that she always felt happier when Carlton was with her, that his kiss had aroused new sensations of excitement in her—but love?

She had not planned to love her husband, had convinced herself that she did not want to love anyone again—that it would be too painful—but now she was not sure. Perhaps this rather odd breathlessness she had begun to experience at the thought of Carlton kissing her was love. And she rather liked it.

If she was loved in return, might not that be the greatest happiness any woman could ever know?

And surely Vincent did love her? He had certainly seemed to be powerfully affected by his feelings for her. She felt a sudden glow of happiness as she hurried upstairs to impart the news to Sarah. How surprised she would be!

Sarah embraced Cassie, assuring her that she thought it all quite wonderful, but adding that she was not in the least surprised.

'I was sure Lord Carlton would make you an offer,' she told Cassie a moment or so after they had hugged. 'I could see it in his eyes when he looked at you. You are very lucky, Cassie. I like Lord Carlton, and I am certain you will be happy as his wife. Any woman must be content with such a man. He is so kind and has such pleasant manners.'

'Yes…' Cassie was thoughtful. All that her friend had said was true, but there was far more to Carlton than he let show. The secret nature he concealed from the world intrigued her, making her want to learn more of the man she had promised to wed—the real man. 'Yes, I suppose so. He does seem to be everything he ought…though can any man really be as perfect as he appears?'

'What an odd thing to say.' Sarah looked at her in surprise. 'You do wish to marry him, do you not? You do not sound very certain.'

'Yes. Oh, yes,' Cassie replied. 'I am quite sure of that. I was merely thinking aloud.' She was just not sure of her feelings! A marriage of convenience was one thing, a passionate love match quite another, and her thoughts were too confused, too private to share with anyone. She smiled at her friend, hiding her doubts. 'Now I am settled, we must concentrate on finding you a husband.'

'Oh…' Sarah sighed. 'I am afraid that will not be so easily achieved.'

'You are so very pretty,' Cassie said, sliding an arm about her waist. 'I am sure someone will fall in love with you instantly.'

'Perhaps.' Sarah blushed, avoiding her gaze. 'You will not go down to Brighton now, I suppose?'

'We shall remain in London for a few weeks, I expect. I am not sure where the wedding will be…but you will stay with me for that, Sarah. Please, say yes! I want you to be my chief bridesmaid. And I am certain we can find you someone you like before that.'

Sarah smiled but said nothing. She knew that her own case was very different from her friend's. She had overheard something Mrs Dorkins was saying to the butler—something she had thought a little strange. However, she was a sensible girl, and she genuinely liked Lord Carlton. Besides, servants' gossip was often misinformed, and to mention a few odd remarks when there was no way of knowing the truth could cause terrible harm. She had no wish to put doubts in Cassie's mind that were not already there, for she was extremely fond of her. No doubt Sarah was mistaken. Mrs Dorkins could not possibly have said that she had given Cassie the rooms adjoining his lordship's, because she knew they had been secretly engaged for years!

Cassie had no notion of her friend's anxieties on her behalf. Life had suddenly become much more exciting. Lady Longbourne had seized on the news of the engagement with delight.

'Oh, I knew how it would be when I first saw you,' she exclaimed. 'Your clothes were wrong, but I could see you had something about you, my dear. You were exactly what Carlton needed in a wife, not a cold, spoiled beauty, but a lady who will grace his household with charm and dignity. Septimus will not be able to scold me in future—nor will his odious brat step into Carlton's shoes. Felicity will be wild with disappointment, of course, but I am so happy! I shall enjoy having you as a daughter, my love.'

Having lived with Lady Longbourne for just over two weeks now, Cassie was well aware of her ladyship's dislike of her brother-in-law and his family. Although she had not yet met the infamous Septimus and his *odious* son, she had heard sufficient to be able to sympathise.

Lady Longbourne presented her with a pair of diamond-and-pearl bracelets as she was dressing for the evening.

'You should have the Carlton diamonds, of course, but no doubt Vincent will give them to you when you marry.'

In fact, Vincent sent her a gift a few minutes later. It was a choker of large creamy pearls with a small diamond pendant in the shape of a daisy. Very suitable for a young lady, but also stylish and obviously of the best quality.

Opening the box to exclaim in pleasure over the

gift, Cassie wondered how Vincent had managed to match the ring so perfectly in such a short time. And how had he known about her love of daises? As a small girl, she had spent hours making daisy chains. She had often crowned both herself and Jack with them.

'One day I'll buy you a real diamond necklace shaped like a daisy,' her brother had told her once. 'When I inherit the estate, you shall have everything you want, Cassie.'

'You will grow up and get married,' Cassie had teased. 'Then you'll forget me.'

'I might marry. I dare say I shall one day,' Jack had said, grinning at her. 'But you're my little sister, Cassie. I shall never neglect you. I shall always be there to take care of you—and when you marry, I shall make sure your husband treats you as he ought.'

'What will you do if he beats me?'

'I shall kill him!'

They had been children then, playing King and Castle in the sunshine, but Cassie had never forgotten her brother's words—or the chill that had run down her spine as he'd said them. She recalled them now in the midst of all the excitement.

Jack was so close to her, in her thoughts, as if she could almost reach out and touch him. She was drawn to her window, looking out into gardens shaded as the sun began to dip lower in the sky. What a glorious summer evening. Just as many evenings had been when she and Jack played together.

'How I wish you were here to give me away,' she whispered as she took a last glance at herself in her dressing mirror. 'But I know you would be pleased for me, Jack. Vincent was your best friend. You would approve of my marrying him. I know you would. You wrote to me about him so often.'

Jack's letters had glowed with praise for his friend. Everyone in the regiment looked up to him, he was always there for them, supporting them, pushing them to do better. Remembering the last letter her brother had sent her from France, just a few days before the war started, Cassie took it from her dressing case and read it through again. Jack had written:

Sometimes I am afraid for my life. More than that, Cassie, I am afraid I shall not acquit myself with honour. I could tell only you this, my dearest one, for I know you will understand. I do not want to die. I want to come home to you and all I hold dear—but if I deserted my friends now (or worse still, under fire) I should never forgive myself. If it were not for Vinnie, I do not think I could bear this waiting—it is the dread of what may happen rather than the fighting itself. God knows, I do not think myself a coward, Cassie—but there is so much good in life. Yet, if Vinnie is by my side, I believe I can face even death. With his help, I shall hope to do my duty and maintain the family honour.

Her poor, darling Jack! Cassie's heart ached for him, knowing how much he must have suffered before writing her such a letter. He was not a coward, could never have been a coward, but the thought of a violent death and the blood shed by his comrades had filled him with horror—as it must any man of sensitivity.

She blinked away her tears, replacing the letter in the secret drawer of her dressing case. She had shown it to no one and never would. Jack had died two days after it was sent. His grave was somewhere in France. She had never known exactly where. One day she would ask Carlton to tell her. Perhaps he would take her there.

Determinedly, Cassie locked her grief away. This was meant to be a happy night. She was about to make her début in society—and she was already engaged to a man who had been hunted by matchmaking mamas since he was first on the town! She was already a success. No one could possibly look down their noses at her now.

Besides, she would be with Lord Carlton, and they would probably dance together. Cassie's heart raced as she thought of being in his arms.

Was she foolish to let herself think of love?

She put away her doubts and fears. This was to be an exciting night—and she meant to enjoy herself!

It would have been impossible for a girl of Cassie's nature not to have enjoyed herself that evening. People were so amazingly kind to her. She had wondered if she would find herself short of partners, for she was already engaged and not on the marriage market. However, after she had danced first with Carlton and then with his brother Harry— who was just as charming and handsome as she had remembered—she found herself besieged with eager partners.

Many of the gentlemen were friends of her fiancé. Some had known Jack and spoke of him as a fine soldier. All were charming, attentive and willing to make her feel welcome in society. She was several times offered felicitations on her engagement, and everyone seemed aware that she was going to marry Lord Carlton.

'He and Jack were such good friends,' said a certain Freddie Bracknell. 'We might have known Vinnie would snatch the prize from under our noses. He always was a lucky devil!'

Cassie laughed, not quite sure of his meaning, but taking it as a compliment. 'We have known each other for years,' she said. 'Carlton was a good friend to me as a child.' She did not mention the incident of the kitten, but the reminiscent look in her eyes and the soft smile on her lips convinced her partner that this story of a long-standing engagement—which he had had good cause to doubt—must after all be true.

Strange, though, that Jack had made all five of them promise that one of them would marry her if he was killed. Freddie Bracknell thought wistfully of the long straw he had drawn. Had he had the presence of mind to have snapped it short, he might have been standing in Carlton's shoes. It was a damned shame! He could have done with the fortune Miss Thornton had inherited from some obscure aunt. Certainly he had had no suspicion of such an aunt, nor had the others...though Carlton was a damned knowing one. And, being Jack's closest confidant, he might have known in advance.

The idea rankled. The more he thought about it, the more convinced he became that he had somehow been cheated. After his dance ended, he went off to share a drink with Harry and commiserate with him over the prize they had both lost.

'What was all that nonsense with the straws?' he muttered, feeling considerably put out. 'If Vinnie knew he was going to marry her all the time?'

'It—it was understood but not spoken of,' Harry replied uneasily. 'I dare say either of them might have changed their minds—indeed, Vinnie was uncertain what to do right up to this afternoon.'

'You mean he hadn't asked her?' Freddie Bracknell frowned. It was months since Jack had been killed. Why had Carlton delayed all this time? 'I should have thought he would have done it an age ago. Damned smoky, ain't it?'

'No, of course it isn't,' Harry replied, uncomfortably aware that once again he had put his foot in it. 'He just wanted to be sure they would suit, that's all.'

'Might have given the rest of us a chance,' Bracknell muttered. 'If it ain't just like Vinnie to draw the short straw, then find out the girl's an heiress. Luck of the devil, that's all it is!'

Harry pokered up. 'If you're going to insinuate there's something havey cavey about it…'

Seeing the glint in his eye, Bracknell backed down hastily. Harry might not have as much skill in the art of boxing as his half-brother—who did!—but he was a damned fine shot.

'No, no, it was just a thought,' he muttered. 'Miss Thornton has obviously been expecting the proposal for years anyway. I gather they were great friends when she was still in the schoolroom.'

If they were, Harry knew none of it but he nodded slightly, allowing his companion to believe what he liked. Since Vincent had obviously decided to let the rumour stand, Harry wasn't going to risk another set down like the last one!

Such is the stuff of rumour and innuendo! Freddie Bracknell's conclusions were much as most other interested bystanders' that evening. And, as always, rumour builds upon rumour.

'I hear it was a love match when they were in leading strings,' one dowager repeated to another as they sat watching the young ones dancing. 'They were far too young to think of marriage, of course, and then circumstances parted them. Now Carlton has honoured his childhood promise to wed her.'

'I heard it was a match made by their parents when she was in her cradle,' replied her friend. 'I think that is more likely. Carlton has spread himself on the town for years, now he has done the decent thing and kept the promise made in his name. It is a matter of honour, Rosalind. Nothing more or less. You can't say she's a beauty.'

'No, she ain't a beauty—but there's something about her.'

'Her fortune? They say she has ten thousand a year!'

'As much as that? I heard it was less. No wonder Carlton made up his mind to have her in a hurry!'

Blissfully ignorant of all the gossip and speculation, Cassie danced on, round and round, enchanted by the music and the glittering jewels reflected in the light of many candles. It was a magic night, a night when sadness was far away and everything seemed dreamlike and wonderful. She wished it might go on and on forever.

Sarah was dancing every dance as well. For the third time that evening with Harry Longbourne! Which was a little unwise, perhaps. Cassie noticed and wondered at it, then forgot as Carlton came to claim her for the dance before supper.

His eyes were soft with amusement as he looked down at her glowing face. 'Are you enjoying yourself, Cassie?'

'Oh, very much,' she sparkled up at him. 'I wish I might go on dancing for ever.'

'You would tire of it eventually, I dare say.'

'Perhaps. But not tonight.' She gave a little gurgle of sheer pleasure. 'I have danced with so many of your friends.' She mentioned a few names, then paused as she saw something flicker in his eyes. 'Is anything wrong?'

'No, nothing at all. Shall we go down to supper now?'

Cassie laid her hand on his arm. She thought he was looking very splendid that evening in a coat of blue superfine that fitted him perfectly, accentuating the wiry strength of his body; his cravat was tied in a magnificent style that she knew was called *à la Fortuna*, and favoured by the more sophisticated dandies: there was some amusing story behind the style, but it was shared only by the gentlemen and no lady had yet been able to discover it!

Cassie was aware of a subtle change in his manner when she had mentioned Freddie Bracknell, or Captain Bracknell to give him his correct title. She knew they must have been in France together, in the same regiment as Jack—so what had caused that wary look in Vincent's eyes? Was there something she ought to know?

'Do you dislike Captain Bracknell?' she asked as he was silent.

'Lord, no,' Vincent said, glancing at her uncomfortably. She seemed to read him too well! 'Freddie is decent enough. He was one of us out there—but not a special friend to me.'

'Not like you and Jack?'

'No, not like that.'

For the briefest time Vincent's eyes took on the bleak, distant expression she had noticed before. She wondered what it meant, but this was neither the time nor the place to ask. One day soon, she would. After they were married, when they had the leisure to really talk of things that mattered.

Cassie became aware that someone was staring at them. A rather tall, statuesque lady, very beautiful in a dark, exotic way. She had the most compelling, magnificent eyes!

'Who is that?' Cassie asked, pressing on Vincent's

arm. 'That very striking, slightly plump lady. She is staring at us rather peculiarly. Do you know her?'

La Valentina would not have been best pleased to hear herself described as plump, and only the foolish or the brave would do so in her hearing. Statuesque was the word usually applied to a figure such as hers.

Vincent hesitated momentarily, then inclined his head towards the beauty. 'Everyone knows La Valentina. She is an opera singer. Her voice is beyond anything you have ever heard.'

'Oh…' Cassie had the oddest feeling he was trying to hide something from her. She waited for him to introduce her, but he merely nodded again to La Valentina in passing and drew Cassie on into the crowded supper room. 'I should have liked to meet her.'

'Another time. She is to sing after supper, and when she gives a performance she likes to save her voice.'

'Yes, I suppose so,' Cassie agreed, but felt that he had deliberately avoided the meeting. 'She must take care of her voice.'

'Forget her,' Vincent commanded, his harsh tone startling Cassie. 'Some things are best left alone. She is not important.'

Cassie was silent. Although largely innocent of the ways of the world, she was not stupid. She knew very well that men sometimes had mistresses, especially when they were unmarried. It was inconceivable that a man of Vincent's age and experience would have lived like a monk. She sensed there had been an intimate relationship between La Valentina and her fiancé quite recently, and she told herself it did not matter. It was over, of course. It must be, mustn't it? Yes, she was certain it was—and yet she could not help feeling hurt. Which was very foolish of her!

It would not do to let Vincent or anyone else see she had been upset by the chance meeting. She lifted her chin, looking about her and waving at Sarah, who was taking supper with Harry and Lady Longbourne.

'Shall we join your mother and Sarah?' she asked, her smile bright, fixed.

'Yes, of course. If you wish it.'

Vincent was frowning. Cassie was a very perceptive young woman. She had picked up the vibes coming from La Valentina at once, and he had spoken more harshly than he had intended in an effort to stop any doubts entering her mind. He had sensed her withdrawal, and knew she had been hurt, as much by his tone as the realisation of what was behind it. He was sorry she had been distressed by the meeting, but it was brief and could not have been avoided for ever. She must have learned of it one day: the gossips would see to that sooner or later. There was no help for it. His main worry was that she would hear something she might find even more disturbing. Cassie had intelligence and a sharp mind. She must know that his relationship with La Valentina had been merely a diversion, and had ended before he had proposed marriage to her.

Vincent had caught snatches of the gossip circulating that evening. People whispered that his marriage was a matter of honour—a promise redeemed at last after years of delay. That was Harry's doing, of course. The damned idiot! Yet had the truth got out…that might have hurt her even more. She had, even before her inheritance made her independent, been angered by her father's cousin's clumsy assumption that she would be glad to marry him. He could not imagine what she might think if she learned that her brother had extracted a promise from his friends that one of them would marry her—and that they had all solemnly drawn straws to see who went first!

She would be both hurt and angry. He had realised that almost at once after meeting her, and it was this that had made him withdraw. He had decided to let things drift, watch over her through her season, and then talk to her if she did not find someone she liked well enough to marry. Harry's blunder had forced him into proposing that afternoon. It was the only way he could think of to protect Cassie from the far more dangerous gossip that would have been occasioned had she not made her début as his fiancée.

He would not harm her for the world! Vincent smiled as he watched her talking and laughing with her friend and his family. Her hurt was easing now. She was coming to terms with the idea that he had had mistresses, as he had known she would. She looked directly at him, shy and yet wanting to believe in him, to believe that he cared for her, would not shame or distress her deliberately.

He felt an odd pain in his heart. What had begun as a duty, as a way of absolving his conscience—of banishing the dreams that sometimes haunted his sleep—had become very much more.

Cassie was so much finer than he had ever imagined. She had been his best friend's sister—a spirited girl he had once rescued from a tree. But now…now she was a woman he had begun to admire very much, and he was afraid he might actually be falling rather desperately in love with her. He was struggling to keep afloat against a flood tide, but thought he might be about to go under.

He believed she liked him very well. She trusted him, looked up to him as a gentleman and a friend of Jack's. The open, warm, sharing glances she sent him sometimes were enough to make him realise that he had never experienced anything like this in his life: it showed him a new world, a new, exciting way to live and he was anxious to explore all that that might mean.

But what if she ever learned the truth? Not just the foolish ceremony of drawing straws to see who honoured the promise to Jack—but the terrible, shameful truth that had overshadowed his life for a long time now, keeping him from seeking her out. The damning, terrifying reality that haunted his dreams and made him wonder if he would ever be free of this crushing guilt!

He had lived with guilt eating at him for months. Sometimes he woke from a nightmare, sweating, calling a name. And there was never a waking moment when he did not wish that he could turn back the clock…change what had happened. Especially now that Cassie had come to mean so much to him.

How would the woman he had learned to respect and care for feel if she ever discovered that he was responsible for the death of her beloved brother? That if it had not been for him, Jack might well still be alive? She would not smile at him so trustingly then. She would turn from him in disgust and horror—and how could he bear that?

Chapter Six

The past ten days had passed in a whirl of pleasure. Mornings were usually spent either driving or walking in the park, visiting the lending library, or shopping; afternoons, either visiting or outings to places of interest. Any of these innocent pastimes was liable to lead to a meeting with some of the new friends Cassie was making, and were all equally enjoyable to both her and Sarah.

Quite often Vincent escorted her and Sarah in the afternoons, and sometimes he took her driving alone in his carriage. She had mentioned her wish for a smart turnout, something that she might learn to drive herself in the country, and he had promised to look into it. Once again, they seemed to be becoming friends and Cassie was well pleased with her situation.

The memory of that look in La Valentina's eyes—which had spoken volumes, letting Cassie know exactly what the opera singer thought of the plain dab of a girl Carlton had chosen to marry!—had lingered like a nasty odour. Despite all her efforts to dismiss it as unimportant, Cassie had not quite been able to put her thoughts aside; they rankled and pricked at her like a stone in her shoe. Because, of course, La Valentina was so beautiful. And Cassie could not understand why any man should prefer her to such a woman. Had Lord Carlton been in an awkward financial position, she would have understood perfectly, and, had he been honest with her, she believed she would still have accepted him—but he was one of the wealthiest men in London. So why did he wish to marry her? She was not exceptional in any way.

The thing Cassie hated above all else was falseness. She had always been a very honest girl herself, and hated lies and deliberate deception.

However, her fiancé had made it plain by his manner that evening that the beautiful opera singer meant nothing to him, and she had tried very hard not to be jealous of his affair with her.

'You must not expect too much,' she told herself seriously when she was alone in her bedroom, gazing into a mirror which refused to lie. 'Why should he have fallen desperately in love with you, Cassie Thornton? You read too much into that look. It is enough that he likes you! He does not have to love you.'

It was and must be enough. Cassie knew there was no turning back, nor did she wish for there to be. Whether Vincent loved her or not, she was sure that they could at least be friends. Besides, everyone took it for granted that she would marry Carlton. Indeed, of late, she had begun to realise that many people seemed to believe that theirs was a long-standing affair. She wondered how the rumour had sprung up. Because of the friendship between Jack and Vincent, she supposed, and the fact that they had been close neighbours for some years.

'It is so amusing,' she told Sarah that morning as they were strolling together in the park. 'People must always gossip and make up stories!'

Sarah was silent for a moment, then, 'It does not bother you that they should say such things?'

'Good gracious, no!' Cassie laughed out loud, causing one or two heads to turn. People smiled to see the two young girls walking together in the park, a maid following just behind should she be needed, as was proper. 'Why on earth should it? I know the truth. We hardly met in those days—except for the time Carlton rescued my kitten. And then we exchanged only a few words before he hurried away to change his breeches.'

'You are wise to ignore the gossips,' Sarah said. 'It is obvious that Lord Carlton cares for you. He would not otherwise have proposed so soon.'

'Yes. I think—' Cassie stopped speaking, gasped and caught her friend's arm as she recognised the man coming towards them. 'Oh, no! What can I do to avoid him? He is coming this way and he has seen us. What a nuisance…'

'Who?' Sarah looked about her, startled by the urgency in Cassie's tone. 'Do you mean that man in the ill-fitting brown coat and grey breeches?'

'Who else would walk in a London park dressed like that?' Cassie groaned. 'It is Kendal Thornton—Father's cousin.'

She looked so dismayed, poised, as if on the verge of flight, that Sarah laughed and shook her honey-gold curls at her. 'You cannot run away from him, even though he *is* sadly lacking in town bronze. He is your only relative, after all. You must at least say good morning to him, dearest.'

'It is not only a sense of style he lacks,' Cassie hissed agitatedly. She would have said much more, but was obliged to desist as Sir Kendal approached, planting himself firmly in her path and clearly determined to address her.

'Good morning, Miss Thornton.' His thick eyebrows knitted in a frown, and Cassie thought he resembled nothing so much as a bad-tempered bulldog. 'Can it really be you? I must confess I am surprised to see you here.'

His eyes went over her, noting her stylish gown and all the accompanying trifles that proclaimed her a lady of fashion.

'Indeed?' Cassie bristled. 'I cannot imagine why anything I choose to do should surprise, or even interest, you. I believed when we last parted we had nothing more to say to one another.'

'Now, now, Cassandra,' he said, giving her his irritating, pompous smile. 'No need to fire up like that. I have realised it was foolish of me to have spoken so soon. I was concerned to set your mind at rest as to your future standing, but did not reckon with your natural grief. You were upset and that was my fault. I shall not hold your rash words against you. In fact, I am perfectly willing to make you another offer here and now, if you wish?'

'You would be foolish to do so, sir,' Cassie replied, eyes flashing. 'I meant what I said the first time. Forgive me if I am rude, but I must make it plain to you that I have no wish to marry you—nor to meet you again. Or at least, only as a distant relative, with whom I am on nodding terms.'

'You are a very stubborn girl, Cassandra. I have no idea where you found the money to come to town, but…'

'That is none of your affair,' Cassie said, very

angry now. 'I have touched nothing that was by law yours. As it happens, I am the guest of Mama's closest friend. Lady Longbourne wrote to me, inviting me to stay with her and—'

He glowered at her, clearly put out by the news. 'That is as may be, but you cannot put a mere acquaintance before kinship. You ought properly to have sought my permission for the visit. You deny it, Cassandra, but as your only living relative, I do have some say in how you conduct yourself.'

'No, you do not!' Cassie said, holding her temper by a whisper. 'My father never liked you, sir. He would never have left me to your care. And if you have anything further to say on this matter, please address it to my fiancé—Lord Vincent Carlton. If you care to trouble yourself, you will soon discover that our engagement is of a long-standing nature, arranged by my father years ago. I am sure Lord Carlton will be happy to put your mind at rest on this matter if you have any doubts about my future.'

Sir Kendal's mouth fell open. Cassie saw her thrust had gone home, leaving him temporarily at a stand, and, taking Sarah's arm, she walked on. He stood, staring after her for several minutes, but made no attempt to follow.

It was a moment or two before she was calm enough to speak, and when she did so, it was of a balloon ascension they were to attend on Hampstead Heath later that day.

'Carlton says it will be an awe-inspiring sight,' she said conversationally. 'I am rather looking forward to it, you know. I imagine it must be very exciting to ride in the basket, don't you?'

'Oh, no,' Sarah said faintly, but with a look of admiration in her eyes. 'I should be terrified.'

'That awful man!' Cassie burst out, unable to hold back a second longer. 'I could not speak of him for a moment, for fear of offending your ears with words unbecoming to a lady. Words Jack sometimes used, you know.' She coloured slightly. 'I should not, of course. But it makes one feel so—so cross. How dare he? Oh, I wish I were a man. I would make him sorry he had ever been so presumptuous as to force his attentions on me when I have already made it plain they are unwelcome.'

'But, dearest,' Sarah pointed out reasonably, 'were you a man, he could not have done so.'

Cassie stared at her for a moment, then began to gurgle with laughter, her anger melting. 'Oh, how foolish of me! Of course he couldn't. I should have inherited the title and estate, shouldn't I?' She sighed. 'Why does he wish to marry me? Do you suppose he knows of my inheritance but is pretending not to? I cannot see why he should persist otherwise, can you? If only Jack had not been killed. I do miss him! He should have been here, sharing this with us, Sarah. He would have loved it so!'

'Yes, dearest. I wish he was, too, for your sake.'

Cassie smiled and hugged her arm. It was very odd, but she had a very strong feeling of Jack being close to her at that moment. She almost expected him to come riding up on his horse, jump down and swing her up in his arms as he was used to when they were together, and the tingling in the nape of her neck was so fierce that she glanced around as if to see him.

She could, of course, see no one resembling her brother. There were several gentlemen walking or riding along the bridle paths, sometimes in small groups, with ladies or alone, but no one who looked in the least like Jack. She caught a glimpse of a beggar hobbling towards her, a crutch under one arm, but just as she was thinking of looking for a shilling to give him, she heard a shout and turned to see Lord Carlton striding towards her. She waved and called his name, and when she looked again, the beggar was shuffling away in the opposite direction.

'Cassie!' Vincent cried as he came hurriedly to join them. 'Mama told me she thought I might find you here. I hoped I should, because the time of the balloon ascension has been brought forward an hour. If you do not wish to miss it, you must come home and change at once.'

'We were just about to do so,' Cassie said as Vincent companionably offered an arm to both of them. 'We would not miss such a sight for the world!'

'No, indeed, we would not,' agreed Sarah. 'We were only just talking of it, were we not, Cassie?'

'Then there is not a moment to be lost,' said Vincent, smiling at them.

The occasion was one of huge excitement that afternoon. A great many fashionable ladies and gentlemen had turned out in their carriages to watch the exciting event. Many had brought hampers with them, intending to picnic on the Heath afterwards. Some intended to follow the balloon's flight for as far as they could in the carriages or on horseback.

'Is this not thrilling?' Cassie asked as she, Sarah, Vincent and Harry sat together on a grassy bank, watching all the preparations. Several men were at that moment engaged on spreading the balloon on the ground. 'How will they ever get such a large contraption to fly? It does not look possible.'

'What are they doing now?' Sarah asked. 'Pray tell me, what is that pump thing for?'

Lord Carlton explained the principles of heating a gas that was lighter than air, which made the balloon float. 'The first balloons were invented by the Montgolfier brothers and flew in 1782 at Annonay near Lyons. They were filled with heated air, but soon after hydrogen was tried successfully. Once the balloon is filled with the gas, they have to tie it down to stop it breaking away. That is what those ropes are for. They have to be very careful or it would float off without them—indeed, that has been known to happen to some amateurs. However, I think our balloonist today is an expert.'

Cassie nodded, watching in fascination as the huge, colourful bag began to inflate. Just as Vincent had said, several men were hanging on to the ropes, pegging them down and shouting to one another as it heaved and tugged this way and that.

'I understand how they get up—but what happens when they want to come down?' Sarah was asking.

Leaving Vincent to satisfy Sarah's curiosity, Cassie moved a little nearer the balloon. It was very noisy and confusing, and she hovered at the edge of a group of excited children, knowing she must not get any closer for fear of getting caught by a stray rope should one break free.

'Cassie…' The sibilant whisper sent a little shock through her. 'Cassie, I need you…I need your help.'

'Jack!' She whirled round, looking for her brother amongst the crowd. That was his voice! She was certain of it. But where was he? She looked and could not see him. People were milling all around her, pressing forward to secure a better view as the balloonist announced he was almost ready to take flight. 'Jack—where are you?'

Suddenly, a rope snapped and the huge balloon lurched drunkenly on one side, scattering those who had ventured too close. Several ladies screamed and a man rushed past Cassie, nearly knocking her flying; the next moment Cassie's arm was caught and she was firmly guided away from the crowd.

'You must not stand so near,' Vincent said, looking at her in concern. 'It is not just the balloon itself which might be dangerous, Cassie. When people panic, others can sometimes suffer. I would not have you crushed.'

'No. It was foolish of me.'

Cassie's voice was breathless, her face very pale. She had scarcely noticed the panic over the wayward rope, which had now been secured while the balloon was righted once more. Surely she had heard Jack's voice close behind her? She could not have been mistaken! That voice had been—was still!—so dear to her. Jack had been there with her. She felt it in her heart. And yet that was impossible. Jack was dead.

'You are distressed,' Vincent said. 'Would you like to go home? Are you feeling unwell?'

Cassie shook her head, forcing a smile. 'No, no, I am perfectly well, thank you. It was just the shock…just the shock.'

The shock of hearing Jack's voice from beyond the grave. She had felt him close to her for some weeks now, but this was the first time he had tried to speak to her. Why here? Why now? Why not when she was lying alone in bed and could listen to him?

'Thank goodness I was close at hand,' Vincent said, bringing her back to the present. 'Are you faint?'

What a missish creature he must think her to make so much fuss over a silly fright! Cassie tugged her composure back into place. She could not tell her fiancé the true reason for her distress, because he would think her mind was wandering—as indeed it must be!—but she did not like him to think her such a sad case.

'Not at all,' she cried, rallying. 'It is all very exciting. Oh, Vinnie, do look! I believe it is going to fly.'

She hugged his arm, looking up at him in such a way that he was moved to kiss her, very gently on the lips. Cassie blushed and smiled at him.

'I could not resist,' he excused himself. 'You looked so much like an excited child.'

Cassie was not certain she cared for such a description, but made no reply. Then her attention was diverted as a heartfelt sighing issued from the onlookers. She looked skyward as the magnificent balloon rose majestically into the air, carrying its wicker basket and two passengers beneath it.

Cassie shaded her eyes to watch as it rose steadily,

then began to move with the currents of air, gradually drifting further and further away across the Heath.

'Oh, it has almost gone…' she said regretfully.

'Do you want to follow?'

'No—not unless Sarah or Harry does.'

'Shall we ask them?'

Sarah having declared herself satisfied with what they had already seen, Vincent popped the bottle of champagne his butler had packed for the occasion and they drank toasts to each other and ate some of the delicious trifles Monsieur Marcel had conjured up for them.

The afternoon passed away in pleasant idleness until at something past the hour of three, it suddenly became much darker overhead.

'We ought to be getting back,' Vincent said as he heard a rumble of distant thunder.

Harry and Sarah had been strolling together a little way from the carriage but, realising there was a threat of rain, came rushing back. Then, all at once, it began, tumbling down in a torrent of huge drops that hit the ground and bounced up again. The sudden downpour made everyone else hurry to pack up picnics and take shelter. Those fortunate enough to have closed carriages gave the order to move off, though the general rush made the narrow roads congested.

It was as they were passing a stand of thick trees

that Cassie happened to notice the figure taking shelter there. He was huddling into a shabby great-coat. An old soldier by the look of him, long, straggling grey hair sticking out beneath the shapeless hat jammed down tight over his forehead. Cassie was not certain why she turned her head to get a closer look as they passed. She had an odd feeling that she might have seen the man before…quite recently.

The beggar in the park that morning? No, she did not think so. Both were obviously vagrants, but this man did not have a crutch. He was just standing there, looking dejected and getting very wet. She could not know him. It was all in her imagination. Just like hearing Jack call her name!

Cassie sat back with a sigh. Of course she hadn't heard Jack call her. How could she? In her heart, she did not really believe it was possible for someone to return from the grave—though it was possible to feel them near you in spirit: that she knew for certain.

'Is something troubling you?' Vincent asked softly in her ear. 'You have not seemed yourself this afternoon.'

'Nothing is troubling me,' Cassie replied, not quite meeting his eyes. When he looked at her that way it made her heart do strange things. And she was not sure she ought to let herself care too much: gentlemen did not always appreciate clinging vines. 'Thank you for taking us to the balloon ascension. It was exciting.'

'You know I would always please you if I could, Cassie.'

'Yes, of course. You are so thoughtful. Please do not worry about me, I am perfectly happy and well.'

Vincent nodded, but his eyes were watchful. Something had seriously disturbed her that afternoon, but she had made up her mind not to tell him what it was that had caused her to come close to fainting. He regretted the fact that she was not inclined to confide in him, but he could only hope that she would learn to do so in the future. Perhaps when they were married, she would feel able to trust him…and then perhaps he could find a way to explain to her what was in his heart.

The pleasures of London continued apace: escorted rides in Rotten Row, visits to Almack's, that hallowed place of patronesses and privilege, the gardens at Vauxhall where the fireworks were only one of the delights on offer, and a succession of private lunches, dinners, musical evenings and dances. Cassie gave herself up to the excitement, forgetting everything else as the day of her wedding came nearer.

Jack seemed to have gone away from her again, and she knew it was time she let go of her grief. She had a new life ahead of her, and she was looking forward to it more and more as the days passed.

Because surely Vincent must care for her? She must forget that look in La Valentina's eyes, the look that had told her she was a mere nothing. Vincent had asked Cassie to marry him—why would he do that if he did not feel some strong emotion towards her?

She must forget she had ever seen his mistress!

And yet he had called her a child the day they had watched the balloon ascension. She wanted him to think of her as a woman he could share his life with, not someone he must always flatter and indulge as he did his mama.

They were to be married from Sir Harry Longbourne's house. A town affair had been discussed and dismissed. It was fitting that Cassie should be married at the village church in which she had always worshipped. After the ceremony, Lord and Lady Carlton would spend a few days alone at his Hampshire estate, then leave on an extended tour of France, and perhaps Italy if they cared for it. When they returned from their trip, their house in Surrey would be prepared to receive its new mistress. Lady Longbourne would have returned to Carlton House, and they would divide their time between the two estates and the house in London.

'It will be very suitable,' Lady Longbourne declared herself satisfied with the arrangements. 'Carlton can take himself off to Surrey for a few days after he has seen us safely to Longbourne, and come back a day or so before the wedding. I am sure he can find somewhere to put up for a night or two. We shall be at Longbourne. It will be almost as if you were being married from your own home, my love.'

'Yes, but much better,' said Cassie. 'For I should not want to be living there now that Sir Kendal has taken it over.'

Cassie had not chanced to meet her father's cousin again since that morning in the park, and was truly grateful for it. She hoped she would not have to see him again, and was at first adamant that he was not to be invited to the wedding.

'But surely you must,' Lady Longbourne said, slightly shocked by this obstinacy in a girl who was usually so amenable. 'I know you do not care for him, and I understand that you would not precisely wish to have such a man present at your wedding feast, but not to invite him—it cannot be done. I heartily dislike Septimus and his family, but I shall invite them. I could not do otherwise for politeness' sake.'

Cassie held out for as long as she could, but was forced to give in when Vincent told her very firmly that in this case his mother was right.

'It would be unforgivable,' he said. 'You must send him an invitation, Cassie.'

'Oh, very well,' she said, realising that her husband-to-be was not quite as easygoing as she had imagined. There was a very firm hand beneath the velvet glove he used to stroke his mama with, and even Lady Longbourne knew that there was a point beyond which she might not go. 'If it is your wish.'

'Sir Kendal is your only family,' Vincent said, giving her an odd look which she was not able to interpret, not having been present at a certain interview with her distant cousin. 'If he upsets you, you may safely leave him to me, Cassie. I will engage to put him in his place for you.'

Cassie said nothing, merely looking at him from beneath her thick, dark lashes. It struck her then that she really knew very little about the man she was so soon to marry. She had seen only his public manners, which were very pretty, but perhaps not a true representation of the real man.

Something in his eyes at that moment disturbed her, making her heart jerk, and she turned from him to Sarah, beginning to talk to her about the ball they were to attend the following evening. It was given by the Duke of Devonshire and his duchess and was one of the grandest affairs of the season.

'Shall we go and try on our new gowns?' she said, then looked at Lady Longbourne. 'Will you come with us, ma'am? To advise whether or not we need any last-minute adjustments?'

Lady Longbourne agreed at once and the three of them went off together. Excluded from their plans,

Vincent sat frowning over his own thoughts. Cassie was keeping something from him, he was sure of it. Something that had disturbed her at the balloon ascent. And since that afternoon, he had felt a slight withdrawal in her. He was sure there was something on her mind—yet what could it be?

She appeared to be perfectly happy with the arrangements for the wedding; however, he had caught an odd thoughtful expression in her eyes at times when she thought herself unobserved. What was worrying her? He would have liked to ask, but found it difficult. She was entitled to her private thoughts, as he was to his—but he could not help wondering whether perhaps he had been unfair to her in proposing to her so swiftly.

Might she have found someone she preferred if she had been free? The question played on his mind, especially when he saw her looking at him as if she did not quite understand why she had promised to wed him. Or was that his imagination? Was there something else upsetting her?

If she would only confide in him. Yet he could not blame her when he carried a far more terrible secret in his own breast—a secret he was not sure he would ever be able to confide in her.

The ballroom was a sad crush and therefore the evening a huge success, just as it had always been meant to be. Cassie was wearing a very elegant gown of saffron yellow with a scooped neckline, a white ruched sash, and little puffed sleeves. A band of white daisies had been embroidered on the hem of her gown, and round the edge of the sleeves. Her dark hair had been swept back into a smooth chignon at the nape of her neck, one shining ringlet allowed to fall on her shoulder. In her ears she wore a pair of magnificent diamond earrings, shaped like daises, and the pendant Vincent had given her on the occasion of their engagement was around her throat.

'You look charming, Cassie,' Vincent told her just as they entered the crowded room. He touched her hand, setting her pulses racing like the wind. 'I am very proud of my fiancée. Please save the supper dance and at least one other for me?'

'Of course.' She smiled up at him, her heart catching as she caught a look in his eyes. 'You may have the first waltz, sir.'

He preferred it when she called him by his name, but she did so only on rare occasions. Usually when she was excited—as she had been at the balloon ascension.

'Enjoy yourself, Cassie,' he murmured as he saw a group of her friends beckoning. 'We have only another few days before we leave for the country, and this is the last ball we shall attend before then.'

'Yes. I have not forgotten.'

'I shall leave you now,' Vincent said. 'But I shall return to claim my dances.'

Cassie nodded as he raised her hand to his lips briefly, then wandered off to speak to various acquaintances. She knew that, like many other gentlemen present, he would probably play a hand or two of cards during the evening. She did not think him reckless at the tables, but amongst his friends gambling was very much favoured, and he would have been thought very odd had he stayed by his fiancée's side all evening.

Nor did she expect it of him, of course, though sometimes she thought privately that it might be pleasant to spend some time alone with him, to really talk to one another. That was not possible, however; they were both engaged with friends every day, and the evenings were often so filled with entertainments of every kind that they were forced to go from one house to another. This evening was one of the big events of the season, and would be spent entirely at the Devonshires' magnificent house.

Cassie was now very much at home amongst these people, having made a large acquaintance and several friends whose company she really enjoyed. So when she was introduced to a gentleman called Major George Saunders, who immediately asked her to dance, she merely handed him her card and forgot him until he came to claim his dance.

'I have only just come to London,' he told her with a frank, open look that was immediately appealing. 'I have long wanted to communicate with you, Miss Thornton, but rather than write I felt it would be better if we could meet in person. Had I not been detained on family matters, I should have called on you in Hampshire months before this. I wanted to tell you that I had the highest regard for your brother. Jack served under my command, and I believe he trusted me. We were certainly friends.'

'Yes, sir. I believe he did mention your name in his letters once or twice,' Cassie said. She liked him immediately. 'It is a pleasure to meet you, Major Saunders.'

'The pleasure is all mine. Jack spoke of you so often, Miss Thornton. He made many a lonely evening by the camp-fire seem brighter by telling us stories about his sister. There were usually five or six of us, including Jack himself, and I must tell you that you won all our hearts. I particularly recall a story about an irate man and a donkey…'

'Oh, no!' Cassie gazed up at him, a wicked sparkle in her eyes. The laughter bubbled up inside her. This man was reminding her of the happy times, and it was good to talk so easily of her brother with him. 'Did Jack truly tell you about that? It is too bad of him! My father was furious with me. I suppose I must have been about thirteen at the time.'

'Did you really steal the donkey from the tinker and smuggle it up to the nursery while your parents were out dining with friends?'

'Yes.' Cassie's laughter rang out. 'But she made such a terrible noise when I left her alone. The servants came running to see what was going on, so I was discovered. And the next morning the tinker came up to the house to claim his donkey; he threatened terrible things but Jack had a fight with him, and then Father had to pay him ten guineas to compensate him for the loss of his donkey. And it cannot have been worth a fraction of the price, for it was half-starved and its hooves needed attention from the farrier.'

Major Saunders was obviously hard put not to laugh as he asked, 'But you kept the creature?'

'Oh, yes! I could not have let the poor thing go back to be beaten and starved again. Especially after my father had made such an investment in its well-being.'

This time Major Saunders let out a bellow of laughter, that caused heads to turn and stare at them. 'What a remarkable young lady you are!'

'My father scolded me for days afterwards, but Jack bought me a fine leather harness and we used to take Miss Carrot Stubbornhooves for walks.' Cassie dimpled naughtily as his eyebrows rose. 'We called her that because sometimes she simply stood her ground and would not move—unless we gave her a carrot.'

'Stubborn creatures, donkeys. I often think some ladies are much the same—at least my dear mama and sisters have very similar characteristics.'

This time it was Cassie's turn to laugh. She was caught by a fit of the giggles and for a moment they were forced to stop dancing until she recovered enough to continue. She gave him a look of warm approval as he stood patiently for her to recover. He was such an amusing, understanding companion. Not a particularly handsome man, of course, rather too large and bluff to be thought fashionable, but comforting to have around one. The kind of man who would always be there in a crisis, she thought.

She was still smiling as they parted. When she returned to Lady Longbourne, she found Vincent waiting for her. He was frowning and she sensed that he was displeased about something.

'Is it our waltz now?' she asked. 'Did you see me dancing with Major Saunders a moment ago? He said that Jack often told stories about me by the camp-fire. We were laughing about a donkey I once stole from a tinker—' She caught her breath at the look in Vincent's eyes. 'Is something wrong? Are you angry with me?'

'How could I be angry with you?' he asked. 'Forgive me if I seemed distant. I was thinking of something…'

Jack had told the story of the donkey the night before he made the five of them promise that one of them would marry his sister. George Saunders had agreed instantly. Indeed, he had seemed disappointed not to draw the short straw later. Vincent had noticed the inquiring look sent his way. Had he guessed then that all the straws were the same length, and that Vincent had snapped his own in half, making certain that he would be the one to ask Cassie first? If so, he had made no comment.

As he took her hand to lead her out on to the dance floor, Vincent decided he must have a word with George later that evening. Saunders was a decent fellow, but apt to say whatever was in his mind. Vincent did not want his fiancée to hear the story of the straws from anyone else but him.

Cassie could not read Vincent's thoughts as they danced. He held her carefully so as not to crush her gown, one hand placed lightly at her waist, his manner slightly distant. When she spoke to him, he looked down and smiled, but answered as if his mind was far away.

Was he angry with her? Cassie wondered. She could not see that she had done anything to upset him. Yet she felt that he was holding back from her. Or was his reserved manner simply indifference? Was this how it would always be between them?

He would be polite, charming, but not really interested in her.

The thought hurt more than she had imagined it could. His proposal had been made with such passion! She had been misled into thinking he really wanted her for his wife, but now she had begun to doubt. But, oh, she must not doubt him now!

Why else would he have asked her to marry him? She simply did not understand his reasoning. If he did not feel any more than liking…why ask her in such a rush? Surely he had not spoken merely out of pity? Had he thought her too plain to ever find a husband unless he offered for her? If so, he was mistaken. No one had spoken to her openly, of course, but had he waited, it might have been different. She knew well enough that one or two gentlemen had shown a decided preference towards her—or her fortune.

'That was very pleasant, thank you, Cassie,' Vincent said as the strains of the music died. 'Please do not forget the supper dance is also mine.'

He escorted her to Lady Longbourne, kissed her hand and walked away. Watching him go, she felt a sense of loss inside her, a terrible aching that threatened to destroy her composure.

To her horror, Cassie discovered that she was feeling weepy. She excused herself to Lady Longbourne, saying that she wished to tidy her gown, but instead of going upstairs to the bedchamber provided for the ladies' comfort, she slipped through a small anteroom into the garden.

It was a moonlit night, the grass, trees and bushes bathed in silver. A night for lovers and romance.

Why had everything suddenly changed? She had gone along blithely in a daze of excitement and pleasure, but now she was feeling oddly empty and a little nervous of the future—but that was so foolish of her! Nothing had really changed. She was letting her imagination run away with her. There was no reason to feel like this, no reason at all.

Just because Carlton had had a mistress, who was all the things Cassie was not and never could be! It was so foolish of her to mind—but she did. Oh, she did! And she had no right, absolutely none.

Cassie searched for her kerchief and dabbed fiercely at her eyes. She was not going to cry! She refused to be so foolish. What a very missish creature she was to be moping over something that could not be helped. She had always known it was unlikely she would ever find true love. Indeed, she had not wanted to love, had been afraid of the pain it might bring; she had expected to settle for a comfortable life—but now she had suddenly realised that it was not enough for her.

She wanted to be loved. Truly, deeply, wholeheartedly loved! She wanted her husband to give up all other women, to forgo his mistress for her sake. But how could she expect that when La Valentina was so very beautiful?

She gave a little sigh, blinking back her tears as she caught the unmistakable scent of cigar smoke.

'Are you unwell, Miss Thornton? May I be of some assistance?'

Cassie swung round, startled as she peered into the gloom of the garden, then she smiled as the rather large shape of Major Saunders loomed closer.

'Thank you, but I am better now,' she replied. 'I…I had a little headache and came out for some air.'

'These large affairs can be overpowering,' George Saunders agreed. 'I much prefer more intimate gatherings—but one cannot be in town and miss the Devonshires' ball.'

'No, of course not,' Cassie agreed. 'I am being very foolish. I shall go back inside now and apologise to the gentleman who was to have been my partner for the dance I have just missed.'

'Are you sure there is nothing I can do for you?' He moved towards her as she would have gone inside, his expression one of grave concern. His hand reached out to touch her, then dropped to his side as she stepped back. 'I would serve you in any way I could, Miss Thornton. If you are unhappy…or in distress?'

Cassie was surprised at the sincerity in his voice.

'No, no,' she said, blushing at this evidence of his concern. 'You are very kind, but I am not at all unhappy. I assure you it was merely a headache, and now it has gone.'

'Then forgive me for having spoken too plainly.'

'No…no such thing,' she said, blushing. 'Of course you have not. You are very kind…'

The look in his eyes at that moment shocked her. They had only just met, but he quite clearly felt attracted to her and she was uncertain what to do, embarrassed.

'Please excuse me, sir. I must go in or I shall be missed.'

George Saunders stood on in the semi-darkness of the garden after she had disappeared inside, still smoking his cigar. He was quite unaware that someone else was there, watching from behind a large bush of rosemary. When he disposed of his cigar and went into the house, the silent observer stayed on.

Vincent had come in search of the major, but having found him indulging in what was clearly a tête-à-tête with Cassie, had waited in the shadows to watch.

It was obvious that both had been affected by whatever had been said between them. Cassie was upset, embarrassed—distressed. And Major Saunders looked thunderstruck, like a man who knew the woman he most desired in the world was lost to him, as of course Cassie was, being engaged and on the verge of marrying another man.

He was reading too much into what might be a chance encounter. Saunders had come out to smoke a cigar, and perhaps Cassie had felt the need of some air. It did not have to be an assignation. Yet if that were so, why had she seemed so distressed?

He knew she had been enjoying herself in London. She had shown every sign of being content with her lot—though she had never indicated by a word or a look that she was in love with him. She had talked of liking, but nothing more. Was it possible that she had suddenly realised how much more there could be in a marriage between two people who loved one another?

It was possible for two people to meet and fall instantly in love, Vincent knew that only too well. What he could not know was whether that was the case here. If it was, then he had ruined the life of the woman he had hoped to make happy.

Chapter Seven

Cassie was feeling very tired when she parted company with her hostess in the early hours of the next morning. Vincent had escorted them home, but, after bidding them a brusque goodnight in the entrance hall, remained downstairs in his study, not having spoken a single word in the carriage.

'I vow I do not know what is the matter with Carlton,' his mama said, vainly trying to smother her yawns as she paused on the landing with Cassie and Sarah. 'I have seldom seen him so out of temper. Why, he almost snapped poor Harry's head off after supper.'

'He has seemed quiet all evening,' Cassie agreed. 'Do you suppose he is worried about something?'

'I am sure I do not care at this moment,' Lady Longbourne declared. 'His father was sometimes very disagreeable, but Vincent has always been even-tempered. This cold reserve is most unlike him.'

'Perhaps he had lost at cards?' Sarah suggested. 'That always makes Papa out of reason cross, though he never plays for anything but pennies. I think perhaps gentlemen do not like to lose at anything.'

'Carlton is not a heavy gambler,' his mother said, frowning. She stretched and yawned behind her hand. 'Well, I am for my bed. I think I shall sleep until past noon.'

Cassie kissed her, then Sarah, and they all went to their various rooms. She was yawning as she entered her bedroom, where Janet was waiting to undress her. Instantly, she was full of concern for her elderly maid.

'You shouldn't have sat up all night, Janet dear. One of the other maids could have helped me.'

'A nice thing it would be if I left you to strangers,' Janet grumbled to hide her emotions. 'Besides, I wanted you to hear about this nonsense from me. At least then you will have the truth and not some garbled version of it.'

The tone of Janet's voice alerted Cassie. She wrinkled her brow as she looked at her. 'Is something wrong? What has happened to upset you?'

'It's all a storm in a teacup, if you ask me.' Janet gave a sniff of disapproval as she began to unfasten Cassie's gown. 'If you ask me, it's the fault of that Monsieur Marcel with his airs and graces! Who does he think he is?'

'What has Tara done?' asked Cassie, feeling a sinking sensation in her stomach. 'Tell me at once, Janet, for I can tell by your face it is serious.'

'She put some salt in a special stock he was making. Apparently it has a very delicate flavour and was ruined, according to his highness! He threw it away, shouted at her for several minutes and raised a right old rumpus in the kitchen. He was heard to declare that he was not appreciated in this house and would return to France.'

'Oh, dear.' Cassie sighed. She had been expecting something of the sort since Tara was introduced into the great man's kitchen. 'That was indeed very bad of her, but did Monsieur Marcel need to make quite so much fuss?'

'One would not think so,' muttered Janet darkly. 'But it seems it was hours of work wasted and he was furious. He said that he would not tolerate her in his kitchen another moment—and the upshot of it is that she has run away.'

'Run away? Oh, no!' Cassie was dismayed. 'Where can she have gone? She knows no one in London. Are you sure she isn't hiding somewhere in the house?'

'We've looked everywhere,' said Janet pulling an odd face, as if she were battling her tears. 'Dorkins had a soft spot for her and he has fallen out with Monsieur Marcel over it. And Mrs Dorkins says she won't stay in a house that's ruled by a mad Frenchie, and now all the servants have taken sides for and against and we've had Bedlam.' Janet shook her head. 'To tell you the truth, Miss Cassie, I think they've all gone mad. All this fuss over a pinch of salt! In my opinion, the stock tasted all the better for it.'

'But it is not up to us to have an opinion, is it?' Cassie reminded her. 'Monsieur Marcel is in sole charge of the kitchen, and Tara was at fault. What she did was as bad as my going to church without a hat or gloves. She broke the rules, Janet. And I do not think Lord Carlton would be pleased to lose his chef, do you?'

'Well, if you put it that way, I suppose she *was* wrong.' Janet frowned. 'But I've grown quite fond of the little lass. I don't like the idea of her being out on the streets, at the mercy of all the nasty folk waiting to pounce on girls like her.'

'Nor do I,' agreed Cassie, vainly trying to smother a yawn. It had been such an exhausting evening! 'I hope she will be found, or that she will think it over and decide to come back to us. It really is very distressing. Especially as we leave for the country next week. We must make an effort to find her tomorrow. No, it's tomorrow now, isn't it?'

'You're exhausted and need your bed.' Janet saw the signs of strain in her face. 'And here's me chattering on about a naughty girl who didn't know when she was well off. Get to bed, lass, and don't worry about Tara. I dare say she'll come back when she's ready.'

'I do hope so.' Cassie kissed her cheek. 'Goodnight, dearest. Thank you for telling me yourself.'

Cassie carried her candlestick to the bed as Janet closed the door behind her. She set it down on the bedside chest before pulling back the covers and climbing into bed, then blew out the flame. She was so tired, but her mind was going round and round in confusion.

There was the problem of Tara's disappearance, and the domestic upset she had caused—then there were the more worrying problems of Cassie's own making. What a very foolish person she was! She had been so happy, swept along by all the excitement of the wedding preparations, her new clothes and the gifts which had been showered on her—but all at once she had begun to really think about what was happening.

Did she truly want to marry Lord Carlton? The answer was yes, but only if he cared for her.

Cassie knew she could be very happy as Vincent's wife, but not if he were marrying her simply to provide an heir for his title and estates. She had thought and thought, and the only explanation she had been able to come up with was his need to satisfy his family's expectations. She was a very suitable candidate for such a position: a plain, complaisant wife who would be content to stay at home in the country and not cause any scandals!

The thought was so painful it made her almost cry out, but she controlled the urge to give way to her disappointment. She had been foolish to allow herself to expect more. It was exactly the kind of marriage she had told Lord Carlton she was looking for, so she could not blame him for offering it. She knew in her heart it was a very sensible arrangement, but she wanted more.

Cassie tossed restlessly in her bed, sighing as she tried to come to terms with her own feelings and could not. Her meeting with Major Saunders had unsettled her, bringing back vivid memories and making her aware that there had been other alternatives. Had she not been engaged to Vincent, she felt something might have developed between her and the major— Oh, but she could not know that! Besides, she did like Vincent so very well.

Liking? Was that truly what she felt for him? Or was it something more? Was that the reason for her restlessness now?

She shifted position and sighed again, then stiffened as she heard the whimpering sound. It had come from somewhere close by. And she knew exactly what it was!

Sitting up, Cassie lit her candle. She got out of

bed, looking about her. Where was the foolish child hiding?

'Come out, Tara,' she said. 'I know you are here, so there's no point in hiding from me. I am not angry with you, so you do not need to fear that I shall punish you.'

For a moment nothing happened, then the frilled covers at the bottom of the bed moved and Tara crawled out from beneath it. She stood up, standing with her head bent, hands clasped in front of her, then raised a tear-streaked face to look at Cassie.

'I never meant to upset him,' she sniffed, wiping the back of her hand across her face and smearing it with fluff from beneath the bed. 'I was interested in what he was doing, and I tasted the stock when he wasn't looking. I thought he had forgotten the salt so I put it in for him. I was only tryin' to help. Honestly, Miss Cassie. I didn't mean to make him cross. I like him. I think he's clever and I like his funny ways.'

'You like Monsieur Marcel?' Cassie was surprised. Everyone else seemed either to fear the Frenchman or think him too full of his own importance. 'You have enjoyed working for him?'

'Oh, yes, miss!' Tara's face lit up. 'I've never bin so happy in me life. He gives me bits of his special stuff to try and talks to me about soul and fings. Only now he hates me and won't 'ave me in his kitchen no more.'

'Would you behave in future?' Cassie asked, looking at her thoughtfully. She had put on a little weight and looked much healthier, her eyes bright and her hair clean. There was, in fact, a vast improvement in her. 'If I could manage to persuade him to give you another chance—would you promise faithfully to do exactly as he says?'

'Cross me heart and hope to die,' Tara said suiting her action to the words. 'Honestly, miss.' Tears welled up and she sniffed miserably. 'Only he won't, because I ruined hours and hours of work, and he's so clever and I'm stupid.'

'Well, as long as you remember that in future.' Cassie smiled inwardly. Was the talented Frenchman aware of the devotion he had inspired in this child? 'I shall speak to Monsieur Marcel in the morning and see what can be done—but what shall I do with you in the meantime? I cannot send you back to the servants' quarters until this is settled. So I suppose you must stay here with me.'

'I'll curl up on the floor, miss, and I won't disturb you no more.'

'You did not wake me,' Cassie said truthfully. 'I was…thinking of something.' She smiled at Tara. 'You cannot lie on the floor all night. I should be awake all night worrying. Get into bed with me, you foolish child! And don't you dare kick or snore, or I shall very soon push you out again.'

Tara laughed, knowing her mistress was only teasing her. She was a right good 'un! Almost as nice, in Tara's opinion, as his lordship himself!

Alone in his study, his lordship sat with a glass of brandy in his hand and stared into space. The truth was hard but he must face it. He had made a mess of this whole affair from start to finish, and there was no point in blaming Harry. Had he gone straight to Cassie on his return from France and made her an offer of marriage as he ought, none of this need have happened.

She would have refused him, of course. But they might have become friends… Vincent allowed himself to dwell on various possibilities, some of them so impossible that only a moonstruck fool would have dreamed them up, which just showed what kind of a state he was in! A rueful smile twisted his mouth, as he saw the amusing side of his situation. He had set out with the wrong attitude, and now he was well and truly caught in a trap of his own making.

What to do about it?

He could of course tell Cassie the whole story now. He could give her the chance to cry off before it was too late. He would have to shoulder the blame, naturally. Far better that he should be branded a jilt than that she should be made unhappy.

He could go abroad, take a grand tour. Perhaps in

a few years he might return. The scandal would have died down, though some would always hold it against him. Or he might decide to settle abroad somewhere…Italy, perhaps.

'Damned fool!'

Vincent got up and began to pace about the room. Live his life alone and in exile? Or as a disgraced scoundrel on the fringes of society! He wanted to do none of these things. His heart and mind were firmly rooted in England—and with Cassie. Yet he could not forget that scene in the garden of the Devonshires' home earlier that evening.

Cassie was attracted to Major Saunders. He had seen them laughing together as they danced. He could not convince himself that she had ever been quite as carefree in his company, or only once or twice. Why should she have gone to meet George Saunders secretly in the gardens? And why had Cassie been so upset?

Was it possible that there was more to this than he guessed? Had they known each other before this evening? Could they have been lovers previously?

For the first time in his life, Vincent was the victim of the green-eyed god of jealousy. He had watched Cassie with George Saunders and for a moment he had wanted to strike out at them both. His anger had been such that he had not spoken a word on the way home lest his temper betrayed him.

It was a new experience for Vincent. He had always managed to see the amusing side of his mother's little ways, indulging her and giving her whatever she wanted—but he had never felt this torment inside before, tearing him apart.

Damn it! He did not want to give Cassie up! Why should he? He wanted to make her keep her promise to wed him—but what if she regretted it afterwards? What if she had fallen in love with George Saunders? If she were to have an affair with him at some time in the future…

No! He would never allow that, never! Vincent's temper, though slow to rise, could be fearful. He did not trust himself in such an event. Much better to let her go now if she wished it.

Leaving his study, Vincent climbed the stairs to his own apartments. His limbs felt heavy and all his nerve ends were screaming, but he forced himself to hold line. If this was to be done, it must be done properly, in a civilised manner befitting a gentleman.

Once inside his room, he took the spare key to the dressing room from a drawer in the military chest which had served him well during his time as a soldier. Cassie might be sleeping, but it was best to get this over and finished before he had time to change his mind.

Opening the door very softly, he went in to Cassie's room, then stopped, frozen to the spot as the glow from his candle fell across the bed. His expression softened, his mouth curving as he saw the protective way Cassie's arms held the sleeping child beside her.

She was so beautiful! They had all dismissed her looks as not being pretty, but now he saw her as she truly was, relaxed and flushed in sleep, and he knew that for him she was the most beautiful woman in the world. For a moment he could not tear his eyes away and he felt an ache somewhere inside him, a longing that he had never known was there deep within his soul.

He had been informed by Dorkins earlier of Tara's disappearance, but of course no one had thought to look for her here. Yet where else would she come but to the woman who had found her in the first place? The one person she had been sure would protect her—and Cassie had not failed her.

He could not disturb them. Returning as silently as he had come, Vincent re-locked the dressing room door and returned the key to its resting place. He knew he would not speak to Cassie now. God forgive him, he could not! He did not have the will. Unless she came to him, asked him for her freedom, the wedding would go ahead as planned.

Monsieur Marcel was making pancakes. Tiny, wafer thin little morsels of deliciousness, which would be flambéed later with brandy and dressed with plump raspberries and orange juice. It was one of his favourite dishes and he was making it because his conscience would give him no rest. Well aware that everyone was avoiding him that morning, he concentrated on his work and did not look up until he noticed that all the others were standing almost to attention, staring at the doorway. Turning to look, Monsieur Marcel saw that his employer's fiancée had entered the kitchen and was looking in his direction.

Such a thing was unheard of in the grand houses of London society! Ladies gave instructions to their housekeepers, who were summoned to the parlour to wait on the mistress. Never, never, did a great lady descend to the bowels of the house herself!

Cassie met his startled gaze and smiled. Monsieur Marcel dropped his spoon on the floor. One of his minions moved to retrieve it, but was stopped by a flick of the artist's hand. He moved out from behind the table and made a surprisingly elegant bow for one of his rather generous stature, and as Cassie came towards him, took the hand she offered and raised it briefly to his lips.

'*Mademoiselle,*' he said, 'I am by your visit, honoured. This ees *magnifique.*'

'So this is where you create all those wonderful dishes I have so much enjoyed,' Cassie said, glancing round in fascination. 'I have often wondered. Tell me, *monsieur*, have you everything you need? Is there anything that can be changed to make your work easier?'

'I have all I require, *mademoiselle*.' He was visibly glowing. 'Yet perhaps the oven ees a little…'ow shall we say…*ancien*? There ees marvels of modern invention to be found now, I believe. I 'ave thought perhaps…?'

'Of course. I shall speak to Dorkins later. He will arrange for you to have whatever you feel necessary.' She gave him a smile that would have devastated lesser men. 'Now, *monsieur*, I have come personally to apologise on behalf of a very silly girl, and to beg you to forgive her.'

'You have spoken to Tara?' Monsieur Marcel's ears went quite red. 'She ees not dead or lying broken and bleeding in the gutters?'

'No, indeed not. The foolish child had crawled under my bed and spent the night with me. She is inconsolable because she knows she has betrayed your trust. And she admires you so much, *monsieur*. Of course she never could, but she would like to follow in your footsteps to be a great culinary artist one day. Alas, I suppose she has lost all chance of studying under your guidance? Or is it just possible that, from the generosity of your heart, you might forgive her? Just this once…'

'She admires me?' Monsieur Marcel blinked his

sparse lashes. He knew these cold English did not understand him or his dedication to perfection. To them, food was merely food; they could not see that cooking was a precise art known only to a few. How could they? They had no soul! But he had taken to the young waif Lord Carlton had introduced into his kitchen and was sorry that he had frightened her. Besides, who could resist the charm of this lady: a very great lady as he would forever after tell anyone who would listen! 'She ees a foolish child, no? But I shall do my best with her. She must learn not to take my rages so seriously—and to respect the food.'

'I have already scolded her,' Cassie murmured, not quite truthfully. 'I am sure she will do better in future.'

'Then she may return.' Monsieur Marcel's graciousness hid the emotion he was feeling. He could not shed tears before these English; they would laugh at him behind his back and they could never understand the passion that was so necessary to an artist of his calibre. Yet perhaps the future Lady Carlton had soul. Yes, perhaps she might just begin to appreciate him for his true worth. 'Tell Tara I am not now angry with her, *mademoiselle*. All ees forgiven in my heart.'

'Thank you. You are very kind, *monsieur*. But I always knew it must be so. No one who could serve such delicious food could possibly be unfeeling towards a child who needs his compassion.'

She did understand him! Emotion welled up inside him, and his eyes blinked rapidly. He abandoned all idea of returning to his native France. He must stay forever here to serve the mistress who had shown such sensitivity: it was his mission in life, his reason for being. He would create a dinner for her this evening such as never before!

As she turned to leave, he was all activity. A clean spoon was fetched, his underlings sent flying about their business, and once more the delicate task of producing mouth-melting crêpes fit for a goddess was continued.

A little later in the small parlour, Dorkins and Mrs Dorkins responded to Cassie's stroking in much the same manner. Dorkins confessed himself to have been a bit hasty, and his wife promised to keep an eye on Tara while Miss Thornton was away.

'Dorkins and me…all of his lordship's people, really. We were wishful to say how pleased we are, Miss Thornton, that you are marrying Lord Carlton. It has been a pleasure to serve you, and we shall be happy to see you back when you next come to town.'

Cassie thanked them for their kindness, said she had been well looked after and went upstairs to Lady Longbourne's rooms. She had risen earlier than usual to sort out the troubles with Tara, and Lady Longbourne was still in bed, a tray set with a dainty porcelain pot of hot chocolate and a dish of soft rolls balanced across her lap.

'Cassie, my love,' she said, smiling up at her as she spread the warm roll with thick honey. 'You are up already. I made sure you would sleep all morning. You were so tired last evening.'

'Yes, I was a little tired,' Cassie replied. 'But I feel perfectly refreshed now. I have just this moment spoken to Sarah, and she is getting ready to go out. We have remembered two books which must be returned to the lending library before we leave town, and we thought a little walk would do us good.'

'Thank you for coming to tell me,' said Lady Longbourne, sighing as she snuggled back against her pillows. 'I think I shall stay here and rest for most of the day. We have a long journey before us tomorrow, and then all the preparations for the wedding.'

Cassie felt a prickle of alarm. Her hostess did look a little fragile this morning. 'Has all this junketing about been too much for you, ma'am? You are not feeling unwell, I hope?'

'No, not at all,' her ladyship replied. 'To be honest, my dear, I have not enjoyed myself so much for ages. It was wonderful to meet so many of my old friends again. I shall be sorry to leave—except that we have your wedding to look forward to, of course.'

'Yes. You will have the pleasure of entertaining your friends at Longbourne.'

She was a little hesitant, which made her hostess frown and look at her. 'Is something wrong, Cassie? You do not seem quite yourself this morning.'

'I am perhaps a tiny bit tired after all,' Cassie admitted, knowing that she could not speak of what was truly in her mind to anyone, least of all her kind friend, who had been so generous and taken so much trouble on her behalf. 'But a walk will do me the world of good. Fresh air always blows the cobwebs away, do you not think so?'

'I must admit I have not always thought so,' said Lady Longbourne, bravely repressing a shudder. 'But if you say it does you good, Cassie, I shall believe you. As long as you do not expect me to walk out at this hour. The streets are hardly aired, my dear!'

'No, no, I do not expect it of you, dear Lady Longbourne. I should not dream of asking you to come with us. Sarah and I will be perfectly safe on our own, you know. We mean to go straight to the library and come back immediately. We shall not even trouble to take a maid with us. I cannot think it necessary, can you? Besides, they are all so busy packing and preparing for the journey tomorrow.'

'There is not the least need for you to be accompanied,' Lady Longbourne said, relaxing against her pillows with a sigh of content. 'Go along then, my love. I shall see you later.'

* * *

'It has been such an enjoyable time,' Sarah said as they were returning from the library an hour or so later, having lingered a while for a last look in the shops. 'I've had such a lovely time, Cassie—and it is all thanks to you. When I am back at home, I shall often think of this visit. I know I may never come to London again, but I shall never forget how wonderful it was. Thank you so much for all you have given me.'

Cassie looked at her thoughtfully, detecting a slight wobble in her voice. 'I am glad you have enjoyed it, Sarah. We have been so busy going here, there and everywhere that we have not had time to have a really good chat, but I was sure you were having a good time.'

'Oh, yes, wonderful!'

She looked so downcast that Cassie squeezed her arm.

'You do not know for sure that you will not come again,' Cassie said. 'You may well do so.'

'I do not expect it,' Sarah replied, avoiding her eyes. 'Papa could not afford it—besides, I've had my turn. My sisters would give anything for a chance like this. No, I shall have to be satisfied to be at home and help Mama. It is truly my duty to do so, Cassie. I have been much indulged of late.'

'As to that, I dare say your papa will let you come

and stay with us sometimes. I shall certainly invite you.' Cassie hesitated, then, 'Did you meet no one you particularly liked? Was there not one gentleman who showed an interest in you?'

Sarah's cheeks were very pink. 'One gentleman— do you recall Mr John Barker? No, perhaps not. I do not believe you ever danced with him. He did show an interest in me for a while, but I did not encourage him.'

'Why?' Cassie stared at her curiously. 'Did you not like him?'

'He—he was quite pleasant, but…' Sarah faltered, not wholly able to prevent a little sigh escaping her. 'I suppose I ought to have encouraged him. It would have pleased Papa if I had found a husband, but…' She stopped, quite unable to continue. She fiddled with her reticule, twisting it round and round her fingers. 'Oh, I am so very foolish!'

'Was there someone else?' Cassie sensed some deep emotion in her. 'I thought you might rather like Sir Harry…oh, Sarah, of course you do! How foolish of me not to have realised it before. Has he not spoken or shown any partiality?'

Sarah bit her lip, tears hovering on her dusky gold lashes. She was such a pretty girl! It would be a terrible waste if she were to live her life out as a spinster.

'He…he has been amazingly kind to me, Cassie. I dare say you may not have noticed, but we have

danced often. And he has fetched me drinks and
little trifles at supper. Oh, you know! But of course
he was only being himself. He is so very charming,
and pleasant to everyone. However, I believe there
is someone else. A lady he is in love with but cannot
marry. He did hint at something once, but I was not
properly sure what he meant.' Sarah's cheeks went
bright red. 'I think she might be his mistress, though
of course he did not say that to me.'

'Oh, I see.' Cassie nodded. 'He would not marry
her, I suppose?'

'His mama would not approve. Harry would never
marry to disoblige her. So of course he would never
ask me to be his wife, even if he was not in love with
someone else.'

'Why ever not? Lady Longbourne likes you,
Sarah. You know she does. It is always you she asks
to run little errands for her.'

'But I am not an heiress.'

'Must marriage always be about property and
money, then?'

'Not always, but it often is. You must know that,
Cassie.' Sarah sighed deeply, her face wistful. 'You
are so fortunate in marrying Lord Carlton. He likes
you very well, and you like him. I shall probably
have to marry Papa's curate, who I do not like much
at all—or stay at home with my mother.'

Sarah's words struck home. It was very likely that

she would have to be satisfied with a marriage of convenience or remain unwed. Even if Cassie settled some money on her, which she intended to do once her capital was her own, there would be few chances for Sarah to meet someone suitable in the quiet village where she normally lived. Had Cassie's circumstances not taken a turn for the better, she might well have been in a similar position.

'Yes, I am lucky,' she replied. 'Lord Carlton is a real gentleman and very kind. I think I shall be comfortable with him.'

'But surely…' Sarah gave her a puzzled look. 'I thought you… I mean, your case is different.'

'Why?' Cassie asked. 'Why do you say that?'

She had stopped walking, and was looking at Sarah so intently that she did not notice the shabby figure lurking to one side of her. Suddenly, he lunged at her, snatching the beaded purse she was carelessly holding by its strings. For a moment Cassie held on, then released it, letting him take it and turning her head to watch as he ran off down the street.

Sarah gasped with shock, her face going as white as a sheet. Cassie was also pale, but more stunned than frightened.

'Cassie…' Sarah caught at her arm, her chest heaving as she fought for breath. 'He—he stole your purse. That terrible old man, he stole your purse.'

Her voice sounded faint and Cassie looked at her in concern. 'Are you all right?'

'Are you?' Cassie inquired, a little worried by her friend's odd colour. Sarah really was shaken by the incident. 'Do you want to sit down? You look quite ill.'

'It was the shock.' Sarah was beginning to recover, her colour coming back. 'You were wise not to struggle, Cassie. Far better to let the purse go than be hurt. Was there much in it?'

'A few guineas,' Cassie said. 'I thought I might purchase a small gift for Lady Longbourne, but we have another two days before we leave. Besides, I dare say I can find something to give her as a thank-you present. I have not worn half of the pretty scarves and shawls I've bought since we came to town.'

'Several guineas!' Sarah frowned. 'It was a considerable loss, then.'

'It doesn't matter,' Cassie said, dismissing it as of no importance. The colour was returning to her cheeks, and though her heart was still beating rather fast, she had recovered her composure. 'I should not precisely want to lose the money, but you know, dearest, I think he must have been an old soldier—and desperate!—to rob me here in broad daylight. We should be grateful to men who have served us so well in the fight against Napoleon. And I can spare the money. Especially to a man who needs it so badly.'

There was an odd, faraway look in her eyes, and

Sarah realised Cassie was thinking about her brother. 'Yes, now you put it that way, I can see what you mean, Cassie. He must have needed the money desperately—but it was still a terrible shock.'

'He did not harm me,' Cassie said, still thoughtful. 'But I am sorry you were upset, Sarah.'

'I am better now,' Sarah replied, tucking her arm through Cassie's. 'I dare say it was our own fault for coming out without some kind of escort. If only Lord Carlton—or even one of the maids!—had been with us. He would not have dared to approach you like that for fear of being pursued and caught.'

The truth of this struck Cassie very forcibly. This *was* the first time she had been out without an escort of some kind. There was usually a maid or a footman to carry parcels if they went shopping, and in the afternoons and evenings both Lady Longbourne and Lord Carlton went everywhere with them.

'No,' she said, an odd, speculative expression in her eyes. 'You are very right, Sarah. This *was* his chance to approach me…he could not do so before. Even if he had wanted to…'

'What do you mean?' Sarah stared at her in bewilderment. 'Have you seen that particular man before? Where? Has he been following you?"

'I believe I may have seen him—once or twice.'

'Oh, Cassie!' Sarah cried, looking over her shoulder in sudden alarm. 'We should have called the watch or something. Supposing he is a—a wicked murderer? Or a kidnapper!'

'If he had meant me harm, he had his opportunity,' Cassie said. 'No, Sarah, I dare say I am mistaken. One old soldier is much like another, I expect—and now the war is over, London has its share of them amongst those forced to beg for their bread on the streets.' She caught her friend's arm. 'You will not say anything of this—to anyone? Not Lady Longbourne, or Lord Carlton—or even Harry. Please? I do not want to make a fuss about this.'

'But surely…'

'Please, Sarah. I should be grateful if you would keep this incident to yourself. I have lost only a few guineas. There is no need for anyone else to know what happened.'

'If that is what you want.' Sarah clearly did not understand but she agreed as she saw the appeal in Cassie's eyes. 'But I do not see why.'

'Let us forget it,' Cassie pleaded, smiling at her. 'Now, tell me about Sir Harry—are you very fond of him? Would you like to marry him if he asked you?'

Chapter Eight

Cassie did not exactly put the odd incident of her purse from her mind, but that evening something happened which pushed it to one side. She had known they were to attend a musical party, and that the opera singer La Valentina was to perform, but had made up her mind not to let it upset her. She would have Vincent at her side, and she did not imagine the singer would attempt to speak to her.

However, at the last moment, Vincent apologised and said that he was forced to cry off. 'I have an appointment at my club I must keep,' he told them. 'Forgive me, but it is a matter of business and I cannot accompany you this evening. I am sure Harry will be pleased to escort you in my stead.'

'That is not the point,' his mama said, frowning her displeasure. 'Cassie will be disappointed not to have you there.'

'I am sure she will excuse me this once.' He smiled at her, asking for her indulgence.

Cassie could do nothing but smile and say she perfectly understood. If it was in her mind that he had deliberately avoided another meeting with La Valentina in her presence, she did not allow her doubts to show either by a word or a look.

'Yes, of course,' she replied and smiled at him. 'You must do just as you think best, sir.'

'Such an understanding wife you will make,' Vincent said, an odd quizzing expression in his eyes that made her heart race wildly. 'I wonder if you will always be so willing to please me, Cassie?'

Since she did not know how to answer, she remained silent. In her turn, she wondered what he might have said if she had expressed her true feelings and complained of his neglect as Lady Longbourne had, as she might well have done.

'Vincent has never been overfond of musical evenings,' his mother confided as they were driven to their host's house. 'I dare say he is going to a boxing match or some equally barbaric sporting occasion. It is all of a piece, and his father was just the same.'

Cassie nodded, but said nothing. She was not exactly dreading the evening, but she did not particularly wish to meet the beautiful woman who had been Vincent's mistress for several months. She had been prey to a few unkind whispers over the past weeks, and certain spiteful ladies had not hesitated to let her know that the opera singer had lasted longer in her position than any other light o' love of Carlton's before her—which surely meant that Vincent must have cared for her.

The evening was begun with a quartet of men singing in harmony; they were followed by a tenor, and finally La Valentina took the centre stage. Her singing was so beautiful that even Cassie was moved to the verge of tears. She could not deny that the woman was both beautiful and talented.

After her performance, there was a general movement towards the supper room. Following behind Lady Longbourne and Sarah—Harry having long ago disappeared to the card room—Cassie felt a firm touch on her arm and turned to find herself being detained by none other than La Valentina.

She had hoped to avoid such a confrontation, and her heart sank as she saw the purpose in the other woman's eyes.

'You wanted to speak to me, ma'am?'

'I know you are to marry soon,' La Valentina said, a flash of fire in those magnificent eyes. She touched a necklace of sapphires at her neck, as if wanting to draw Cassie's attention. 'This was *his* gift to me. Now I shall give you a gift, Miss Thornton. For the moment he is yours alone. Carlton is too much a gentleman to keep a mistress while he courts his wife. You may have him for as long as it takes you to produce the heir he needs, but he is mine. When you are with child, he will come back to me.'

Cassie's throat was too tight to speak. Besides, what could she say? If she denied La Valentina's words, she would be treated to one of those condescending smiles. And if she did what she really wanted and slapped her, it would cause a scandal, which was very probably what the singer had hoped to provoke.

She nodded her head, then moved off, her back straight. She was the very picture of dignity. It was the best she could do. As long as no one knew how much she was hurting inside, it could not matter.

She had almost reached the supper room when Harry came up to her. He looked at her white face and swore.

'What did that witch say to you, Cassie? Whatever it was, ignore it. She was hoping Vinnie would marry her, which he never would, of course—and she was trying to hurt you.'

'She did not tell me anything I did not know,' Cassie said, forcing a smile. 'Forget it, Harry. I intend to—and I would be obliged if you would not tell Carlton that you saw her speak to me.'

He looked at her for a moment, then nodded. 'Just as you like, but had Vinnie been here she would not have dared to speak to you like that. He finished it, you know—before he even asked you to marry him. If she is hoping he will go back to her, she will be disappointed. Stands to reason. No man would be fool enough to leave your bed for hers—' His ears went bright red with embarrassment. 'Forgive me. I ought not to have said that…'

Cassie laughed and tucked her arm through his, smiling up at him. 'Oh, yes, you did, Harry. You have made me feel very much better, I assure you.'

'Vinnie is no fool,' he said. 'Shall we go into supper now, Cassie?'

'Yes,' she replied. 'I think we ought…'

Alone in her bed that evening, Cassie allowed herself a few tears. She was so foolish to have let the little incident hurt her. No doubt Harry was right. Vincent had done the honourable thing and finished his affair. La Valentina had merely been trying to get her own back. She must be sensible and ignore her spite.

Her mind turned to the moment when her purse was snatched. She thought about it for a while, trying to decide whether or not she had seen something in the man's eyes that had reminded her so much of her brother she had let go of her purse. Or was that just her imagination?

Oh, of course it was! She dismissed it as

nonsense, thought again about La Valentina's spite, then turned over and closed her eyes.

It was their very last day before leaving for the country. Cassie, Lady Longbourne and Sarah had spent a very enjoyable morning doing their last-minute shopping, and Cassie had managed to buy a little silver-beaded evening purse as a gift for her hostess while her back was turned. She was feeling very pleased with herself for managing to keep her gift a secret, when she heard herself addressed from behind and jumped.

'Miss Thornton?' a gentleman's deep voice said. 'How pleasant to meet you. I understood you had left town.'

'Oh, no, not until tomorrow,' Cassie said, her cheeks pink as she saw who had spoken to her. 'I hope you received your invitation to the wedding, Major Saunders?'

'Yes, I did, and have written to accept,' he said. 'I wondered…have you thought about who is to give you away, Miss Thornton? If you have by some chance not decided, I hope it would not be too forward of me to offer my services—as Jack's friend?'

Cassie felt herself blushing. She supposed she ought to have asked Kendal, but it had not actually occurred to her until that moment.

'It is not forward at all,' she said. 'Indeed, I should

be grateful, for there is no one else I would rather have, sir.'

'Then I shall come down a day or so earlier,' said Major Saunders. 'I have friends near by where I may stay. And I shall take the liberty of calling on you to discuss the arrangements. It will give me great pleasure to be of service to you, Miss Thornton.'

'You will be most welcome.'

Cassie gave him her hand, blushing as he raised it to his lips. She could not mistake the very real warmth in his eyes as he looked at her. It was quite clear that he liked her very well.

'Who was that gentleman, my love?' asked Lady Longbourne a moment or so later. 'I was not quite sure.'

'Major Saunders,' Cassie replied, avoiding her curious gaze. 'He was Jack's friend and has offered to give me away. Do you not think that was kind of him? He says he will call on us a day or so before the wedding to make certain of the arrangements.'

'Yes, very kind,' said her ladyship, frowning. 'Although, had you thought, you might have asked Harry.'

'But will he not stand up with Vincent as his best man?'

'Carlton could very well have found someone else,' said Lady Longbourne. 'But since it is arranged, I dare say no harm will come of it.' She glanced at the gold watch pinned to her gown. 'And now I think we really must go home…'

Some twenty minutes later, Cassie took off her bonnet and handed it with her gloves to Mrs Dorkins, who was attending her in the hall of Lord Carlton's house.

'His lordship was asking for you, Miss Thornton,' the housekeeper said. 'He asked most particularly that you would oblige him by going to the study as soon as you returned home.'

'Thank you,' Cassie replied. 'I shall go to him now.'

She left Sarah talking to Mrs Dorkins and went through the house to the study, which was at the back and looked out at the gardens. Her knock was answered by an invitation to enter and she did so, pausing just inside the door. Vincent had been staring out of the window and she was at leisure to observe that he was dressed for riding before he turned and smiled at her.

For a moment her heart stopped, then raced on wildly.

'Ah, Cassie, you have returned. I trust you enjoyed your shopping? The air is very fresh this morning, is it not?'

'It was pleasant,' she replied. 'One cannot but enjoy shopping, sir.'

'One of the privileges, I presume?'

Cassie laughed at the long-standing joke between them. 'Oh, most definitely, sir! Though I must admit it can be wearing if one has to visit too many shops to find what one particularly wants.'

His eyes were bright with amusement. 'Yet you seem to enjoy walking for its own sake?'

'I believe I prefer to walk in the country, especially when the dew is still upon the hedges, but the town has many pleasures to offer, does it not? For gentlemen as well as ladies.'

'I have always thought it enjoyable to be able to divide one's time between the two,' Vincent said. 'I dare say we shall visit London often when we are married—if you would like that?'

His eyes seemed to watch her intently. Cassie flushed and dropped her gaze. Why did she feel that there was so much more behind the simple question?

'Yes, of course,' she murmured. 'I am sure we shall find an agreeable routine that suits us both if we try.'

'Monsieur Marcel has told me you paid him a visit the other morning.' Cassie's eyes flew to his as she heard the new note in his voice. 'He came to the study, to discuss the week's menus with me as has been our custom, you know. He told me he was honoured to be consulted by my future wife as to his welfare. I believe you promised a new oven or some such thing?'

'Oh, yes. I hope you do not mind?' Cassie was

slightly awkward beneath his probing gaze. Was he annoyed with her for interfering? 'I dare say it will be expensive, but one must always strive to keep one's people happy—don't you think?'

'Undoubtedly.' Vincent's eyes danced with suppressed mirth. 'I am only too glad to be relieved of all domestic responsibility and shall in future be glad if Monsieur Marcel receives his instructions from you. Particularly as you seem to have him eating out of your hand, Cassie. Yes, you may deal with him in future if you please. I confess I found the man's tantrums a little wearing.'

'Oh, no, did you?' Cassie smiled, relieved as she saw he was teasing her as usual. His odd mood of the other evening seemed to have left him. 'I think he is feeling rather lonely here and misses his own people. But I shall be happy to take over the task. I know you have much to concern you. Besides, gentlemen do not care for such things—settling domestic disputes is what you would expect from your wife, is it not, sir?'

'Must you call me sir?' Vincent asked, a hint of irritation in his voice—or was it agitation? 'I think I would prefer Carlton, as Mama says—or Vincent, as you once promised.'

Cassie was surprised at his tone. 'Forgive me,' she said. 'I shall do better when we are married, I promise.'

'Shall you?' The expression in his eyes was unreadable. 'When we are married...'

'Do you not find our present situation a little strange?' she asked, meeting his frowning gaze with her own, which was clear and candid, putting him to shame. 'We have known each other for several weeks, and yet we are no closer to truly knowing one another than we were at the beginning. I think…I believe that must change when we are husband and wife.' She paused, giving him a shy look. 'Do you not think the same, Carlton?'

'Yes, Cassie.' Vincent smiled, making her heart race. He came towards her as a breeze lifted the curtain at the open window, standing so close that her heart fluttered like the rippling silk of the drapes. She felt suddenly breathless yet expectant. 'I believe many things will change then—and I am looking forward to having you as my wife.'

Cassie trembled as she heard the husky, intimate note in his voice. He was going to kiss her! She sensed it, welcomed it, standing very still as he reached out to draw her a little nearer. Then she was in his arms; he was holding her pressed close against his body, his eyes compelling her to look at him. A tiny shiver of anticipation ran through her as he lowered his head and touched his lips to hers.

At first it was a gentle kiss, but then his arms tightened about her and his mouth became demanding, wrenching a response from her. A response that shocked and disturbed her by its very force. Oh, she was going to swoon! It was so very, very exciting and—and terrifying to be kissed in this manner. Very different from the chaste kisses he had given her before. It aroused all kinds of new sensations in her: feelings and longings she had never dreamed of experiencing.

When at last Vincent let her go, Cassie was so confused she could hardly bear to look at him. He had aroused such longing in her, such need!

'So,' he said. 'We *shall* be married, Cassie.'

'Yes, of course. In ten days from now.'

She was puzzled. He had spoken as though it had been in doubt but was no longer.

'In ten days.' He nodded, as if he had something on his mind. 'I am sorry to have to tell you that I shall not be able to escort you to Longbourne, Cassie. I must leave almost immediately for Surrey. Some estate business needs my attention. I have asked Harry to accompany you and Mama. He has promised to do so, and you may rely on him to see you safely there.'

'You must attend to your business, s…Carlton.' Cassie hid her disappointment that he would not be with them behind a smile. 'I am glad your brother is to come with us. It will ease the leavetaking for Sarah. She likes Sir Harry, I believe.'

Vincent nodded. 'I have noticed the attraction. Well, why not, if it suits them both?'

'Would Lady Longbourne agree—if a proposal was made? And I must make it clear that none has as yet. I have been told of Sarah's preference in confidence—but I know nothing of how Sir Harry may feel about the situation.'

'It would not surprise me if his feelings were much the same as Miss Walker's. I believe he would hesitate to ask a girl of no fortune, for fear of distressing Mama. She might not be pleased at first—but I believe she might be brought to see the advantages,' Vincent said, a little smile playing about his mouth. 'Sarah is a country girl at heart and I do not think Mama will return to London for a while. I had hoped she might find someone to share her exile—but I have seen no sign of it.'

'No, nor I,' Cassie admitted with a little frown. 'But she will have us now. We shall visit her and she may like to come to us sometimes. Indeed, I am sure she will.'

'Well, we shall see what transpires.' Vincent took out his gold pocket watch and checked the hour. 'I must ask you to excuse me, my love. I shall see you again two days before our wedding.'

'Yes, of course.' Her cheeks flushed as she remembered that kiss and the response it had evoked in her. 'I shall be waiting for you.'

Cassie remained in Carlton's study after he had left. She sat down at his desk, glancing idly at the menus Monsieur Marcel had brought him, picking up various objects and turning them over in her hand. The blade of a silver paper knife had an inscription. She read it without thinking and her heart caught as she saw it had been a long ago birthday gift to Vincent from *'Your friend Jack'*.

'Jack…' The word stuck in her throat. 'Jack…'

Cassie's eyes clouded with tears. She blinked them away. It was so very odd. She could not explain the feeling that had come over her that morning when her purse was stolen. She had been determined not to let go, then, for one brief moment, she had looked into the eyes of that old soldier and her heart had almost failed her. She had thought for one brief second that it was Jack.

It could not be. Of course it could not be! The man was years older than her brother. He had a scar on his cheek and his hair was long and grey. But his eyes… Oh, his eyes were so like Jack's. Surely she could not be mistaken? She knew those eyes as well as she knew her own.

She had since that morning told herself she was wrong again and again, but gradually the feeling had taken root that she had not been mistaken. The old soldier's eyes were Jack's eyes.

Yet how could that be? How could she have seen her brother, when she knew very well that he was dead?

But if by some chance, some wonderful miracle,

Jack had not died on the field of battle, why had he not come home to her? Why had he not claimed his inheritance?

Oh, this was madness. To let herself hope, knowing that hope must founder on the rock of disappointment!

She knew it could not possibly have been her brother who had snatched her purse. And yet the same man *had* been following her in London, waiting for his chance to approach her. She was almost sure of it—sure she had seen him at the balloon ascension. The afternoon when she had thought she heard Jack's voice call to her.

'Cassie, I need you…I need your help.'

Had her brother been there in that crowd of on-lookers? Had he tried to reach her?

She remembered hearing the voice, then the rope snapped, panic followed and Vincent took her arm, leading her back to Sarah and his brother.

The old soldier had been there, too, that afternoon. She remembered seeing him sheltering from the rain, the shabby coat pulled up around his ears. Surely it was the same man? She was almost certain of it.

Could he possibly be her brother?

His eyes had been so like Jack's. The scar could have been gained in battle—but the hair and the way he had aged?

Actors on the stage were sometimes aged by the

*paint they put on their faces—and a grey wig would
make anyone look older.*

It could be done, she realised. If Jack wanted to
disguise himself, to hide his identity, he could
change his appearance—but not his eyes!

'Why, Jack?' she whispered to herself as she sat
on in Vincent's chair, playing with the paper knife
he had given to a friend. 'Why snatch my purse? I
would have given it willingly. I would share all I
have with you. You must know that? You must!'

Cassie would like nothing more than to have her
beloved brother home again, to share her fortune
with him. Jack must know that, so why not come to
her openly?

If it was Jack—and of course she was most
probably catching at straws!—but if it was, why
was he in some sort of disguise? What could keep
him from revealing himself to his sister and friends?

The only answer she could think of was that he
was in some kind of trouble…

That evening seemed to Cassie the dullest they
had spent for an age. It was just the four of them to
dinner, and Sir Harry left immediately afterwards
for reasons he did not disclose.

'How delightful to spend an evening quietly at
home,' declared Lady Longbourne, sighing with
content as she lounged negligently on the sofa.

'Would you play for us, Sarah? You have such a sure touch. Something restful if you please, my dear.'

Sarah obliged with a sad, melancholy piece that reflected her mood. Cassie saw the tears she could not hide and, feeling restless herself, got up and went over to the window. To make matters worse, it had begun to rain. She blinked hard, telling herself sternly not to be so foolish. All she had wanted was a comfortable marriage, much like her own parents' had had, but now she longed for something vastly different.

Carlton's kiss that morning had awoken a fierce hunger in her. She felt as if she had been sleeping all her life, waiting for this moment in time. And now Carlton had gone away, leaving her to a burning frustration that could not be satisfied until she was in his arms again.

Oh, how tiresome it was of him to choose this moment to abandon her! What business could possibly be as important as furthering their relationship?

If he had gone on business, of course.

The unworthy thought wormed its way into her mind. Gentlemen did not always tell the exact truth to their wives and sweethearts. Carlton's business could easily be a race meeting at Newmarket, a bare-knuckle fight at some secret location—or an assignation with a lover.

No, no, she would not believe that last of him!

Jealousy tore at her heart, wounding her so deeply that she could not prevent a gasp of pain escaping her.

'Is something the matter, my love?'

Cassie avoided the searching gaze turned on her by Lady Longbourne. 'No, nothing is wrong, ma'am,' she lied. 'I am a little tired, I suppose.'

'As well you might be,' her hostess replied. 'You do not rest as you should, Cassie. We have all been racketing around with no thought of our health.' She yawned behind her hand. 'It is past nine, my dears. Why do we not dispense with the tea tray this evening and go to bed?'

All three ladies agreed on an early night, though, knowing she would not sleep, Cassie had the forethought to fetch a book from Carlton's study. She spent a few minutes looking at the variety ranged in the bookcases, then settled on a small, leather-bound volume of Shakespeare's sonnets lying on the desk. It seemed to have been well used, and when she opened it, she discovered that Carlton had marked his place with a piece of straw.

How very odd! She smiled, imagining him using it for want of something better. He must have carried it with him while campaigning in France, and just holding it seemed to bring him back to her. She clasped the book to her breast, feeling once again the strange but very exciting sensations his lips had created in her earlier that day.

'Oh, bother,' she said and, sighing, went to bed.

* * *

The return journey—first to Carlton House, where they rested for a night, and then to Longbourne—was uneventful. There were no highwaymen to frighten them, or gypsy women lying at the point of giving birth by the side of the road to be rescued.

For some obscure reason, Cassie was almost inclined to agree with Lady Longbourne when she complained that travelling was tedious.

Sir Harry was just as attentive and considerate as his brother, but somehow nothing was quite the same. Even his mama told him that Carlton had procured better rooms for them at the inn where they stayed one night, and that the supper was barely tolerable after the culinary delights Monsieur Marcel had prepared for them.

However, once they arrived at the Hall, things took a turn for the better. Sir Harry had decided not to relet after his previous tenants had taken themselves off to an archaeological expedition to Greece. He had, without telling anyone, given instructions that the whole house be modernised and refurbished.

'Oh, Harry!' his delighted mother exclaimed. 'You have made it comfortable at last. I believe it compares favourably with Carlton's house now.'

Harry looked pleased with himself. 'I am glad you like it, Mama. I—I shall quite possibly spend more time in the country in the future, and naturally I hope you will visit me from time to time.'

'Oh, I shall, my dearest,' said Lady Longbourne. 'What a good son you are to go to so much trouble on my behalf!'

Harry's ears went red and he looked oddly guilty, but did not deny that his efforts had been meant solely to gratify his mother.

Cassie wondered. However fond a son he might be, she thought it unlikely that he would have gone to so much effort unless he had another, more personal reason. Was it possible that Sir Harry was considering marriage—and if so, to whom?

Sarah did not look like a young woman nursing a happy secret. Indeed, she seemed in danger of falling into a sad decline.

Cassie was not surprised when on the morning following their arrival, she said that she felt it her duty to return home to the vicarage.

'Oh, but I thought you would stay with me until after the wedding,' Cassie cried. 'Please, do not leave me just yet, Sarah. We both need another fitting for our gowns, just in case they need a slight adjustment. Besides, I need you to keep me company. And there is the dance two nights before the wedding. You will have to come and stay for that!'

Sarah was persuaded, but insisted she must visit

her parents that morning. Cassie agreed and, since it was a lovely day, decided to walk to the vicarage with her friend.

'It will do us good to have a really long walk,' Cassie said. 'I shall come in to greet your parents, of course, Sarah, then go on to visit Nanny Robinson at her cottage. We can walk home together later.'

Mrs Walker greeted her daughter with a loving embrace and a suspicion of tears in her eyes. She would not hear of Cassie leaving without a glass of her own raspberry wine and a slice of seed cake. So it was at least half an hour before she set out for Nanny's cottage.

Her old nurse greeted her with smiles, accepting the basket of small gifts she had brought and plying her with questions about her forthcoming marriage.

'I remember his lordship well,' she said, a gleam in her eyes. 'He and Master Jack were always up to some lark or other.'

'Yes, they were good friends, Nanny.'

'And now you are to wed Lord Carlton.' Nanny Robinson nodded her satisfaction.

Cassie was silent for a moment, then, 'You still have Jack's things? In the trunks I sent?'

'I stored them in my barn,' Nanny replied. 'I have not looked recently, but I am sure they are still there.'

'I shall send for them as soon as we go to Carlton House.'

'Just as you wish, Cassandra.' Nanny shook her head. 'Though no good will come of clinging to the past, my dear.'

'I couldn't let anyone else have them.'

'No, of course you couldn't.'

The subject was dropped. Cassie spent another half an hour chatting to her old nurse, of whom she had always been fond, then set out to return to the vicarage. Her walk led her through secluded country lanes and past the drive of Thornton House. She glanced towards the house, which was just visible through the trees, but had no thought of visiting. However, just as she was about to pass by, she heard her name called, and, turning, saw Sir Kendal hurrying towards her.

Dressed for riding, he looked more at home in the country than he had in town. Cassie would have avoided him if she could, but in her heart she knew that would be impossibly rude of her.

'I was just coming to visit you,' he said as he came up to her, slightly out of breath. 'I am sorry, but I must report something unpleasant to you, Cassandra. Something I imagine must cost you some pain.'

She stared at him in dismay. 'Whatever can you mean, sir?'

'When I came into your late father's estate, it was my intention to be a good custodian. And though you chose to think ill of me, I asked you to be my wife because I thought it wrong that you should be driven from your home.'

Cassie blushed for shame. She realised that, despite his irritating manners, and thoughtlessness in making her an offer so soon after her brother's death, he had meant well. She had never really given him a chance to explain himself.

'I have misjudged you,' she admitted. 'Please forgive me if I have been impolite.'

'Well, we need not say more of this,' Sir Kendal said. 'His lordship assured me that I need have no fear for your future, so all that remains is for me to wish you well…as I do.'

'Thank you, sir. You are most kind.'

Oh, how very lowering! She still could not like him, but she knew Vincent had been right to insist on an invitation being sent.

'I shall naturally attend your wedding,' Sir Kendal went on. 'But first I must acquaint you with the shocking news…' He paused to give importance to his next words. 'There has been a burglary at Thornton House.'

'A burglary?' Cassie was startled. 'Oh, how very shocking! Was anyone hurt?'

'Fortunately, no one was injured. I myself disturbed the rogue, having risen to investigate a noise I heard. I sleep very lightly, Cassandra. Had I not gone to see what was wrong, I fear the damage might have been worse. As it was, only a pair of your father's pistols and a silver tankard were taken.'

'A pair of pistols?' Cassie stared at him. 'Oh, yes, I remember them. Father never used them because he said they were not reliable. I should think your thief would be very disappointed to get so little.'

'Then they were not of sentimental value to you?' Sir Kendal looked relieved. 'I am glad of that. I was afraid you would blame me for not taking care of your father's estate. Since it is unlikely that I shall marry, it is probable that Thornton House will one day return to your son, Cassandra, and I should not want you to blame me for any neglect.'

Cassie discovered she was touched by his concern. Seemingly, he was not so very odious after all.

'No, no,' she said. 'You must do just as you wish with the estate, Kendal. I shall not blame you for anything. Indeed, I think you very brave to investigate strange noises at night. Had it happened when I was there alone, I should have put my head under the covers and ignored it.'

She would not have, of course, but wished to make up for her former curtness to him.

'Well, as to that, I had a blunderbuss with me. And I fired it out of the window after the rogue.'

'Did you actually see him?'

'Not his face—just a glimpse as he ran away. He was wearing a shabby greatcoat and I took him for an old soldier, for there was a military look about his clothes.'

Cassie's heart jerked. Her mouth went dry, and for a moment she could not speak. 'Did—did you hit him with your shot?'

'I doubt it,' Kendal said regretfully. 'He was too swift for me. The scoundrel! Fellows like that deserve to be hung.'

'He was probably desperate,' Cassie said, not daring to say what was truly in her mind. 'Indeed, he must have been to break into the house.'

'Well, he will not try it again in a hurry,' Sir Kendal said, a gleam of satisfaction in his eyes. 'He knows I shall not hesitate to shoot if he does.'

Cassie murmured something complimentary, though she hardly knew what she said as she parted company with him. Her thoughts were tumbling over themselves in confusion.

The old soldier who had taken her purse and the intruder who had broken into Thornton House—were they the same man? It was such an odd coincidence!

Yet not so strange if that man were Sir John Thornton. Her brother Jack!

Cassie could not help the well of hope that all at once sprang up in her. Jack was alive! She was suddenly so sure of it that she felt like screaming aloud for sheer joy.

Jack had not been killed in France. He was here in England, perhaps near by. She glanced over her shoulder as if expecting to see him following her, but he was not here at this moment: she could not feel him. Somehow she knew that he had been here in order to break into the house—presumably because he was in need of money.

Cassie thought about the times when she had sensed Jack trying to contact her. Once she had thought there was someone following her in Carlton's woods—but then she had found Tara crying. Then she had heard Jack's voice at the balloon ascension, but Vincent had come to drag her away. And the incident of the purse…when her brother had been so desperate he had been driven to steal from his own sister.

'Why, Jack?' she whispered to herself. 'Why not come to me? Why steal Papa's pistols when they belong to you?'

Cassie was now quite certain in her own mind that her brother was alive but in trouble. He must be afraid to reveal his identity to her—or to any of his friends. It was the only possible reason for his behaviour.

'Jack,' she said, urgently willing him to hear her, drawing him to her by the power of her thoughts. 'Come to me, dearest. Come to me. I shall help you. Come to me and I will help you—whatever you've done.'

In that moment, Cassie longed for her fiancé. If only he were there, so that she could confide her thoughts to him! Even though her feelings were in such a turmoil over her coming marriage, she knew that Vincent would have understood her fears and shared her excitement.

No one would be more pleased if Jack really had come back to them, and she knew that he would help her find her brother. He was the one person she could truly trust…

Chapter Nine

Cassie had collected her composure by the time she reached the vicarage. Sarah was waiting for her, and had clearly recovered her spirits. The visit with her mother had done her good, and she chattered happily enough about the wedding as she and Cassie walked back to Longbourne Hall, besides telling her lots of news about her own family.

As they drew close to the house, they stared in surprise at the rather antiquated coach which had just drawn up outside the front door. A portly gentleman was getting out. He was followed by a small dog which jumped down and proceeded to yap excitedly at the footman who was attempting to help a tall, thin lady and a spotty-faced boy of perhaps nine years from the coach.

'Whoever can that be?' Cassie said, then, turning to Sarah as they both laughed, their eyes met in shared mischief. 'Do you think it is the dreaded Septimus?'

'And the odious Archie!' cried Sarah, clapping her hands. 'Oh, dear, we must hurry to poor Lady Longbourne's aid. She was hoping they would not arrive for at least another two days.'

Entering the house a few moments later, the two girls looked at the piles of luggage littering the spacious hall. Judging from the amount Sir Septimus and his family had brought with them, they were intending to visit for far longer than the week leading up to the wedding.

'It looks as if they mean to stay a month at least,' Cassie whispered, forcing poor Sarah into a fit of the giggles, which she did her best to hide behind her kerchief. 'Poor Lady Longbourne! She will be driven to despair.'

Sir Septimus was loudly directing the disposal of the baggage when Cassie and Sarah encountered him. All hope of escape vanished as he turned and saw them.

'One of you will be Miss Thornton, no doubt?' He eyed them both with barely hidden disapproval.

'I am Cassandra Thornton, sir.' Cassie lifted her head proudly and went forward to offer her hand. His reputation had gone before him, but she was not a coward and would not let him browbeat her as he did Lady Longbourne. 'And I believe you must be Carlton's uncle Septimus? I, too, have heard much of you, sir.'

'Humph!' His narrow-set eyes fixed on her

intently. 'I had heard you were a plain, sensible, no-nonsense sort of girl. I dare say you will do. It is high time Carlton did his duty by the family. I was afraid he might marry one of these sylphlike, fair girls. No good for breeding. You look to me as if you might be capable of producing an heir. And high time, too.'

Cassie blinked. Was she meant to take that as a compliment? He was surely the bluntest man she had ever met!

'I hope I shall do all that my husband expects of me,' she said, and turned as his wife and son came up to them.

'Lady Felicity and the sprig,' Sir Septimus said, looking sourly at his wife. 'I'll leave you to get to know each other. Where is that damned butler of Longbourne's? Is nothing ever ready in Emmeline's house?'

He was, of course, referring to his former sister-in-law. Cassie knew at once why Lady Longbourne lived in fear of his visits. His loud voice was almost guaranteed to bring on one of her headaches.

'I believe you were not expected until tomorrow at the earliest,' Cassie said. 'However, I am sure I speak for Lady Longbourne when I say you are most welcome whenever you choose to visit. If you would all care to go into the green salon, I shall arrange for refreshments to be brought to you immediately.'

'And what about all this?' Sir Septimus waved his hand at the piles of luggage.

'I am sure the servants will manage better alone, sir. I know you would naturally wish to help, but I am sure Lady Felicity is exhausted and would be glad to rest.'

'Yes, I would.' The lady in question glared at her husband and pushed her son in front of her. 'Archie, say how do you do to Miss Thornton, if you please.'

Archie extended a hand that looked suspiciously sticky. Cassie smiled and bent to kiss his cheek, which was marginally more presentable. She also kissed Lady Felicity, then firmly directed her towards the front parlour. By this time Sir Harry's butler had arrived and was directing several strong, young footmen to carry up the luggage. Sir Septimus, suddenly discovering himself superfluous to requirements, followed behind his son and heir.

Cassie set herself to making their visitors comfortable, and a tray of sherry wine, biscuits and comfits was brought in. So, when Lady Longbourne arrived looking flustered some minutes later, she found there was nothing for her to do but kiss her relatives and sit down with a restorative glass of wine.

'Forgive me for not being down to receive you myself,' she murmured faintly. 'But there has been so much to do and—and I was resting.'

'You do not take enough exercise, in my opinion,'

commented Sir Septimus with a frown. 'Do you good to ride out with the hunt as Felicity does.' He glanced at his wife, who Cassie could not help thinking looked much like a horse herself with her long nose and prominent teeth. 'Shake yourself up, Emmeline.'

'Poor Lady Longbourne has had an exhausting few weeks.' Cassie jumped in to save her. 'We have been simply everywhere. And the Devonshires' ball—such a sad crush. I am sure it is no wonder we all needed some time to recover from it.'

Sir Septimus turned his piercing gaze on her. His nostrils quivered and his ears pricked as if sensing a more worthy adversary.

'Humph! I do not approve of too much racketing about town. No time for it, nor has Felicity. Too expensive—but I dare say you won't care for that. An heiress, aren't you?' He tossed that one into the conversation with the air of a gladiator entering the arena.

'I believe I am,' Cassie said, a faint curve about her mouth as she prepared to give battle. 'And, no, I do not mind what I spend. Money is so boring, do you not think so? One either has none, in which case it is a worry, or so much that there is not the least point in thinking about it.'

Lady Longbourne gasped in admiration. Cassie was so brave! She herself had never dared to use Septimus's own weapons against him, and it afforded her not a little satisfaction to see him—however temporarily—at a loss for words.

He made a recovery, scowled and said, 'A fool and his money are soon parted.'

'Yes, indeed,' Cassie agreed, giving him one of her devastating smiles. 'You are so right, sir. I could not agree more with that sentiment—but there is a difference between spending money for the good of oneself and one's friends, and throwing it away. I do not care to see money wasted, naturally. But to hoard it as a miser! Can anything be so ridiculous? I am persuaded that no person of sense could wish to waste life's opportunities in such a sad way.'

Unknowingly, Cassie had hit upon Septimus's besetting sin. Although not as rich as Carlton, he had inherited an estate that provided him and his family with a satisfactory living. But he lived in fear of exceeding that income and would never spend a penny more than necessary.

'A penny saved is a penny gained.' He glared at her as if daring her to deny him, but a warning look from Lady Longbourne to Cassie saved the day.

'Oh, I am sure you are right there, sir,' Cassie said, 'and now I really think Lady Felicity's rooms will be ready for her.'

'Oh, yes, I am sure they are,' said Lady Longbourne, rising hurriedly to her feet. She had sensed a storm brewing and felt much too fragile.

'Do please come up, Felicity, for I am perfectly sure you need to rest after such a tiring journey.'

Cassie excused herself as they went out, leaving Sir Septimus to turn his attention to his son, who had been steadily eating his way through the almond comfits and now looked slightly green.

'If you are going to be sick, Archie, you may go outside,' his father said. 'Indeed, you should go out anyway, for I am fed up with the sight of you. And take that miserable dog with you! Why your mother should want to own such a puling creature I do not know. I have put up with it all the way here and cannot do so any longer!'

Cassie fled up the stairs before either Septimus or his son could come out and delay her. They really were too awful for words. Beside them, Kendal was a perfectly pleasant man!

Thinking about what Kendal had told her earlier, Cassie frowned to herself. Was she jumping to conclusions? Letting herself believe there was a chance of Jack coming back to her, when there was really no hope? It would be so foolish to build her expectations if it was all in her head!

If only there was someone she could talk to about all this!

Cassie realised with a little shock that the one person she could possibly unburden herself to was Vincent. Insensibly, she had come to rely on him to share her thoughts. She saw now that she ought to have mentioned her suspicions to him. She should have told him about what had happened the day her purse was snatched, but she had been foolishly determined to keep the peculiar incident to herself.

And the next time they had really talked, he had kissed her and everything else had been driven from her mind by her longing to have him hold her in his arms again.

'Oh, why are you not here when I need you?' she muttered to herself as she hurriedly changed into a fresh gown for luncheon. 'I miss you, you wretched man. I do wish you would come home!'

Vincent closed the estate books with a sigh. He had been in his library at Hamilton Manor, poring over them for hours and he was not sure why. His manager was always so efficient that he had no real need to go through them, except that it had become a habit from the days when he had needed to watch the pennies in order to bring himself and his family back from the edge of ruin.

The agents and managers sent in after his father's death to look after the Carlton estate, until he reached his majority and could take over, had near bankrupted him, and it had taken a lot of effort and some skill to put the estate in good heart. Indeed, had he not been left the Hamilton estate by his maternal grandfather in its entirety, he doubted it could have been done. But over the years he had acquired more and more land, building up his wealth by careful husbandry and some inspired investments, and now he knew he could afford to sit back and enjoy his life.

One thing he was sure of, his son would not find himself close to ruin when the time came for him to inherit.

His son. A smile curved Vincent's lips as he remembered the moment he had walked into Cassie's bedroom and discovered her with her arms about that wretched child Tara. It had made him realise he wanted to see his children—his son—in her arms.

'Sentimental fool,' he spoke aloud as he got up and walked over to the sideboard to pour himself a glass of brandy. It was a warm night and he had left the long windows to the garden open to get what breeze there was. 'She doesn't love you, why should she? She merely wants a comfortable marriage.'

Behind him a rustling sound at the windows alerted Vincent. He froze as a prickling at the nape of his neck alerted his sixth sense and warned him he was not alone.

'Stay where you are,' the voice commanded. 'I've a pair of pistols pointed at you and, by God, I'll use them if I have to!'

The chills ran down Vincent's spine. He was

going mad! He had to be. That voice…it could not be. Jack was dead. He had killed him. As sure as if he had held the gun to his head and fired himself. He knew he had to be dead, there was no way he could have survived such an injury.

'Jack…' Vincent turned slowly, the colour leaving his face as he saw the man standing just inside the open windows. He was holding a pair of old-fashioned duelling pistols and they were both levelled at Vincent's heart, cocked and ready. 'Good God, man! It can't be you. You were dead. I saw the blood gushing from the wound to your head. The shot was fatal. I was sure you were dead.'

'Damned nearly.' Jack's eyes glinted with anger. 'For all the help you gave me, Vinnie, I might as well have been. You left me for dead. You led me into that blasted ambush, and then left me there to die.'

'No! It wasn't like that,' Vincent cried hoarsely. The guilt, grief and regret he had been nursing for months flared up in him. 'You know it wasn't, Jack. You were in a blue funk, on the verge of running when I found you. I couldn't let you do that. I couldn't let you desert the field of battle. I had to make you go back and face the enemy again. You would never have forgiven me if I hadn't—or yourself.'

'You threatened to shoot me yourself if I didn't go with you,' Jack said, still angry. 'You took me into that ambush, and then you abandoned me to my fate.'

'I thought you were dead,' Vincent said. 'I was on a mission for Wellington. He told me to pick my own man to back me up—and you were about to run. It was my duty to ride on once you had fallen. Had I stopped to make sure you were really dead, I should have been killed and the documents I carried would have been captured by the enemy.' He turned away as the emotion surged in him. 'Good grief! Do you think I haven't been to hell and back since then? Blamed myself a thousand times for forcing you to go with me! I returned later, when the fighting was over, to search for you. I searched for days, everywhere. I went to all the field hospitals, convents, churches, wherever they told me the wounded had been taken. I scanned every list of the injured and dead. There was not a trace of you anywhere.'

'No, there wouldn't be,' Jack said, some of the tension draining out of him as he read the truth in Vincent's eyes. 'Louise found me. Apparently a finger twitched when they were going to put me on the dead cart, and she believed I was still alive. She had me carried to her home. I was more dead than alive, I promise you—and when I finally came to myself some weeks later, I did not know who I was. My memory had completely gone. I could neither walk nor speak, though I was not paralysed. I had to be taught to use every bodily function all over again, as if I were a child. If it had not been for that angel…'

'Louise? A Frenchwoman?' Vincent's eyebrows rose. 'She took you in and nursed you back to health? From what I heard, you were more likely to get a ball through the heart to finish you off.'

'Louise is not like that, she helped all those she could. She fed me, bathed me, taught me how to walk again. She is an angel, Vinnie.' Jack stepped further into the room and took off his hat. His hair was very short, as if it had been shaved close to his head and there was a deep scar and indentation near his temple where the bullet had lodged in his skull, saved from entering his brain by bone. He smiled as he saw the stunned expression in Vincent's eyes. 'They tell me my hair will grow again eventually, but it has gone grey from the shock of my illness. When you get that close to dying, it does strange things to you. I think I was near mad for a time.'

At first glance he looked an old man but, as Vincent looked into his eyes, he realised that the friend he had cared for so deeply was still there inside.

'You look awful,' he said gruffly, to hide his emotion. 'And your clothes—have you been living rough?'

'Sleeping under the stars, near starving at times. I came back six weeks or so ago,' Jack said. 'Louise gave me what she could, but she has nothing, poor darling. I intended to see Cassie as soon as I got home. In fact, I went to the house one night, and she leaned out of her window. I think she sensed someone was there, but when she looked out I lost my nerve.'

'Why? You must have known she would be glad to see you. She grieved for months over your loss. Indeed, she has hardly got over it now, though she is trying to rebuild her life.'

'I was afraid to just walk in on her looking like this,' Jack said. 'I mean, she would probably have screamed blue murder and sworn I was an impostor.'

'You know Cassie better than that,' Vincent said. 'So what was your true reason?'

'Why did you try to shoot me about a month ago?' Jack answered his question with another. 'After I couldn't bring myself to face Cassie, I came to Carlton House. She was walking alone in your woods. I followed for a while. I had almost made up my mind to speak to her then, but backed off when she found that child crying. So I decided to follow you to London…'

'That was you?' Vincent stared at him in stunned disbelief. 'Why the hell did you skulk in the trees like that? I thought you were a damned highwayman!'

'I was very nearly reduced to it.' Jack pulled a wry face, lowered his pistols and tossed them on to the desk. 'They aren't loaded. Father always said they were lethal. I wouldn't have taken them if that idiot Kendal hadn't come blundering in the way he did—

I was looking for something decent to wear, but Cassie must have thrown all my clothes out.'

'I believe she sent them to Nanny Robinson for safekeeping,' Vincent said apologetically. 'She wasn't going to let Kendal get his hands on anything of yours, apparently.'

'If that isn't just like her!' Jack chuckled, obviously relieved that his sister hadn't decided to sweep his possessions out the door. 'I was pretty cut up when I thought she couldn't wait to get shot of my things. I mean, it seemed as if she had forgotten me.'

'Oh, no,' Vincent said. 'She hasn't done that. She told me you had come back to her a few weeks ago— Good grief! She was right, wasn't she? Is that when your memory returned, just a few weeks ago?'

'Yes.' Jack was smiling now, at ease. 'It came in bits and pieces, then it was suddenly all there and I thought of Cassie, willing her to think about me. Until then, I hadn't really thought much about her. Once I remembered, Louise told me I had to come back. I was reluctant, but she insisted. She said I must at least let Cassie know I was alive.'

'Surely you will reclaim your inheritance?' Vincent looked at him hard.

Jack shrugged. 'There isn't very much, you know. I suppose I could sell the house, but my life is in France with Louise now.' His mouth softened into a smile of tenderness. 'She lives in a dreadful old château with her grandmother Madame Moreau. The roof has holes in it, and when the rains come we have to put out buckets to catch the drips. They have lost most of their land over the years, but there is a decent little farm and a vineyard. I worked with the grapes when I was recovering my strength but still did not know who I was. It was good, satisfying work, Vinnie. I think I could be happy there. Besides, Louise would never leave everything to come to England—and I love her.'

'But what if you change your mind in a few years?' Vincent said with a frown. 'Besides, there's your family to consider. Cassie…'

'She will be fine,' Jack said. 'She was always able to cope with anything life threw at her. I came back to make certain. But when I realised she was engaged to you, I knew everything was all right. So I thought I would tell you the whole story and go back to France. You can tell her when you're ready. You can bring her out to see us when you've prepared her for the shock.'

'You're going without seeing her?' Vincent was suddenly angry. 'No, damn you! You shan't do that. I shall not permit you to hurt her like that, Jack. I cannot believe you would even consider such a course of action.'

'I have seen her,' Jack said, looking awkward. 'I've been close to her a couple of times, but she…well, you couldn't expect her to see me as her brother, could you?'

'But does she know you're alive?'

'Well, as to that, I'm not sure. I think she might have started to suspect. When I stole her purse a few days ago she looked at me a bit suspiciously—'

'When you stole her purse?' Vincent was thunderstruck. 'Where did this happen? I've heard nothing of it.'

'She didn't tell you? I thought she would be sure to.' Jack frowned. 'Why *did* you ask her to marry you, Vinnie? Was it just because of that stupid promise I forced you and the others to make?'

'That's none of your damned business!'

'Forgive me.' Jack stared him out. 'But I think it is my business. Because so much time had passed, I imagined you had become friends, got to like one another—but if she didn't tell you about losing her purse she doesn't trust you much. If this isn't a love match, I want to know. I want to be sure Cassie is happy with the arrangement.'

Vincent controlled his very great desire to give him a bloody nose. 'Then you will just have to stay around for a while, won't you? Claim your rightful place in the world and stop running around stealing other people's property.'

'Come off it, Vinnie! Cassie wouldn't grudge me a few guineas. Besides, I was desperate. I had no money. I was hungry—and I'd caught a chill at that damned balloon ascension.'

'You were there!'

'I almost spoke to Cassie then, but you took her away. I can tell you, Vinnie, you've been a thorn in my side these past weeks.'

'What I cannot understand,' Vincent said, 'is why you did not come to me? If you were afraid your appearance would upset Cassie—why not come to me and let me break the news to her?'

Jack's gaze fell away. 'You must know why I hesitated, Vinnie.'

'I'm damned if I do!'

'You knew I was a coward. You knew I had run from enemy fire. I thought you had abandoned me to my fate. I thought you must hate and despise me.' He looked up suddenly, a glint of anger in his eyes. 'Damn it, Vinnie! You had tried to shoot me once. I thought you might make a thorough job of it if I came to you, that's why I brought Father's pistols with me this evening. After all, I couldn't blame you if you did decide to shoot me. I am a disgrace to my name and family.'

'What you are is a numskull,' said Vincent, a flicker of amusement in his eyes. 'Do you think I could turn against you because of a moment's panic? You're no more a coward than any of us, Jack. We were all scared out there, believe me.'

'Not you,' Jack said, frowning. 'Nothing ever frightens you.'

'You would be surprised,' replied Vincent, a wry smile on his lips. 'Quite a few things terrify me—but I shan't tell you what they are.'

'So you don't despise me? You haven't told anyone I ran under fire?'

'Do you take me for a gabblemonger? I blamed myself for forcing you to return with me. I was your murderer, Jack—and I have had your death on my conscience these many months. I thank God that you are alive, and I am very glad to see you again.'

Jack stared at him. 'Then I can come back? I can give Kendal notice to quit and claim what is left of the estate?'

'I believe you will find Mr Thornton pleased to be relieved of the burden,' Vincent said. 'But whatever you decide, you must speak to Cassie first. And before you do that, we must make you look presentable. We are much the same size. I can find you something decent to wear. If I were you, my friend, I should take a long soak in the hot tub and then we'll have supper and talk about the future.'

Cassie paused on the stairs as she heard the voices coming from the rear of the entrance hall at Longbourne. Surely that was Vincent? She had not expected him for another two days at least and her heart took a flying leap. She ran down the last few steps and saw him removing his capped greatcoat.

'Cassie,' he said, coming towards her with his hands outstretched. 'How are you, my love?'

'Very well,' she replied, blushing at the warmth in his eyes. 'I am very happy to see you returned sooner than you thought.'

She offered her cheek and he kissed it. 'My business took less time than I had imagined,' he said. 'Besides, I wanted to see you. We must talk—'

'Ah, there you are!' Sir Septimus boomed, coming into the hall from the parlour. 'Couldn't stay away from her, eh? Well, I cannot say that I blame you. You've got yourself a spirited filly there, Carlton. More spunk in her little finger than your mother ever had.'

Vincent frowned. He did not mind his uncle's blunt manner towards himself, but was not about to countenance an insult to his mother, even if it was meant to be a compliment to Cassie.

'Lady Longbourne's health has never been as good as it might be,' he said stiffly.

'You mean she uses it as an excuse to twist you round her little finger,' Septimus crowed, looking for all the world like a Bantam cock shaping up to a full-sized cockerel. 'You won't get that from your wife. I'll wager a hundred guineas on it!'

Vincent's mouth went hard, but Cassie jumped in before he could answer.

'You should not gamble so wildly, sir,' Cassie quipped, a sparkle in her eyes as she saw Vincent's hands clench at his sides. 'You told me yourself last night that I am a wicked jade, and there's no saying what I might do to get my own way.'

'Damned if you ain't right again!' Septimus looked startled. 'Don't know what's come over me of late. You'll have me tipping my blunt like a regular gamester if I don't watch it!' He laughed as if hugely amused at the idea, nodded to Vincent and walked into the parlour, where he could be heard telling his son to take himself off to the garden and keep out of his way.

'What was all that about?' Vincent asked Cassie, looking bewildered. 'Was that really my uncle—or have I walked into the wrong house? I have never heard him talk that way to anyone. He was almost good humoured.'

'Yes, it *was* Septimus,' said Lady Longbourne, coming down the stairs to greet her son. She smiled at Cassie as Vincent kissed her cheek. 'This fiancée of yours has bewitched him. I vow I have been near hysterics at the battles between them these past two days—but it seems your uncle enjoys having her stand up to him. I have never seen him so mellow.'

'He seems just as rude as ever,' Vincent remarked drily.

'Oh, but that is just his way,' said Lady Longbourne. 'However, he has not been half as horrid to me as usual. In fact, he called me his dear Emmeline yesterday—*and* he squeezed my hand.' The look in her eyes spoke volumes to Cassie.

'Oh dear, did he?' She gave Lady Longbourne a sympathetic look. 'How very uncomfortable for you, dearest Mama.'

'Well, it was,' replied Lady Longbourne. 'For I have not been used to it and it gave me quite a turn. But I am better now and I shall not feel so—so odd next time.'

'You cannot expect it to happen again? This is merely the shine of the new,' Cassie murmured wickedly. 'I dare say he will be himself again before you are aware of it.'

'Do you think so?' Lady Longbourne laughed. 'Well, I suppose I had better go and find Felicity. She was talking of going through the linen cupboards to make sure there were enough clean sheets to make up all the guest rooms. I am persuaded Harry's housekeeper has already seen to it so I must try to divert Felicity if I can.'

'Mama seems to have more energy than usual,' Vincent said with a lift of his eyebrows as she went off.

'There is so much to do,' Cassie said. 'I was about to walk down to the church to make sure there are enough vases—for the flowers, you know. Mrs Walker says they have plenty, but I think we might borrow some from Sir Harry's storeroom to be safe.'

'You are *very* busy,' Vincent said, feeling a little disoriented by what was happening around him. 'I do have something important to say to you, Cassie. If I shall not be in your way—perhaps I could walk down to the church with you?'

'Yes, of course.' She smiled at him. 'If you would not find it too boring. I should like to have your company. I too have something I have been wanting to discuss with you.'

'Have you, Cassie?' His eyes met hers searchingly but learned nothing. She was adept at hiding her thoughts.

They left the house together, walking through the formal gardens at the front of the house and entering the wood beyond. Neither of them spoke for several minutes, then both began at once.

'It is about Jack—' said Cassie.

'Cassie, prepare yourself for a shock. I do not know how much you have guessed but—'

They both stopped speaking and stared at one another. Cassie gazed up at him, her eyes wide and dark with emotion. 'Jack is alive, isn't he? Have you seen him, too?'

'Yes, I have seen him. You knew, didn't you? Somehow, you sensed him near by. And then you recognised him when he snatched your purse.' Vincent looked at her steadily—how frightened she looked. He wanted to comfort her but knew what he had to say would hurt and upset her. 'He thought you might have done.'

Cassie nodded, looking thoughtful. 'I had been aware of him for some time. He had gone, you know—out of my head. We had always been so close in thought, but then I thought he must be dead because he was no longer with me.'

'He nearly did die,' Vincent said gently. 'He was very ill. For a long time he could not remember anything. He had to learn to walk again.'

A sob rose to her lips. 'Oh, my poor Jack! No wonder he is so changed.' She gasped. 'Is that why he did not come to me? Was he afraid I should reject him?'

'Something like that,' Vincent agreed. He could not, would never tell her the true reason for Jack's hesitation. 'I believe he needed time to come to terms with what had happened to him. However, I shall let him tell you his own story himself. I have arranged for him to come to the house this evening, and will engage to make sure that no one disturbs you. You can meet after everyone else has gone to bed. It will be easier for him that way. And for you, I think.'

'Oh, how thoughtful of you!' Cassie frowned. 'Is he much changed—other than his looks?'

'I think him quieter, not so ready to laugh,' Vincent said and frowned. 'He is not as he was, Cassie. You could not expect it.'

'No,' she said, looking sad. 'No, it is not to be expected.'

'I assured him you would be happy to see him.'

'Yes, I shall—whatever the changes.'

'I was sure you would.'

'I want to share Aunt Gwendoline's fortune with him. I am not sure how things stand now.'

'The marriage contract?' Vincent stared at her in mild astonishment. 'Did you not bother to read it before you signed it, Cassie?' She shook her head. 'I have, of course, made a settlement on you, which should cover your needs, and is I hope generous. But should you require anything more, you may have the bills sent to me. I am well able to provide for my wife, and wish to do so. Your inheritance remains your own. Once we are married, you can dispose of the capital as you please.'

'And you will not mind?'

'I shall not mind,' he assured her gravely. 'I am not marrying you for the sake of your fortune. Indeed, it would not matter to me if you had not a penny to your name.'

'This is the first time we have talked properly,'

Cassie said, her eyes searching his face. It was not easy to read what was in his mind. 'Indeed, we have scarcely been alone like this before.'

'No, we have not,' Vincent said. 'Perhaps we ought to have taken more time for such walks, Cassie?'

'Yes,' she said, a shy but determined look in her eyes as she gazed up at him. 'I hope you will not think it impertinent in me if I ask you why you asked me to be your wife?' He was silent and she saw that she had shocked him. He had not expected her to ask such a question, but she needed to know the answer. 'I am not particularly attractive, and you do not need my fortune. People said it was a matter of honour, but...'

'In a way it was at the start,' Vincent said, knowing he must be honest with her. If he did not speak now, it might be too late. 'After the news of your father's death, Jack was greatly worried about what would happen to you...'

Cassie's face went white as she guessed what he was about to say. She took a step away from him, the pain of her disappointment sweeping over her so fiercely that she hardly knew what she said as she cried out, 'No! Do not say it, I beg you. Jack made you promise to ask me, didn't he? I know it, so do not try to deny it.'

'I cannot deny it,' Vincent said. 'He had asked me before and I would not, but that night...'

'You promised to ease his mind, didn't you?' Her face had drained of colour. 'And then when he died…'

'Cassie, it was just at the beginning…'

'No! Do not come near me.'

Cassie gave a little cry of despair as he held out his hand to her in silent appeal, then she turned and ran from him. At first she ran in blind panic, not caring where she went or what she did, wanting only to get away from this pain inside her.

She had to get away from him. She could not bear to hear his excuses. La Valentina had been right, he wanted her only as a means of securing his heir.

She gathered speed, her heart pounding as the tears streamed down her cheeks. Oh, it hurt so much—so much that she felt she would like to die. Nothing penetrated her misery, though she knew Vincent had begun to follow. Not at once but for some seconds now. He must surely catch up with her soon.

She redoubled her efforts. Then, after she had been running for a moment or two, she heard a scream. It was the cry of a wounded animal, a terrified scream that made her turn cold inside, and instinctively she turned towards it, her own hurt pushed aside as she followed the sounds of terror and pain.

'Cassie! Wait! You must wait for me…'

Vincent's cry only served to spur her on. Her instincts told her she must hurry or it would be too late. She knew Vincent was following her but she did not want him to catch her. Nor could she bear that some woodland creature should be in such agony. Its pitiful cries were tearing her apart.

Suddenly, she stopped dead as she saw the poacher bending over his cruel trap. He had caught a young deer by the leg and was about to beat its head in with a thick cudgel.

'Stop! Stop that at once!' she cried.

She ran straight at the poacher, throwing herself on him so that he was knocked off balance. He was taken by surprise and hit out with his stick, striking her a glancing blow on the head. It felled her instantly. She lost consciousness at once and was not privy to the violent scene that took place as she lay senseless on the ground.

'My God! You've killed her. You will hang for this.'

The poacher dropped his stick as he saw Vincent, recognising authority and fearing it. 'No, sir. It were an accident. Honest. I never meant—'

'Be quiet, sirrah! You are a murderer and a poacher,' Vincent said, his face white with anguish. 'I promise you this, if the hangman doesn't get you, I shall.'

With one furious blow, Vincent knocked him to the ground, where he lay whimpering, dazed and writhing in pain from a dislocated jaw. He did not attempt to move. To run would be useless. He was doomed. He knew it as Vincent took a tiny pistol from his coat pocket and shot the deer through the head, to put it out of its pain from the leg which had been nearly torn through and could never heal. The next shot would surely be for him if he dared to so much as flick a finger. But it did not come. He might not have existed for all the notice the aristocrat took of him.

Kneeling down by Cassie's side, his pistol back in his pocket, Vincent touched her face, which was still warm. She whimpered slightly and his heart stopped. She lived! God be praised, she lived. He spoke to her softly, willing her to open her eyes and know him, but she did not move even as he lifted her very gently in his arms.

Then he turned on the rogue who had struck her. The man was standing now, fear stamped all over his cowardly face. Vincent would have liked to kill him there and then, but he knew he must take care of Cassie. Revenge could be sought later, for now her well-being was his only concern.

'Run for your life, coward,' he muttered, eyes blazing. 'For if I find you in this life I shall kill you. You would sooner love the hangman's touch than mine if she dies.'

And with that he strode away, Cassie lying limp and still within his arms.

Chapter Ten

Cassie was just beginning to stir as Vincent carried her into the hall. He had been seen coming towards the house, and besides a worried-looking footman who was foolish enough to offer to take her from him, thereby getting his head snapped off, he was greeted by a small reception committee.

'What *have* you done to her?' cried Lady Longbourne, giving him an angry stare. It was obvious that she blamed him. 'Oh, my poor, dear Cassie!'

'Knew you were a pugilist,' Septimus said with a beetle glare that hid his concern. 'Didn't think you practised on ladies, Carlton. What happened?'

'Out of my way,' came the curt reply. Vincent glared at no one in particular, his face as black as thunder. 'If any of you has the least semblance of sense in your heads, someone see that her bed is ready. And send for Janet!'

Cassie moaned, her long, dark lashes fluttering

against her unnaturally pale cheeks. 'My head…it hurts. Please do not let him…do not let him…'

'You are quite safe now, my love. Your poor head will be better very soon,' promised Lady Longbourne as Vincent carried her past and on up the stairs. She followed him but at a discreet distance, looking distressed. The anger and despair in her son's eyes had shocked her. What could be the matter with him? She had never, never known Vincent to be so abrupt—or to look so out of control.

Janet was waiting with the bedcovers drawn back when Vincent swept into the room a fluttering maid had hurriedly indicated as Cassie's. He laid his precious burden down very carefully, frowning as she uttered a little cry of pain.

'What happened, sir?' asked Janet, shaking her head over her mistress.

'There was a trapped fawn and a poacher in the woods.' Janet nodded and clicked her tongue in dismay, understanding perfectly. She had no need to be told whose fault it was. 'I called to her to stop, but she would not listen. She just ran straight at him, unheeding of her own safety. He was taken by surprise and hit her. There was absolutely nothing I could do…'

'No, sir, of course not. If that isn't Miss Cassie all over. She is always so impulsive. Especially where animals in pain are concerned. It has always been the same.'

A cry of anguish issued from Cassie's lips. Her eyes opened, reflecting her pain as she looked directly at Vincent. 'The fawn…what happened?'

'I was forced to shoot it. It was too badly injured, Cassie. There was nothing else to be done but put it out of its misery.'

'No! Oh, no…' Tears welled up in her eyes. 'Too cruel…too cruel.'

'You were more important,' Vincent said, his face set in an unreadable mask, which she took for anger—or indifference. 'I did not know how badly you were hurt. I had to get you home.'

Cassie made a murmur of denial. She turned her head so that it was away from him, tears running down her cheeks.

'It was hurt, you should have helped it…'

The words were little more than a whisper, but they struck Vincent to the core, because they held so much meaning for him. If she cared so much about an injured animal, what must she feel if she knew he had been the cause of Jack's being injured and brought near to death? If she knew that he had been forced to leave her brother wounded on the ground and ride on? She would surely hate him!

'Cassie, I am sorry…please forgive me.'

She kept her face averted, a little sob escaping her.

'Perhaps it would be best if you left her to me, sir?' Janet suggested. 'I know how to look after her. She'll be better in a while.'

Vincent stared down at Cassie, his eyes dark with anguish. Her words and the way she held herself were rejecting him. He sensed that just at this moment she could not bear to have him near her, and it cut him to the heart.

'I shall fetch the doctor to her,' he said to Janet, then turned and walked from the room, his face so stern that Lady Longbourne felt a little faint. Her heart was racing quite madly, and she was sure she was on the verge of swooning.

However, this was not the time to give way to her own sad health, so instead she went into Cassie's room and sat down on the edge of the bed, holding the girl's hand in her own and kissing it.

'There, there, my dearest one,' she soothed, taking the cold cloth Janet had finished soaking in water and laying it on Cassie's forehead. 'I dare say you will have a nasty bruise, and I am sure your poor head hurts, but we must hope no more harm will come from this.'

Cassie smothered a sob, turning her head to look at her. 'It does hurt,' she said, 'but not so very much. What makes me cry is the thought of that poor creature…it was in such pain. I wanted to help it, but Vincent shot it. That was so unkind of him—he should have done something to help it.'

Lady Longbourne replaced the cloth with another supplied by the anxious Janet. 'You know I do not always agree with Vincent,' she said. 'But on this occasion I believe he acted for the best, my love. It must have been quite difficult for him, you know. A wounded creature in a trap, a dangerous poacher—and you unconscious. I imagine he did what he felt right in the circumstances.'

'His duty, you mean?' Cassie sounded almost bitter. 'Yes, I dare say he did the right thing—but not the kindest.'

Lady Longbourne saw the tears well up in Cassie's eyes once more. 'I think you are wrong, dearest. In this case it was kinder to act quickly. He could not help the fawn and you—and you were naturally more important.'

Seeing that Cassie was in great distress, Janet touched her ladyship's arm. 'Forgive me, ma'am, but I think it would be best if you leave her to me now. She's fretting and she needs to have a good cry, get it out of her system. I've seen her like this before, ma'am, and I know what to do.'

Lady Longbourne bowed to the experience of the woman who had nursed Cassie through many a crisis. 'Yes, perhaps I should leave her to rest.' She bent to kiss Cassie's cheek. 'Try to sleep, dearest. I shall visit you again after the doctor has been.'

Janet closed the door after her. Cassie had pushed herself up into a sitting position against a pile of pillows. Her face was pale and stubborn, her eyes dark with hurt.

'Why don't you just lie still and rest, child?'

'I hate lying in bed,' Cassie said. 'I think I shall get up.' She swung her feet over the side of the bed, then moaned as her head spun giddily. 'Oh, I feel dizzy.'

'What would you expect after a bang on the head?' Janet glared at her. 'Lie back at once, you foolish girl! I've warned you what would happen time and time again. If this isn't the outside of enough. Causing all this fuss—and with the wedding only three days away! What did you think you were doing? Poor Lady Longbourne must have had a dreadful fright. To say nothing of his lordship. You were very unfair to him, Miss Cassie, and so I must tell you. You did not thank him once for helping you. And that was very rude. I am surprised at you, and I do not mind telling you so.'

'Please do not scold me, Janet.' Cassie lay back against the pillows. Her maid's sensible tone had calmed her more than all the fussing and sympathy ever could. 'I know it was very foolish of me to do what I did—but that awful man was going to hit the fawn and I couldn't bear that. So I rushed at him and…I do not recall what happened then.'

'He hit you instead of the deer.' Janet's expression was grim. 'If you ask me, it was a blessing his lordship was there with you. Had you been alone, goodness knows what might have happened…' She shook her head over the thought, her tongue clicking in distress. 'You might have been killed—or worse.'

'That would have been very shocking, wouldn't it?'

'It would have caused a lot of people a lot of grief,' Janet said severely, secretly pleased that her scolding was working. Miss Cassie was coming out of the mopes. 'There are several of us who would have found that very difficult to bear, I might add. If you do not care for yourself, you should care for others.'

Cassie saw that her maid was battling with tears and was touched. She made an effort to stop feeling sorry for herself and smiled, holding out her hand.

'Yes, I know. I do not know why you should love me, when I have been so very much trouble to you, Janet—but I know you do. I am very grateful for it.'

Janet sniffed hard. 'Well, as to that—I am not the only one. There's Miss Sarah, Lady Longbourne—and his lordship, naturally. And I dare say a few others.'

Cassie closed her eyes for a moment. She knew Vincent did not love her. Oh, he liked her well enough. They often shared the same jokes and they were comfortable together. He was concerned for her welfare, as he would be for any lady of his family—but he did not love her. Not as she wanted to be loved.

She opened her eyes and looked at Janet. 'Jack loves me,' she said. 'At least I have him.'

'Now, Miss Cassie.' Janet seemed alarmed, as if fearing that the bang to her head set Cassie's wits a-wandering. 'You know poor Master Jack was killed in France.'

'No, he wasn't,' Cassie said, and now she was smiling, her own hurts temporarily banished. 'He *was* terribly wounded, Janet. Everyone thought he must have died of his injuries, but he wasn't killed. I do not yet quite understand what happened, how it came about that he was reported killed, but I shall soon. He is coming here to see me tonight. I am to meet him in the library, so that we can be private together.'

Janet stared at her. She laid her hand on the girl's brow, but it was cool. She didn't think Miss Cassie was feverish, but it sounded too good to be true. 'How do you know all this?'

'Lord Carlton told me just before...' Cassie paused, swallowing hard. 'I had seen Jack once or twice in London, but he is so changed I did not know him. Do not look so disbelieving, Janet. I have not gone mad. I promise you, it is true. Jack is alive and coming here tonight.'

'God be praised!' Janet sat down on the edge of the bed with a little bump. Her legs had turned to jelly and she was all of a quiver. 'Oh, my goodness me. I'm all upside down. Master Jack not dead. It's a miracle, Miss Cassie.' She crossed herself. 'A miracle… I do not know how to take it in, and that's a fact.'

'Yes, I know. It is so wonderful. I can hardly believe it myself—but it is true.'

'And he's coming here tonight?'

'Yes. I shall meet him after everyone else has gone to bed—because he feels a little awkward about the way he looks, you see. He has a scar at his temple, I think—and his hair may be grey, though I believe he was wearing a wig when I saw him. He followed me in London, waiting to get his chance to speak to me, but in disguise. He did not want me to know him until he was ready, you see. I think he was afraid that I might reject him. But he has since revealed himself to Lord Carlton—and now he is coming to see me.'

'Mercy on us!' Janet cried. 'Well, if that's the case, miss, you lay your head down now. If you want to be up to seeing Master Jack later, you had best get some sleep now.'

'Must I?' Cassie pulled a wry face. 'Oh, I suppose you are right—and I do have a bit of a headache.'

Cassie did her best to sleep that afternoon. The doctor had visited, pronounced her lucky to have got off so lightly, and left her something to help her sleep if her head hurt too much. She thanked him politely, but the medicine remained untouched. Her head did indeed feel rather sore, and very tender where the bruise was coming through, but that was not the reason for her restlessness.

She could not forget what Vincent had told her just before she ran away from him. He had asked her to marry him because of a promise he had made to her brother! Jack had been worried because their father had brought the estate almost to ruin, then shot himself, leaving her to manage alone.

It was so typical of Jack to seek to protect her, but he should not have done it. She did not want to be married for such a reason! It was humiliating—to think that Vincent had pitied her! And he must have done or he would not have made such a foolish vow.

Oh, how could he do that? How could he allow her to believe he truly cared for her when all the time it was a sham?

Cassie tossed restlessly from side to side. She would never, never have consented to be his wife had she known. Oh, it was all too hurtful and too confusing. She did not know what to do about the situation: it was such a tangle!

She could withdraw, of course. That would be so very shocking. The wedding was only a few days away, the guests invited, presents received. What a scandal it would make if she cancelled everything now. She shuddered to think of all the upset it would cause—but it would give great offence to Lady Longbourne and it would also hurt her deeply. No, it was not to be thought of!

Cassie smothered a sob. She felt wretched and very weepy. She was truly fond of her kind hostess, who had done so much for her. After the tiring visit to town Lady Longbourne had undertaken for her benefit, her advice and genuine concern! It would distress her terribly if Cassie withdrew now.

Oh, what a mess it all was! Cassie's mood gradually changed to anger as she lay staring at the ceiling. It was all Carlton's fault. He had deceived her, allowing her to believe he truly cared for her. His proposal had misled her. Why had he been so emotional that day? Oh, he was so very tiresome! She was extremely cross with him.

And yet she liked him so well, had missed him when he went away for a few days.

Who was she fooling? Cassie forced herself to face the truth. She was head over heels, helplessly in love with Vincent. It would break her foolish heart if she were never to see him again. Yet how could she marry him, knowing what she did?

It was an impossible situation, and kept her tossing from side to side as she sought a way out and could not find one. No matter what she did now, she was destined to be miserable.

* * *

Cassie must have slept for a while. She woke feeling tired and listless, lying in the darkness for a moment or two, then suddenly remembered why she had not wanted to fall asleep. She jumped out of bed, in a frenzy of nerves mixed with excitement. As she stood, she was relieved to find that she no longer felt dizzy. A quick wash in cold water from a jug on her washstand left her refreshed and wide awake.

The house seemed very quiet. There was no sound from downstairs. She thought it must be very late. Perhaps Jack was already here, waiting for her.

She tidied her hair, wincing a little at the soreness of her temple, then pulled on a fresh gown Janet had left ready. It was an old one, which fastened at the front and was easy to manage. Taking a last glance at her reflection, she went out into the hall and hesitated, listening.

There were still candles burning, so perhaps not everyone had yet retired. Cassie moved softly along the carpeted landing and down the stairs, not wanting anyone to hear her and come out to ask what she was doing at this hour. She knew that all her friends would urge her to return to bed, and she was determined to see Jack. Nothing must stop her! She prayed that he had not been and gone already.

A clock striking midnight somewhere in the house

made her jump and look guiltily over her shoulder. Reaching the hall, she fled through it to the green salon. It was empty as she had hoped, and led directly into the library. The connecting door was opened slightly, and she could see light coming from inside. Jack must be here!

Her heart began to race, and she went swiftly towards the open door, her mouth dry with a mixture of excitement and fear. She wanted to see Jack so desperately, and yet she was afraid of the changes she might find—not in his looks, which did not matter, but in the essential core of him.

As she paused outside the library door to gather her nerves, she heard their voices: Jack's and Vincent's. They appeared to be arguing—and about her! She knew she ought to go in at once, but somehow she lingered.

'How could you let it happen?' Jack demanded in outrage. 'Damn you, Vinnie! What were you about to let that ruffian hurt her? It was your duty to protect her. You should have done something. Stopped her! Good grief, Vinnie, you must have known she was in danger. She could have been killed!'

'She was too far ahead of me,' Vincent protested, sounding guilty. 'I called her to stop, to wait for me, but she carried on unheeding. I was not close enough to prevent what happened. She simply would not listen to me.'

'I should just imagine she would not listen after what you'd said to her. Why on earth did you tell her about that stupid promise? You must have known how she would react? Why blurt it out like an empty-headed fool?'

'I felt I owed her the truth,' Vincent said. 'Naturally, I said nothing about the others—or that we drew straws to see who went first. And I would be grateful if you kept that to yourself. Goodness knows what she would think then. Your sister is a very independent woman, Jack. And headstrong. I tried to explain, but she would not give me a chance. When she ran away from me in the woods I hesitated, and then I could not catch up with her. Now she is angry with me for shooting that wretched creature—but what else could I do? I had to get her home, and deal with the rogue who felled her.'

'Well, at least he got his just deserts.'

'I've not finished with him yet, believe me.'

'Let it go,' Jack advised. 'Revenge is empty. Besides, you'll have your hands full with Cassie.'

'I dare say you are right. She does seem to have a mind of her own.' A husky laugh escaped him. 'As I am beginning to learn to my cost, Jack.'

'You don't know the half of it,' Jack said. 'She has the devil of the temper, though you might not think it to look at her.' He sighed. 'Oh, well, I suppose it cannot be helped.'

'I shall apologise, of course, and hope she will forgive me.'

'And you think she is too unwell to see me?' Jack said. 'I had best go and—'

Cassie pushed the door wide. Both men swung round, their faces white with shock and guilt.

'My God!' Vincent looked horrified. 'How long have you been standing there?'

'Long enough.' Cassie was furious. With both of them. She took a few steps into the room, her whole body bristling with temper. 'How dare you! How dare you make plots behind my back? I am not a piece of baggage to be disposed of over a casual chat by the fire.' Her gaze fell on Jack. ' How dare you beg your friends to marry me, Jack? How dare you tell my brother to go away because I am too ill to see him, Lord Carlton?' She gave him a freezing look. 'Who gave either of you permission to dictate my life?'

Neither of them uttered a word. Caught in the act like two schoolboys with their hands in the toffee jar, they simply stared at her. She was too angry for them to try and soothe her ruffled feelings. It was clear that she had heard every word of their discussion and was outraged, as well she might be. Cassie had every right to feel aggrieved after the way they had been discussing her.

For several seconds there was complete silence, broken only by the monotonous ticking of the mantle clock. Outside, a branch rattled against the window as the wind rose. Vincent found his tongue first.

'Forgive me. I was told you were sleeping and must on no account be disturbed.'

'You were misinformed, sir. As you see I am awake, and perfectly recovered from what was merely a slight bump on the head. I really do not know what all the fuss has been about.'

'It was a little more than a slight bump, I think.'

He received a scorching look and retired from the field gracefully.

'Sorry, Cassie.' Jack ventured a sortie next. 'It was my fault and mine alone. I just couldn't bear to think of you all alone in the house if anything happened to me—and at the mercy of that bore Kendal. I meant it for the best, but I realise now that I was mistaken.'

'I was at no one's mercy,' she replied, her face beginning to soften as she looked at her beloved brother and saw the scars. Her poor, dear Jack! How he must have suffered. And she was not there to help or comfort him. 'You could not know, of course, but Aunt Gwendoline died and left me her fortune. I am of age, and financially independent. So I may do as I please.'

'Did she have a fortune?' Jack looked startled. 'I swear I never knew of it. I don't think I ever met her. Besides, I wasn't myself out there, Cassie.

Everything seemed upside down. I had a terrible feeling that I was going to die. Forgive me, please? After all this…I came to see that I had made a wretched tangle of things…' He touched his temple. 'I am a bit of a mess myself, I'm afraid.'

'Oh, Jack…' Cassie's outrage faded as she saw the uncertainty in his eyes and realised how vulnerable he was. He really had thought she might reject him. 'Oh, my dearest darling…what a fool I am for pinching at you for such nonsense. It is wicked of me. Of course I forgive you. Nothing matters except you. I am so very glad to see you, Jack. So very, very glad you were not killed after all.'

She rushed towards him and was caught up in a bear hug. Tears began to run down her cheeks as she took his face between her two hands and kissed him, over and over again on his cheeks, his lips, his temple, until he began to protest.

'Hey, come on, Cas!'

'I love you, I love you, I love you. And don't you dare to doubt it ever again!'

'No, no, Cassie, don't eat me. You are as bad as that spaniel we once had! Do you remember Roxy?'

'Yes, yes, of course I do,' she cried and slipped her arm through his, glowing up at him as the memories came flooding back. 'She was forever licking one's face. You once said it wasn't worth washing after Roxy had finished licking you because there couldn't possibly be any dirt left—and Nanny Robinson dragged you off to the bath and scrubbed you. You are unkind to liken me to Roxy, Jack.' She gurgled with laughter. 'I should be cross with you, but I am so very, very glad to see you.'

'I am glad to see you,' Jack said. 'Vinnie had to dragoon me into coming, fool that I am. I thought you might disown me.' He glanced over his shoulder. 'Where is he?'

'He must have slipped out,' Cassie said, looking towards the door and frowning. 'How odd—I did not hear him go.'

'Well, if that isn't just like him. Wouldn't you know it!'

Cassie frowned. 'I suppose he thought we would prefer to be on our own for a while. And he was right. I want to hear everything, Jack—and don't leave anything out. I shall know if you do.'

'Yes, you would,' he said, looking rueful. 'It doesn't make very pretty hearing, Cassie.'

'As if I should care for that! I want to know how it happened—and why everyone thought you were dead.'

Jack pulled a wry face. 'Vinnie reported me dead. He saw me fall and thought the shot must be fatal, as it should have been, of course.' He grinned and touched the indentation at his temple. 'Louise says my skull must be made of iron. That ball should have entered my brain, but it merely splintered the bone. I can only think that the shot did not have a full charge of powder. Had it penetrated a fraction further, I would certainly have died.'

'You always were a bonehead,' his sister said, teasing him in her old way. 'So who is Louise—and how was it that Vincent thought you were dead? Did he not stop to make certain?'

'He could not,' Jack said, frowning. 'We were on a mission for Wellington and he carried vital papers that he dared not let fall into enemy hands.' He flushed as he recalled the way Vinnie had found him cowering in the baggage tent. Had his friend not dragged him with him on that mission, he would have been drummed out of the army for cowardice—and perhaps shot as a deserter. There would have been no Louise to save his life then. 'I—I should have been on the field of battle that day, but Vinnie had chosen me to ride as his escort. It was my job to draw enemy fire if we were attacked, while he went on. We rode into an ambush, and I was shot, but he escaped somehow.'

'And he left you to die? How could he?' She frowned and seemed about to condemn Vincent once more.

'No, no, it wasn't like that. Please listen before you jump to conclusions, Cassie. Vinnie did the right thing. Had I been carrying those papers, I must have made the same choice. It wasn't easy for him, but that's the way it is in war. Vinnie had to ride on, he could not do anything else.'

'Yes, I suppose so,' she admitted, slightly reluctant. 'But surely…afterwards?'

'I wondered after I recovered my memory,' Jack said. 'But in my heart I knew Vinnie would not have simply forgotten me. He did go back to where I was shot, Cassie. He searched for me everywhere, but Louise had already found me. She took me to her home, an old château hidden away in a hollow, which is not easy to find unless you know of it. Vinnie told me there were a lot of fresh graves in the woods near where I was shot. The French peasants had been out burying any bodies they found, their own countrymen or English. Vinnie thought I must have been found and buried by someone who did not know who I was. Indeed, had it not been for Louise, I dare say that would have been the case.'

'Yes.' Cassie reached up to stroke his face, as she began to see how it must have been out there in the aftermath of a bloody war. 'I do sort of understand, Jack. I suppose he could not have done anything other than what he did. It seems very hard to me, but in war these things must happen.'

'Be thankful that you did not have to make such choices. Louise faced them more than once.' Jack's expression was grim. 'I believe it cost Vinnie some grief,' he said. 'He blamed himself for taking me with him on that mission, but it was not his fault. He did the right thing at the time. Promise me you will not hold it against him?'

'No, I shall not blame him for something he could not help,' Cassie said, an odd look in her eyes. She knew in her heart he had done the only thing he could when he shot the wounded deer, though it had hurt her deeply. 'But now you must tell me everything else, Jack. Who is Louise—and what is she to you?' A smile touched her lips. 'I think she must be rather special.'

'Yes, she is. Very special,' he replied, the look in his eyes giving him away. 'I owe my life to her, Cassie—and my sanity. If it were not for her, I should have been buried alive. She saw my finger twitch and made her people carry me home. She nursed me when everyone else said it was hopeless and I should, for pity's sake, be allowed to die.'

'And is she pretty?' Cassie asked, her feelings mixed. Jack had never loved anyone else as much as her, but he did now.

'She has hair like dark honey and greenish eyes,' Jack replied. 'But she isn't pretty like Sarah Walker—I think she's beautiful, but that isn't it either. She has…soul.' He blushed and looked embarrassed, as if ashamed of having spoken so openly of his innermost thoughts.

'Then I am glad you have her,' Cassie said, her feelings of slight jealousy banished by her love for him. If Louise had touched him so deeply, she could only be pleased for his sake. 'Now, tell me the whole of it, dearest.'

Jack's story was long in the telling, for he left no detail out, and Cassie's throat was tight with emotion as she lived through her brother's terrible ordeal. By the time he had finished she knew that she owed a debt of gratitude to the French girl that she would never be able to begin to repay, and she had already begun to love her for her true kindness and generosity of soul.

'So you love her,' Cassie said, smiling as she reached for his hand. 'And she loves you?'

'I cannot see for the life of me why,' Jack said with a self-conscious laugh. 'But it seems she does.' He smiled at his sister. 'Do you know, you and she are very alike. I think I would have loved her had I known her, even if she had not saved my life.'

'I am so glad, my dearest.'

'You will love her, Cassie.'

'I already do, for what she has done.' She looked into his eyes. 'You will be married?' He nodded. 'And you will live in France, of course. Louise could not leave her family or her home. And you will be happier in a new life, more comfortable amongst strangers who accept you as you are and do not pity you.'

'How well you know me,' Jack said and bent to kiss her cheek. 'I shall miss you, of course.'

'As I shall you,' she replied. 'But your life will be with Louise now. You must think of her first. That is only natural.'

'But you will visit us,' Jack said. 'Vinnie will bring you. I am going to sell the family house. With the money from the sale, I can at least make the château comfortable for us all.'

'You will share Aunt Gwendoline's fortune,' Cassie said. 'I want you to have half of it, Jack.'

'Not half,' he said. 'You were always too generous, Cassie. A thousand or two to set me up, if you like—but not half.'

'Half,' she replied, a glint of determination in her eyes. 'Do not argue, Jack. I have already discussed it with Carlton, and besides, I have made up my mind.' She gave him such a glare that he burst into laughter. 'It is not a laughing matter!'

'Miss Stubbornhooves!' Jack cried, grinning at her. 'That donkey was nothing to you, Cassie.'

'Well, yes, in this instance I am prepared to be stubborn,' Cassie replied and laughed. 'Major Saunders told me you used to recount those stories about me round the camp-fire. That was too bad of you, you know.' She reached out to touch his face lovingly. 'You really shouldn't have asked your friends to make that promise. It wasn't fair—to them, or me.'

'I know. I am sorry. Honestly.' He arched his brows at her. 'Forgive me?'

'Perhaps…oh, of course!'

'Well, it turned out for the best, did it not? I always thought you and Vinnie would suit.'

Cassie dropped her gaze. 'I am not sure, Jack. I am not certain I wish to marry Carlton after all…'

Outside the library, Vincent froze with his hand on the door handle. He had been about to enter, having left them together for nearly an hour, and had imagined they would have had time enough to say all they needed to one another. It seemed he had returned too soon—or perhaps too late.

'Not marry him?' Jack cried in astonishment. 'What on earth are you talking about, Cassie? Have you lost your senses? Your wedding is only three days away. You cannot change your mind now. It is impossible. Only think of all the fuss and turmoil it would cause! The gossips would have a field day…'

Vincent walked in before Cassie could answer. She glanced at his face, her heart pounding wildly as she saw the expression on his face. He was so angry! She has never seen him look that way before, his eyes bleak and cold…so cold! But surely it was more than anger…something else she did not understand. Was it pain she saw reflected there? Guilt? Or regret? She could not be certain, but she knew it had struck an answering chord in her.

'The scandal does not matter,' Vincent said quietly. He was looking at her and it was concern for her she saw in his face now. It smote her like a blade in her heart. 'I will not have Cassie forced into something she does not want for the sake of people's tongues. Let them do their worst. I shall naturally accept the blame—'

'Damn you, Vinnie!' Jack jumped to his feet, bewildered and angry himself at this sudden and disturbing turn of events. 'Are you saying you don't want to marry my sister? By God! If you dare to jilt her, I'll give you a bloody nose.'

'You could try, of course,' Vincent replied, a smile on his mouth. 'I very much doubt you could do it—unless you have been taking lessons, of course.'

'I damned well will!' Jack put his fists up. 'Come on, you scoundrel. I'll give you a run for your money, if no more.'

'Stop this!' Cassie stepped between them, her eyes blazing with temper. 'Stop acting like a pair of fools. You will not fight, either of you. I never heard of such nonsense. I refuse to allow it. If you are not careful you will rouse the house—and I dare say neither of you would care for that.' She saw by their faces that she had struck home. 'You may settle this amicably if you please.'

'If he jilts you, I'll kill him,' Jack muttered. 'I don't know what he has done to make you unhappy, Cassie, but I won't have him disgrace you like this.'

'He has done nothing wrong,' Cassie said. 'Oh, stop looking at Vincent like that, Jack! He is your best friend. Besides, he isn't jilting me. I am just not perfectly certain I want to get married after all. I think I might like to wait a while and think things over.'

'You don't want to do that,' Jack muttered, still glowering at his lifelong friend. 'Get left on the shelf if people think you're contrary. Men don't like that sort of thing.'

'Being a wife is not necessarily the only way for a woman to live.'

'Getting cold feet, Cassie?' Vincent's eyes glittered as he looked at her flushed face. 'Want to cry off, make me look a fool? That would give me my own again, wouldn't it?' He smiled oddly as she hesitated, her expression revealing her uncertainty. 'The only thing is—it makes you look bad. You might find some of your friends would not want to know you when you next go up to town, unless you were thinking of retiring to the country.'

'Oh, you impossible man!' Cassie cried, catching the note of mockery in his voice. 'Can you never be serious? Pray what is all the fuss about? I merely said I was not sure I wanted to marry you—and then you offered to jilt me. I must suppose that I have given you the excuse to cry off.'

'I've changed my mind,' Vincent countered promptly, his eyes challenging her. 'You shall be the one to decide, Cassie. I'll give you until the evening of the dance to make up your mind, whether you wish to be my wife or not.'

'That's not fair,' she said, flushing angrily as he turned to leave. 'Where do you think you are going, sir? You just cannot walk out. We have too much to discuss.'

'I shall be at Carlton House,' Vincent replied. 'You can send word if you want me to return.'

'You cannot do that!' Cassie cried, distressed and confused by her own emotions. 'Vincent! You surely cannot mean it?'

'Give me one good reason why I may not?' His brows rose, his eyes daring her to answer him.

'Because…because I refuse to jilt you,' Cassie said, her face pale. 'I cannot be the cause of so much pain to Lady Longbourne. It is not fair of you to make me do it, Vinnie. You must see that it would be quite impossible.'

'Why?'

Cassie shook her head, face flushed as she wrestled with pride and common sense. 'You are putting me in an awkward position. I must appear foolish or contrary. What will everyone think of me?'

'That you are very wise to have cried off before it was too late?' He looked at her hard.

'No, of course they will not. Why should they? Anyone who knows you would think I had gone mad.' Cassie said, turning to her brother for assistance. 'Tell him, Jack!'

'You have to marry her, or jilt her. Vinnie, you know you must do one or the other. You cannot possibly make Cassie jilt you. No, no, you must see it!'

'I do not see why,' replied Vinnie, a flicker of amusement in his eyes. 'Cassie is the one who changed her mind. I am still perfectly willing to go ahead with the wedding. Indeed, I consider myself the injured party. If I were a vengeful man, which I am not, of course, I should go to court and sue for breach of promise.' He turned his intent, wicked gaze on her. 'So—what is it to be, Cassie? Will you marry me or not?'

'Oh, you…you awful man!' she cried, her eyes sparkling with suppressed fury. 'I dislike you very much. I should be out of my mind to marry you, but I cannot see what else to do as you are so very disobliging. Very well! You win, though by methods I cannot think anything but disreputable. I shall marry you, sir—but only because it would cause so much fuss if I didn't. Besides giving grief to Lady Longbourne, of whom I *am* fond.'

'That's told me, hasn't it, Cassie?' Vincent was unrepentant. 'A matter of honour, then?' His mouth quivered at the corners, and it was obvious that he was enjoying himself. 'I would have this quite clear if you please, my love. You are consenting to be my wife, because you do not want to let everyone down?'

'No—yes!' Cassie glared at him. 'If it were not for the harm it would cause to people I care for, I would jilt you this instant. You are an impossible man and—and I do not like you. At this particular moment, I detest you!'

'But you will marry me?'

'Yes, I shall marry you,' Cassie said, giving him a look that would have felled any other man. 'If only to make your life utterly unbearable. And do not think I cannot do it, because I assure you I can—and will!'

With that, she gave a choking cry of despair and ran from the room, leaving her brother and Vincent to stare after her.

Jack was silent for a moment, then he looked at Vinnie. 'What do you make of that? Damned if I've ever known her to be quite so contrary. Not sure why…'

'I seem to remember telling you earlier that your sister was both headstrong and stubborn.' Vincent's eyes gleamed. 'Perhaps you had forgotten?'

'Yes, I remember,' Jack said mournfully. 'Dash it, I know it all too well! You wouldn't think she had such a temper, would you—not in the general way. She is usually the sweetest creature, but if she gets a bee in her bonnet it is best to steer clear for a while.

Regroup and come about another day, that's my best advice. You would do well to heed it.'

'Do you think so?' Vincent smiled to himself. 'I find it all rather interesting.'

'That's because you do not know how far she can go to get her own way. You'll come off worst, old friend. I'm warning you—Cassie will get her way in the end.'

'No, do you say so?'

'Women always do,' Jack said ruefully. 'You should have heard the language Louise used to get me off my back and stop me feeling so damned sorry for myself—and *she* is a milk-and-water miss compared to my sister. You have no idea what you are taking on, Vinnie.'

'Oh, I think perhaps I do. Cassie is capable of many things,' replied Vincent a hint of satisfaction in his eyes. 'I have always believed temper and passion go together.'

Jack's gaze narrowed. 'Damn it, Vinnie! You had no intention of jilting her—or of letting her jilt you, had you?'

'No, of course not.' Vincent chuckled. 'I merely gave her her head, to see what came off it.'

A long, low whistle escaped Jack. 'Well, blow me down! You *are* in love with her, aren't you?'

'Desperately,' Vincent admitted. 'Until a few minutes ago, I believed the passion was all on one side, that she wished only for a comfortable marriage. But do you know, Jack, I think…I really think that she might just care for me a little.'

'She is in love with you, of course!' Jack said. 'That's why she was so cross.'

'Yes…' Vincent nodded, a smile in his eyes. 'But do you think she is prepared to admit it?'

Chapter Eleven

Alone in her bedchamber, Cassie threw a few cushions around before tearing off her clothes and depositing them on the floor. She then pulled back the covers, fell into bed and burst into a flood of frustrated tears, ending at last with her face buried in the pillows. Her heart was aching and she felt both exhausted and miserable.

What was she to do? Carlton had turned the tables on her and she was caught in a trap largely of her own making.

Oh, that wretched, wretched man to make her so unhappy! She disliked him very much. Indeed, she wished she had never set eyes on him. It would be the greatest pleasure to her to tear him limb from limb. She pounded at the pillow, which had become unaccountably wet and lumpy, then turned onto her back. For some minutes, she lay staring at the ceiling.

'Oh, bother,' she said and sighed. 'Why should I

care? He is a complete shamster, a liar and a cheat and I shall make him pay for this. Oh, he will be sorry! To deceive me so—and then refuse to do the decent thing and jilt me!'

If there was a tiny bud of satisfaction deep within her that he had refused to jilt her, Cassie was not yet ready to allow it room to grow. Her feelings had been badly bruised by what she had heard as she eavesdropped outside the library door—which only went to show that Janet was right when she said listeners never heard good of themselves! And it just served her right for not going into the library at once.

Cassie reached for her kerchief and blew her nose. She was not exactly sure of how she felt about anything at this precise moment. She had been very close to telling Carlton she would not marry him, but at the last moment something had stopped her. And in her heart, she knew it was because she loved him.

'You are a complete idiot,' she scolded herself severely. 'If you love him and he does not love you, you will be miserable. You had much better run away now, tonight!' But she did not want to, of course.

She knew that she would not be able to bear it if, after she had conceived the child she knew would be expected of her, her husband left her to return to his mistress.

But she would be desperately unhappy without him. Cassie realised she was caught in a trap.

Whichever way she turned, she could not escape the feelings inside her. Besides, she had for the second time that evening promised to marry Carlton.

Why had he been so ungallant as to insist she must jilt him? Cassie could not be sure. If he had wanted to change his mind about marrying her, it would have been easy for him to insist that he did the honourable thing and stood aside. But like the wretch he was, he had turned it all back on her— even saying that he might sue for breach of promise!

And now she had a throbbing headache.

'Bother, bother, bother!' Cassie said, and put her head under the bedclothes. 'I am sure I do not care what you do, my Lord Carlton. You are quite odious, and I want nothing to do with you!'

Despite her fears that she would not sleep a wink, Cassie was awakened from her uneasy dreams by a young maid pulling the curtains back. She sat up, yawned and blinked in the bright sunlight pouring in at the window.

'What time is it?'

'Past eleven, Miss Thornton. We were given orders that you were to be allowed to sleep in a little this morning.'

'Oh…thank you. I was tired.' Cassie wondered who had given the order, but did not ask. 'Where is Janet?'

'She was feeling a bit under the weather, miss,

so she stayed in her room this morning. She thinks
she may have taken a summer cold, and was afraid
of passing it on to you. What with the wedding so
soon and all. It would be shocking if you were to
take it, miss.'

'Janet ill?' Cassie was suddenly wide awake. 'I
must go to her as soon as I am dressed. She is rarely
ill. She must feel dreadful if she has kept to her bed.'

'It's just a cold, miss. Best you stay away from her
for a day or so. You do not want to catch a cold
before the wedding.'

'Nonsense! I shall visit her as soon as I am
dressed. I would not dream of doing otherwise.'

Nothing would do for Cassie but that she must
make sure Janet was not in danger of neglect.
However, she soon discovered that it was only a
chill. Her maid had stayed away from her for
safety's sake, and was sitting up in a chair nursing
a hot drink.

Cassie kissed her, despite Janet begging her not
to, and promised that she would make sure she was
supplied with lemons, brandy, hot water and sugar
until she was feeling better.

'For I know that is what you would prescribe for
me, dearest—and you must take care of yourself. I
could not go away without you to look after me, so
you must be better in time for my wedding.'

'Now don't you go troubling your head over me,'

Janet scolded. 'You will have lots to do, and I can manage very well.' She sneezed into her handkerchief. 'There, you would not be told! Now you will catch it and the wedding will have to be postponed.'

'I never catch colds,' replied Cassie blithely. 'If you are sure you have everything you want, I shall go downstairs now. I really must walk down to the vicarage and see about those vases.'

'You should sit quietly with a book,' Janet advised, frowning at her. 'But I suppose you will not be told. So if you must go to the village, take Lady Longbourne's carriage. If there are poachers about, you should not walk in the woods.'

A flicker of pain showed in Cassie's eyes as she recalled the incident of the previous day. She could not bear that a creature should be hurt in that way, though she knew deer must be culled sometimes, but poaching was barbaric.

'Yes, perhaps I shall take the carriage,' she said. 'Do not worry about me, Janet. I shall be quite safe. That particular poacher will not dare to return.'

She was thoughtful as she walked down the stairs. She had been too upset after the incident to really think about what must have happened after she was knocked unconscious. Vincent had shot the fawn—had he shot the poacher, too? Oh, dear! She did hope not, though she also hoped he had been punished for his crime. She rather wondered from something Jack had mentioned the previous evening whether Vincent might have knocked him down, since it would appear that he was quite handy with his fists.

She was thoughtful as she reached the bottom of the stairs. hearing voices in the front parlour, she was about to turn away when Lady Longbourne came out to her.

'Ah, Cassie, my love, how are you this morning?'

'I am much better,' Cassie replied. 'Quite well—except for this horrid bruise, which looks so unsightly.'

'Well, I dare say we shall manage to cover it for the wedding—if we pull a little of your hair lower.' Lady Longbourne looked at her, seeming oddly uneasy. 'Now, my dear, there is someone waiting to see you. I believe you were expecting Major Saunders to call? Some idea of his giving you away, I think?'

'Oh, yes, I was,' said Cassie, remembering that he had been kind enough to offer his services. 'Yes, I must certainly speak with him.'

She went straight into the parlour. Major Saunders had been perched uncomfortably on the edge of his chair, but he sprang to his feet as she entered, coming at once to greet her.

'Miss Thornton,' he said, obviously very concerned. 'Lady Longbourne has been telling me that you met with an accident yesterday. Are you well enough to come down? I wondered if you might decide to postpone the wedding?' He could not quite conceal his eagerness. 'Just for a while, you know…'

'No, I shall not need to do that,' Cassie said, her cheeks slightly flushed. His admiration for her was quite obvious and she wondered if she had been wise to accept his offer to stand up with her. 'How very shocking that would be of me, to upset all dear Lady Longbourne's arrangements for the sake of a little bump on the head.'

'Far more than that from what I have been told,' he said, looking at her with undisguised approval. 'You were quite a heroine, it seems—though perhaps impetuous.'

'To no avail, I fear,' Cassie said on a sigh. 'Carlton was forced to put the creature out of his misery. All I did was cause a lot of fuss and distress for everyone.'

'You are too hard on yourself.'

'No, I do not think so,' Cassie replied seriously. 'It is time I ceased to rush in without thinking. I am no longer a child to be playing foolish tricks. I should have waited for Carlton to act.'

'I think you were brave,' said Major Saunders. 'I like you very well as you are, Miss Thornton. You were not in any way at fault in my estimation.'

She felt that he was implying some criticism of Lord Carlton, but could not imagine what. 'Thank you, sir.' She blushed. 'You are too generous.'

'I only wish I might always be of service—there to champion your cause with my support.'

She wished he would not look at her quite so intently. He was a companionable man and she liked him well enough, but there could never be more than friendship between them. Surely he must know that? He could not think that she had a preference for him?

'It was good of you to call,' Cassie said, getting up and walking over to the window to cover her blushes. 'I was so very grateful for your offer to give me away, but I regret I must now refuse. You see…I shall ask Jack to do so. He will naturally expect it—'

'Jack?' Major Saunders rose and came over to the window to stand beside her. She glanced at him and saw he looked thunderstruck. 'What are you saying? Jack alive? Impossible! Carlton told me himself. He was certain he was dead.'

'It seems I made a mistake,' Vincent's voice drawled from the doorway, causing both Cassie and Major to swing round sharply. Vincent smiled his lazy smile. 'Good to see you, Saunders. I'm glad you could come down for the wedding.'

He crossed the floor to shake hands with the visitor. Cassie moved away and sat down on the sofa.

'Carlton…' Major Saunders shook hands, but was still shocked, still frowning over the startling news. 'Asked for you earlier, of course, but they said you were out. I had hoped to give Miss

Thornton away, but…' He shook his head. 'This is wonderful news, of course. Hard to credit—but wonderful.'

'Yes, it is.' Cassie smiled, her happiness shining out of her. 'I could hardly believe it at first, but we have talked. Where is Jack at the moment, Vincent?'

'We rode over to see Kendal together,' he replied. 'I am afraid it was quite a shock for Mr Thornton. He was embarrassed and wanted to move out at once, but Jack wouldn't hear of it, of course. He has arranged to stay there until the wedding, and I think they may come to some arrangement between them as to the purchase of the property. However, both Mr Thornton and Jack will be dining with us this evening.' He raised his brows as he looked at the Major. 'I know you were invited to the dance, but perhaps you would care to dine beforehand?'

'What? Oh, yes, delighted. Thank you.' He looked at Cassie, still seeming stunned by the news. 'Well, I am disappointed you will not be needing my services, Miss Thornton, but very pleased for you, of course. It is excellent news, excellent.'

'Yes, I think so.'

'Well, I shall not keep you. I am sure you have a great deal to do.'

'Yes, I am afraid we do,' Cassie agreed. 'I have to see Mrs Walker about some vases…'

After the Major had taken his departure there

was silence for a moment, then, as she turned to leave, Vincent laid a hand on her arm, his eyes seeking hers.

'You will take the carriage, Cassie? Please, as a favour to me. I do not believe there is any danger now—but just to be certain?'

Cassie bit her lip, then lifted her head to meet his dark gaze. She flushed, still feeling bruised from the previous night. 'Yes, I shall take the carriage, thank you—but only because Janet had already made me promise her I would.'

Vincent nodded, his face grave. He knew at once that she was still angry with him and felt it best not to push it further at that moment. Cassie was both stubborn and proud, and if they were to come to an understanding, he would need to be patient.

Cassie blinked hard as she went out, finding that she did not like to be at odds with him and missing their old, comfortable companionship. How very foolish she was!

She knew she had been unnecessarily rude and wished her retort unmade. Yet she was irritated by the restrictions laid on her. She had always enjoyed the freedom to walk alone. But of course she had never expected to come across a poacher in broad daylight!

Had she known it, poor Harry had already been taken to task over the incident by an angry Lord Carlton.

'If your gamekeeper had been doing his job properly, it could not have happened!'

'I never dreamed…' Harry was seriously disturbed. 'I hadn't bothered to employ a keeper, because I was not in residence, but now I see I must do so in the future. It could have been…' He hesitated and coloured. 'I mean, it might have been worse if you had not been there.'

'No, be honest, Harry! You meant it might have been Miss Walker, did you not?' Vincent raised his brows as his brother flushed guiltily. 'I do not imagine that she would have reacted to a poacher in quite the same way as Cassie. But if you want your woods to be safe for your future wife and family, you must take the proper steps to safeguard them. It is the price you have to pay for the privilege of your position.'

'Yes, I take your point.' Harry frowned. 'Vinnie, do you think Mama…I mean, would you have a word? About Sarah? See how she feels about the idea?'

'You should properly speak to Mama yourself,' Vincent replied. 'But I shall of course back you up if she cuts up rough over it. Miss Walker seems a very pleasant girl to me—and she is Cassie's best friend, which makes things comfortable for the family. I see no reason why you should not marry her if it is your wish. I'll settle a few thousand on her so you need not fear the expense of a wife.'

Harry's ears went purple. 'Good of you, Vinnie. I didn't expect it—or want it, come to that. But it might help persuade Mama that I do not need to look for an heiress.'

'Consider it done.'

Cassie was not there to hear their discussion, of course. She was not aware of many things going on behind the scenes, and so her doubts continued to plague her as she was driven to the village in Lady Longbourne's comfortable carriage.

On her return home, Cassie went straight up to her room. She discovered a small package on her dressing table and opened the attached card.

'To my future wife. Love, Vinnie.'

Cassie opened the box and discovered a tiny silver statue of a deer and its fawn lying together. She gasped with pleasure as she picked it up and saw how beautifully it was fashioned and marked.

In the bottom of the box was another card, its message brief.

'Forgive me. You were and are more precious.'

Cassie's eyes stung with tears. How thoughtful Carlton was to give her this. She would treasure it more than all the Carlton jewels—just as she did the ring and pendant she was sure had been made specially for her.

Jack must have told him she liked daises, of

course. He must have commissioned them long before he had asked her to marry him. She wondered why he had waited so long if it were merely a matter of honouring his promise to her brother.

Lady Longbourne was secretly shocked by Sir Jack Thornton's appearance, but she was of course too polite to let anyone see her feelings. She presided over the dinner table that evening, her curious eyes noting certain changes in the people gathered there.

Vincent seemed in a better humour than of late. He and Jack had slipped into their old, comfortable companionship and spent most of the evening insulting one another. It was very odd, but she had frequently noticed that gentlemen who were the best of friends saw this sort of behaviour as the greatest fun.

She could not herself see what was so amusing about calling one's friend a great oaf or a madhammer, out and outer over the fences. But it caused a great deal of hilarity from the two friends, and Cassie seemed to approve of their banter.

There was something different about Cassie that evening. Lady Longbourne could not quite put her finger on it, but the girl seemed quieter somehow. She laughed, but her eyes were thoughtful and her manner oddly shy when she looked at her fiancé.

Perhaps that was not so very surprising, thought

Lady Longbourne, wondering if she ought perhaps to have a quiet word with Cassie about the intimate side of marriage. She did after all stand in place of a mother to her, and although she was certain Carlton would be gentle with his wife on their wedding night, it was always best to be prepared. If Cassie were nervous, it might help her to set her mind at rest.

Her thoughtful gaze travelled down the table to Major Saunders, and then she frowned. If ever she had seen a man in love struggling against his feelings, it was him. He did try, but somehow could not keep his gaze from straying to Cassie again and again, and his eyes betrayed him.

He looked extremely agitated, as though he found the situation intolerable, as of course he must in the circumstances. She did hope he was not going to do anything foolish!

Lady Longbourne was well aware that Cassie had found the Major attractive when they first met, and she could not help the prickle of alarm that started at the nape of her neck and trickled down her spine. She would not be surprised if some trouble came of this before the night was out. Lady Longbourne was quite aware that her elder son was possessed of a violent temper when roused, though he had never treated her to a display of it—at least, not since he was a small boy and had defied his father over some trivial matter.

For which he had been soundly thrashed, despite all her pleas in private to her husband.

She dreaded to imagine what Carlton would do if Major Saunders attempted to seduce Cassie, and by the growing desperation in his eyes she knew it was a definite possibility.

She would have to keep a very strict eye on things that evening! If at all possible, she would make sure that the Major never had a chance to be alone with the object of his infatuation!

Cassie met Lady Longbourne's eyes down the table and smiled. She was too caught up in her own private thoughts to have noticed the burning glances directed her way by the love-sick Major Saunders. Her wedding day was approaching very fast, and she had begun to think more and more of the moment when Vincent would come to her as a husband.

She was, despite Lady Longbourne's fears, perfectly aware of the things every young girl should know at such a moment, and her nervousness was not because of what would happen. The kiss Vincent had given her before they left London had made Cassie realise how much pleasure she could know in his arms, and she was torn between her longing and her pride.

It was too bad of Carlton to have made a promise to her brother—and then to have drawn straws! What would he have done if he had lost? Or perhaps he had! Wasn't it usual for the loser to draw the short straw? Oh, it was too bad of him! What was she? A wooden spoon or a consolation prize?

A sudden thought occurred to Cassie. Had Major Saunders been one of the officers who had drawn these infamous straws? She glanced down the table and smiled at him, making up her mind to ask him if she got the chance to speak to him alone that evening.

It could not make any difference, of course. The wedding must go ahead, but at least she would know what had happened.

After dinner was over, the guests drifted into the long gallery. The room had been cleared of furniture, the carpets rolled back for dancing. A group of musicians was already beginning to play rather romantic background music.

Some twelve persons had sat down for dinner, and another twenty had been invited for the dancing and supper. It was more than the gallery could comfortably hold. But card tables had been set up in a salon adjoining the temporary ballroom and no doubt some of the older guests would find their way there before too long.

'I shall join Felicity at the tables for a rubber or two,' Sir Septimus informed Cassie. 'But you will save at least one dance for me, I hope, m'dear?'

'Yes, of course, sir,' Cassie said and handed him her card.

It was Cassie's special night. She looked radiant in a gown of pale green, the hem embroidered heavily with silver daises, and she was wearing the daisy pendant and of course her engagement ring, having spurned the more expensive diamonds which were a part of the Carlton heritage. Her simple gown, together with her natural air of modesty, was much remarked upon, and more than one gentleman congratulated Carlton on his choice of a bride that evening.

She and Vincent opened the dancing together. They were alone on the floor for a minute or two, their guests clapping their approval before joining in.

'Thank you for your gift,' Cassie said, gazing shyly up at him. 'It is beautiful, and I shall always treasure it.'

'You are beautiful,' he replied, bringing a flush to her cheeks. 'I am very proud of you this evening, Cassie—but will you forgive me?'

'For acting as you did over the injured fawn?' Cassie nodded, not daring to look up at him. 'I believe you had no choice. The poor little thing was in pain. It would have been cruel to let it suffer, I see that now. Had I not been so foolish as to rush in the way I did, you might have driven off the poacher and had the leisure to see what could be done. I am as much at fault in this as you—perhaps more so.'

'Thank you. You are generous.' Vincent frowned. 'I can promise you that you will never be at risk of such an occurrence in my woods. I have keepers whose main function is to make sure they are safe.'

'Then you will not mind if I walk there alone sometimes?' Cassie felt relieved. 'You will not expect me to stay always within the formal gardens?'

'That is your choice, though I hope you will allow me to accompany you on your walks sometimes?'

'Yes, of course.' Cassie blushed and dropped her gaze.

'Have you forgiven me for other things?' Vincent asked. 'Or is what I did unforgivable?'

She raised her head to look at him with wide, serious eyes. 'I am not sure. I am hopeful that I may find understanding when I have thought more on your reasons. When we have the leisure, perhaps we could discuss them?'

'You are very right, Cassie. This is not the moment for what I must say to you.' He smiled down at her as the music ended. 'Let us agree simply to be friends for the moment—if you can bear that?'

'Yes, of course,' she replied, giving him a look that was more powerful than she could ever have guessed. 'I think we have always been that, at least. Even when I made you climb the tree twice to rescue me.'

Vincent chuckled, his laughter warm and husky. He led her back to the side of the floor where Jack was waiting to claim her for his dance. He himself was engaged to dance with Sarah, and after that his aunt Felicity and his mama. There were also Sarah's sisters and her mother. Sighing inwardly, he prepared to do his duty as the host.

Cassie was enjoying herself very much. She had danced several times with Jack, twice with Harry, twice with Sir Septimus, who had surprised her by his agility, once with Major Saunders and a second time with Vincent. It was now almost time for her to dance with the Major again, but before that she wanted to go upstairs and freshen herself.

She took a few minutes to tidy her hair and gown, and was about to leave when Sarah came into the bedroom. Her face was alive with excitement, her eyes glowing. Cassie guessed her news before she began to speak.

'Harry has proposed!'

'A few minutes ago,' said Sarah, twirling round in a surge of happiness. 'He is speaking to Papa now, but I am sure—I know he will agree!'

'I am so happy for you, dearest,' Cassie said as the two girls embraced. 'Has Lady Longbourne been told?'

'Harry says Lord Carlton prepared her and she was not surprised. It seems she would prefer him to be happy than to marry simply for money.'

'Then everything will be comfortable for you,' Cassie said and embraced her again. 'We shall be sisters, and you must persuade Harry to bring you to visit us often. I am not sure, but I think we may ask Lady Longbourne to make her home with us, but of course she will divide her time between us. I do not think she should be allowed to live by herself again—do you?'

'Oh, no,' Sarah agreed. 'There is no need for it. She is so good at arranging things and telling one who one ought to invite and what one ought to wear. I do not know how I should manage to entertain all Harry's friends and relatives without her.'

Cassie nodded her approval. She had not yet spoken to Vincent about her plans for his mother to have her own rooms permanently in all of their homes, but she would find the right moment—after they were married—and hoped to persuade him of its convenience.

She left Sarah to refresh herself, knowing that the next dance must have already started. Major Saunders would be thinking that she had abandoned him!

However, when she reached the hallway leading to the ballroom, it was to find Major Saunders sitting on a hard-seated chair. He sprang to his feet at once and came towards her, his manner so urgent that Cassie was startled.

'I am sorry to keep you waiting, sir,' she apologised. 'I meant to be only a minute or two, but was delayed.'

'The dance is not important,' he replied, his face flushed with colour. 'Please, Miss Thornton, may I beg your indulgence? Just a few moments of your time to speak privately with you?'

Cassie hesitated, some instinct warning her against this private tête-à-tête. 'What can you have to say that needs to be said in private, sir? I do not think that—'

'Something of great importance,' he replied. 'Please, I beg you, give me a hearing. Will you not step across the hall into the green parlour? I give you my word as a gentleman that you will be quite safe.'

He seemed so very agitated. Cassie allowed herself to be persuaded against her better judgement. She nodded and turned towards the parlour, feeling slightly apprehensive.

'Well,' she said, turning to face him after he had followed her inside. 'What can be so important, Major Saunders?'

'I could not allow you to marry Lord Carlton without being sure you understood the situation…'

'I beg your pardon?' Cassie stared at him in surprise. 'You could not allow… Forgive me, but I fail to see of what concern my actions are to you, sir?'

'Forgive me! I was too abrupt.' His agitation grew visibly and he took a hesitant step towards her, his face going from red to white and back again as if he were suffering some extreme emotion. 'You think me impertinent, as perhaps I am, but I shall risk your displeasure for the sake of your future happiness. No, no, do not look at me so! I beg you to listen for your own sake.'

'Very well, sir. Since you think it is so important, you may speak.' Cassie's heart was pounding frantically. What on earth had he to say to her?

'I must tell you first that I am devoted to your service, Miss Thornton. If you wished to—to leave this house, I would escort you safely wherever you wished to go. And to guard your honour with my life.'

His dramatic statement made her frown. 'I am indebted to you, sir, but why should I wish to leave? I am about to be married—'

'To a man who does not love you,' said Major Saunders. 'He asked you to marry him only because of a promise to Jack. There were five of us that night around the fire. Jack made us all promise. Carlton drew the short straw…' He looked at her as if this news must make her turn pale or faint. 'I am sorry to tell you this…but I felt you should know before it is too late.'

Cassie stared at him, her expression giving nothing away. 'Why are you telling me this, sir? If you also drew a straw…you were equally at fault. And it was ridiculous, of course. Five grown men drawing straws to determine who had the dubious honour of asking a woman none of them really knew to marry him. I must tell you, I can think of nothing more foolish.'

'No, no, you much mistake the matter,' Major Saunders cried, his eyes flashing fire. 'For me it would have been a prize beyond anything. I was even then halfway in love with you. And when we met, I knew what I had lost...what Carlton had cheated me of!'

'Cheated you?' She was bewildered. 'What can you mean, sir? I do not know how you could have been cheated.'

'Carlton presented the straws, but they were all of the same length. I saw him break his own behind his back, so that he made sure of winning. He was determined to be the one to ask you first.'

'I see...' Her face gave nothing away of the turmoil inside her. 'Thank you for telling me this, Major Saunders. I am much indebted to you for your concern. However, it changes nothing. You see, I already knew about the straws, and that foolish promise.'

His face registered shock and disappointment. 'You already knew? Did someone tell you?'

'I heard the story from Carlton's own lips,' Cassie said. She lifted her head, looking at him proudly. 'Both he and Jack have confessed their parts in this foolishness, and we have laughed over it together. It was all nonsense, of course. And completely unnecessary. Carlton and I have had a private understanding for years. I thought everyone knew that. It was mere liking and friendship when we were children, of course. But it has blossomed into—'

She was allowed to go no further. Major Saunders gave a cry of despair, then grabbed at her in what was clearly a frenzy of disappointment and blighted love.

'No! No, do not say it,' he cried desperately. 'I cannot bear to see you so deceived. He has a mistress still. I dare say you do not know her, but everyone thought he would marry her. Do not waste yourself on this loveless match. Please listen to me, Miss Thornton. Come away with me now. I beg you…'

Cassie averted her face, giving a cry of distress as he tried to kiss her. She pushed against his shoulders with both hands in an effort to hold him off.

'Please, sir,' she cried. 'I must ask you not to do this. Let me go this instant!'

'Take your hands off her, Saunders, or by heaven I'll kill you!'

Vincent was suddenly there in the room with them, but this was not the polite, smiling gentleman Cassie had come to know and love. He was so angry, so violent! Old Carter, one-time landlord of the Hare and Hounds, might have recognised this grim-faced avenger, as might a certain poacher who had not yet stopped running for his life—but Cassie did not know him. As Major Saunders hastily let her go, she gasped and stepped back, watching with wide, scared eyes.

'You damned scoundrel!' Vincent yelled and hit out furiously.

One punch was enough to send his victim to the floor, but not in this case enough to knock him senseless. He lay on the floor, shaking his head and staring up at Vincent with every appearance of being every bit as angry himself.

'You will meet me for this, Carlton!'

'With pleasure,' Vincent replied. 'Name your seconds, sir.'

'No!' Cassie cried, her heart leaping with fright. They must not fight! Something might happen to Carlton, and she really could not bear that. 'Please do not fight over this. It does not matter. I am not hurt. Major Saunders merely forgot his manners for a moment.'

'Be quiet, Cassie,' Vincent said in a harsh voice she had never heard before. 'This is a matter of honour. It will be settled between gentlemen in the proper manner.'

'I say, what's going on?' Jack asked, coming into the room. He watched as Major Saunders rose somewhat unsteadily to his feet and rubbed his chin. 'Vinnie? Did you knock George down? What for?'

His eyes narrowed suspiciously as he saw Cassie's flushed face and sensed her distress. 'Did he offer you some insult, Cassie?' Her uncomfortable silence was enough to answer him. He fired up at once. 'By God, sir! You will answer to me for this, Saunders. Name your weapons—pistols or swords.'

'Hold your heels!' Vincent growled. 'I am before you here. Cassie is engaged to me. I shall teach this bounder a lesson.'

'She's my sister, damn it!' Jack muttered angrily. 'You aren't married to her yet. You can take your place in line. I want first go at him.'

'She is my fiancée. And my wife the day after tomorrow.' Vincent glared at him. 'If I do not manage to kill him—if he should kill me—you can finish it for me.'

'Why do you not draw straws for the privilege?'

Cassie's sarcastic tones stopped them mid-argument. They both turned to look at her in surprise.

'You may as well. Why not, you have done it before, I dare say?' she said, her eyes flashing with temper. 'It is all of a piece, I am sure. I have never heard such nonsense. You will neither of you fight a duel over something which is nothing but foolishness. I will not have either of you risking death or injury before my wedding.'

Or there might not be a wedding!

'Cassie…' Jack said warily, seeing the jut of her

chin. 'You don't understand. A challenge has been issued. It has to be answered for the sake of honour.'

'I do not see why. You can all apologise to each other, shake hands and forget it,' Cassie said. Oh, how foolish they all were! Could Carlton not see that she was terrified of something happening to him? 'Major Saunders can apologise to me, and then he can take himself off and put an end to this. He has been very foolish, but I am prepared to forget the incident. And I might forgive both of you—if you are sensible.'

Jack looked at his best friend's face. Cassie had thrown down the gauntlet in no uncertain manner, but it was not wise to challenge Carlton in such a public way.

'Cassie, I think you ought to be a little careful—' he began but got no further.

'I shall not be dictated to in this manner,' Vincent said coldly, his face stiff with pride. 'You are my fiancée and—'

'I shall not forgive you if you do this,' Cassie cried, her face pale but determined. 'If you persist in this foolishness, Carlton, I shall never, never be your true wife!'

She would threaten anything to stop this happening. It must not happen, because she could not bear the thought of losing him. Until this moment, she had not really understood the depth of her feeling for him—the agony she would feel if she lost him.

Cassie had never believed anyone could mean as much to her as her brother, but Vincent did. Without her truly realising it, he had become a part of her, so much so that she could not bear the thought of life without him. And she would do anything, even run the risk of losing his affection, rather than see him badly wounded or dead.

'Cassie, my love! Not be Carlton's wife?' cried Lady Longbourne, stumbling in mid-scene and misunderstanding what was going on. 'You mean to call the wedding off? Oh, no, my love, do not say so!' For a moment she looked bewildered, then her accusing eyes turned vengefully on Major Saunders. 'This is all your fault, sir. Oh, you wicked creature! How dare you try to seduce Cassie away from us? Viper! I know your motives. I know you covet her fortune, besides being head over heels in love with her, I dare say.' Her eyes filled with tears. 'Oh, Cassie, you cannot leave us. I do not know how I should go on without you. Please, Cassie, if you love me, you must not run away with this awful man.'

'I am not going anywhere with anyone,' Cassie said. 'Indeed, I think I would be far better off staying here with you, Mama. I doubt it is ever worth a woman marrying anyone.'

'But, Cassie dearest, you must marry Carlton. Everyone will be so shocked if you do not.'

'Really, Mama,' Vincent said looking exasperated. 'I think Cassie and I can sort this out between us—'

'But she said she would not marry you…she will never forgive you for…well, I am not perfectly sure why, but you must have done something to upset her if she will not marry you.'

'I did not say I would not marry him,' Cassie said. 'Just that I shall never forgive him if he kills Major Saunders all over a silly misunderstanding.'

'Kill…!' Lady Longbourne gave a shriek of despair. 'You *are* in love with that viper!'

'No, of course I am not. I have never thought of the Major as anything but an amusing friend of Jack's,' replied Cassie. 'But I will not stand by and let Carlton murder him. I am, of course, perfectly prepared to marry Vincent—but if he persists in this wretched duel—'

'*A duel?*' Lady Longbourne gave a yelp and clutched at her son's arm. 'Carlton, I feel most unwell. Forgive me, I am afraid I am going to faint…'

'Mama?' Vincent looked at her frowningly. 'Do not be foolish. This is not the time, Mama…Mama? Mama!' He was shocked into action as she began to crumple before his eyes. 'Mama dearest. Forgive me. Please do not faint!'

Lady Longbourne was not a sylph. It took both Vincent and Jack to carry her to the sofa, where she lay limply until Cassie waved her vinaigrette under her nose. She moaned a little, opened her eyes and promptly burst into noisy tears.

'Do not leave me, Cassie,' she wept. 'I cannot bear it. You have become more dear to me than my own. If you go away, I shall simply have nothing left to live for…'

It was barefaced blackmail and they all knew it, but how could Cassie resist such an appeal? She bent over her soon-to-be mother-in-law, patting her hand comfortably.

'Do not upset yourself, dearest. This is all Carlton's fault. I am sure he will on reflection see the error of his ways, and this can all be brought to a satisfactory conclusion.'

Lady Longbourne's eyes flicked on her son, giving him a warning he would be wise to heed. 'Go away, Carlton. If you care for me at all, you will do the right thing.'

Vincent knew when he was being offered a way of escape and silently blessed his rather clever mother. 'As you wish, Mama.' He glanced at the other gentlemen. 'Perhaps we should retire to the library and discuss the matter further?'

Lady Longbourne clung relentlessly to Cassie's hand as she made a movement to go after them. 'No, no, you must stay with me. They will resolve their differences, my dear, as gentlemen do, in their own rather peculiar way.'

Cassie's eyes sought and held Vincent's. 'I meant what I said. I shall not easily forgive you if you fight a stupid duel over this.' Surely he must know what she was really saying to him, with her heart?

Do not risk your life…I cannot bear it.

Vincent inclined his head, but said nothing as he went out. But she noticed an ominous glitter in his eyes as he glanced in her direction once more before closing the door behind them.

'Have they gone?' Lady Longbourne asked faintly, holding her lavender-scented kerchief to her lips.

'Yes.' Cassie looked at her in concern. 'Do you feel very ill? Shall I send for the doctor?'

'Fiddlesticks to the doctor!' said Lady Longbourne, sitting up with a sudden display of energy. 'I never felt better in my life. But you know, my love, you should not have issued an ultimatum to Carlton like that, not in front of the other gentlemen. It is always a mistake. He could not back down, his pride would not allow it. They would have thought he was petticoat-led!'

'But I do not want either Carlton or Jack to fight. Nor do I particularly wish Major Saunders to be killed. He did startle me with his declaration, but only for a moment. If he had not come in, I could have settled it myself. I was never in the least danger. I am very cross with Vincent for making all this fuss.'

'But you do wish to marry Carlton, don't you?' Lady Longbourne looked at her in bewilderment. Cassie nodded, her cheeks flushing. 'Then I am not sure what can be done. They will fight, you know. There is no possibility of Carlton backing down from a challenge.'

'Oh, no! I must stop them…' Cassie looked anxiously over her shoulders towards the door, the fear catching at her once more. 'Why must men be so foolish?'

'There is not the least need to worry,' said Lady Longbourne, a little smile on her lips. 'They will probably choose pistols and fire in the air. I dare say they are all feeling a bit silly by now, but for the sake of their honour, they will go through the motions.'

Cassie looked at her in surprise. 'Do you think so? That is rather foolish, is it not? How can you be sure they will not try to kill each other? Vincent was very angry. He knocked Major Saunders down—and he looked fit to murder.'

'The same thing happened once to me. Vincent's father was very angry, as I recall,' said Lady Longbourne reminiscently. 'He caught me kissing Sir Bertram, you know. We were in love for years, long before we were free to marry, but did not…well, I was not Bertie's lover. It was just a silly kiss under the mistletoe. But Carlton—my husband then, of course—insisted on fighting him. Bertie told me years later that they both fired into the air, then went off and got drunk together. They were friends, you see, and in the end they saw how foolish it was to fall out over a kiss.'

'No? Really?' Cassie looked at her, then began to laugh as she saw the ridiculousness of it all. 'Do you think Carlton…? Oh, no! It is too bad of him. Of them all…to make such a scene when they know it is no more than a storm in a teacup.'

'You will marry him, won't you, Cassie?'

'I think—'

She was interrupted as the door opened and Sir Septimus came in. He glared at Lady Longbourne as he saw she was sitting on the sofa.

'I might have known I should find this. What are you sitting there for, Emmeline? Everyone is waiting to go into supper.'

'Oh, dear,' said Lady Longbourne and stood up at once. 'That is too bad of me. Do forgive me, Septimus. I only came for a moment…my poor head, you know. But then, I am such a silly goose. I wonder you can put up with me at all.' She tucked her arm through his, then turned back to wink very naughtily at Cassie. 'Come along dearest. It was good of you to rescue me, but we really must not keep our guests waiting for their supper.'

Chapter Twelve

It was some considerable time later. Jack and Vincent were sitting together in the library, sharing a bottle of Sir Harry's very tolerable brandy. Sir Harry had been with them for a while at his half-brother's request, but had now returned to the dance, having played his part as Vincent's second.

'This is an awkward situation,' said Vincent as he poured brandy into two glasses. 'What do you think she means to do, Jack? Will she marry me and then keep me at a distance—or will she throw me to the wolves?'

'I did warn you,' Jack pointed out as he took the glass Vincent had refilled for him. 'There's no denying Cassie is a little contrary at times. She can fly off the handle for nothing…well, very nearly nothing. She does have a mind of her own.'

'Yes, I recall you saying so before.' A faint smile curved Vincent's mouth as he sat down in a rather worn leather armchair and stretched his long legs out in front of him. The window was open, silk curtains moving gently to and fro in the light breeze. 'She was rather magnificent, wasn't she—and completely in the right of it. I should not have lost my temper in front of her. I ought properly to have taken Saunders outside and thrashed him in private.'

Jack nodded wisely. 'Much the better course. What the fair ones don't know, don't hurt them. Of course, you couldn't back down in front of the ladies,' he said, waving his hand expressively as he took a sip of his brandy. 'Good stuff, this! Louise has a few bottles of excellent cognac in her cellars. You must sample it one day, Vinnie.

'As I was saying, a challenge issued has to be met. One couldn't look oneself in the mirror otherwise, naturally—and for two pins, I should have shot Saunders between the eyes. Still, he's not such a bad fellow. I suppose he couldn't help falling for her—and he did the honourable thing. Firing into the air when you had held your own fire and might have shot him had you liked. You could do no less, of course—bad form to shoot a man down after that.'

'Oh, very…' Vincent chuckled, his good humour long restored. 'It would have ended after I'd knocked him down if he hadn't been such a fool and challenged me in front of Cassie. Once I'd thought about it, I had no desire to kill him. To be honest with you, Jack, I've seen enough bloodshed to last me a lifetime.'

'Lord, yes!' Jack looked at him thoughtfully. 'Do you suppose she means what she said? She can be too stubborn for her own good—doesn't like to back down. Makes her pinchy.'

'Yes, so I have observed,' Vincent replied, recalling a young girl stuck in a tree, who would not let him take her down until he had first taken her kitten to safety. He had been obliged to give in to her on that occasion, and to retire with some loss of dignity after discovering his breeches were torn in a very revealing place. 'So what do I do now? I called my trump card the other evening. I cannot use it again.'

Jack thought for a moment. 'Cassie might respond to persuasion,' he suggested. 'If you can make her see the amusing side of all this, she would probably come down off her high horse. Especially when she knows neither of us is actually harmed. It was her anxiety for us that made her explode like that, you know.'

'Yes, I do know.' Vincent's eyes smouldered. He was finding this situation rather amusing and not a little intriguing, and was using Jack as a sounding board for his thoughts rather than seeking advice. 'I am not sure whether I should seek to persuade or use a more masterful approach, Jack. Show her who is in charge?'

'Doomed to failure!' Jack looked alarmed. 'She will simply stick her hooves down and refuse to budge.'

'Like that damned donkey she stole, I suppose?'

'Very much, only worse,' Jack said gloomily. 'You don't know Cassie if you think you can push her. Much better use the velvet glove, Vinnie.'

'You might be right,' Vincent said, a glint in his eyes. 'But for some unaccountable reason, I am reluctant.' He took a thoughtful sip of his brandy. 'Do you know, I think it might be far more amusing to see just how far Cassie will go to defy me?'

'Brave man,' Jack said and finished his brandy. 'Rather you than me, that's all I can say.'

The next morning, Cassie rose, feeling heavy-eyed after a night spent tossing restlessly from side to side. She had regretted her impulsive words to Vincent almost as soon as she had uttered them; if Lady Longbourne was right, her stance against the duel had been quite unnecessary. Indeed, she had begun to feel a little foolish and apprehensive. What if Vincent had taken her at her word? Supposing he decided he did not wish to marry such a temperamental woman? It would just serve her right if he did call off the wedding.

She wanted to apologise to him and yet how could she climb down from her principles? He was very much at fault, but she wished she had not made such a thing of it all.

'Bother!' she muttered as she got up and went over to the window. She was just in time to see Vincent mount his horse and ride off. Now where was he going? They were due to be married the following day and nothing was resolved between them. They had so much to say to one another. 'Oh, you wretched man! How dare you just go out riding as if nothing had happened?'

Cassie's mood swung back to indignation. It was not for her to be sorry! Vincent must apologise for his bad behaviour the previous evening. If he did so, she might forgive him. Yes, certainly she would do so, for it would make everything so uncomfortable if she did not… Bother! Bother! Bother!

Her indignation kept her going until she was met by a rather anxious Lady Longbourne downstairs in the parlour.

'Oh, there you are, Cassie,' she said, fluttering about like a distracted moth. 'I spoke to Carlton not half an hour ago. Oh, my dear! If ever there was such a contrary man! He is in a fit of the blues and says the quarrel between you is all his fault and he perfectly understands why you do not wish to marry him. He has taken himself off to Carlton House and says he shall stay there unless you send for him. He says he would not for the world force you into a marriage you could not like—and that the blame is all his. If you will not have him, he will own to having jilted you by reason of fighting the duel you forbade.'

'Oh, the provoking man!' cried Cassie, irritated beyond bearing by such a message. How could he be such a wet goose as to send his mother to tell her such a sorry tale? It was ridiculous, and most unlike him. 'How could he do this to me? And to ride off like that! He might at least have waited to talk to me.'

'I do not think he could bear to face you,' said Lady Longbourne, dabbing her eyes with her kerchief. She gave a little sob, hoping she was not doing it too brown. 'I have never seen him in such a way. It seems to me he cares for you very much, my dear—and I dare say he will do something quite dreadful if you do not tell him he may come back and marry you.'

Cassie gave her a darkling glance. 'If he gave you that impression, ma'am, you may depend upon it that he was bamming you. I do not believe that anything I said to him last night would cause Vincent to contemplate suicide. No, no, he has sent you as his ambassador in the hoping of forcing me to relent, but I am up to his tricks, and I shall not yield.'

'Oh, Cassie,' her ladyship said, looking disappointed. 'Do you not think you might? Perhaps he is not so very low as I led you to believe, but I am certain he cares for you deeply. Besides, ladies are supposed to be yielding. Men expect it, and one can always find some method of getting one's own back later, you know.'

Cassie giggled as she saw the mischief in her friend's eyes. 'You are a very wicked woman, Mama.'

'I know…but I prefer a comfortable life to confrontation,' said Lady Longbourne with a sigh. 'Do you not think you might forgive him, my love?'

'He should have waited to speak to me. Had he done so, I might very well have forgiven him, this time.' Cassie tossed her head, her eyes sparkling.

'Shall I send someone to fetch him back—so that you can discuss the situation?' Lady Longbourne looked hopeful. 'Just to talk, Cassie. You need not give in just at once.'

'No, indeed, you shall not,' Cassie said. 'He may come if he wishes or not. I have an appointment with Mrs Walker to arrange the flowers in the church.'

'But why arrange flowers if there is to be no wedding?' asked a bewildered Lady Longbourne.

'Because I enjoy it,' countered Cassie blithely, then kissed her. 'Do not worry, dearest. I am sure Carlton will return as soon as he has thought things over.'

Lady Longbourne watched as she walked away, seemingly unconcerned. Then she went inside the house and penned a rather incoherent note to Cassie's brother, begging him to use his powers of persuasion on either his sister or her son.

For if they cannot be brought to see sense, they will throw away something precious—and beside, what am I to do with all the wedding food?

Vincent was lounging on an old-fashioned wooden settle in Jack's parlour when the note was sent over to Thornton's House. Jack passed it over to him, frowning as it was read and returned without comment.

'You've really put the fox amongst the hens now,' he said. 'Cassie will never ask you to return. She is too proud to beg. Besides, why should she? You should have spoken to her yourself this morning, Vinnie.'

'I had a fancy to have her send for me.' Vincent's expression was unreadable, but there was a glint in his eyes.

'Well, she won't. I know Cassie. You can whistle until the cows come home, but she won't send.'

'Why do you not try to persuade her for me?' Vincent fixed him with a winsome smile. 'Ride down to the church, Jack. Tell her you think she ought to marry me even if she does not want to— then come back and tell me what she says.'

'Are you mad?' Jack stared at him suspiciously. Vinnie was a great one for pulling the wool over one's eyes and he had a nasty feeling he was doing it now. 'If I did any such thing she would very likely box my ears. And, besides, it would not serve. She won't change her mind—unless you ask her, of course.'

'Beg her?' Vincent's eyes flashed with fire. 'Would you have me go down on my knees?'

'Well, perhaps you need not go as far as that…' Jack stared at him in exasperation. 'Damn it, man! The wedding is tomorrow, you cannot risk it.'

'There is plenty of time…'

'You always had a steady nerve,' Jack said, admiring him. 'Well, I wish you luck.'

'And you will truly not try to persuade her for me?'

'No, damn it, Vinnie. This is something you must do for yourself.'

'Yes, I dare say you are right.' He glanced at his watch, which was a very fine gold one and engraved on the back. He listened to it chime the quarter hour, then replaced it in his waistcoat pocket. 'I should imagine Cassie has left the church by now, and since she is walking, I shall catch up with her on her way home if I leave at once.'

Jack stared at him, eyes narrowed in suspicion. 'You intended that all the time, didn't you?'

'Of course.' Vincent smiled his lazy smile. 'I believe Cassie may have had time to think things over and will very likely have cooled down by now…'

Cassie took a last look round the church before leaving. She was pleased with her work. It truly looked quite beautiful and the lilies she had arranged everywhere had a pervading scent which seemed to waft pleasantly round the ancient building. The sun was pouring in through a stained-glass window high above her, shedding a rainbow of colours on the worn flagstones. It was such a peaceful place to be and she was sure that just being here for a while had helped her to sort out her confused feelings.

At least, there was no doubt in her mind now. She knew exactly where she was going in her life and why.

Tomorrow she would take her vows here as Vincent's wife. She was smiling as she left the church. For a while she *had* been ruffled by Vincent's message but, thinking it over, she had come to the conclusion that it had been meant to say something far different than it would at first appear. Vincent might well have decided not to marry her, but had he done so, he would not have sent his mother with such a message.

No, he was testing her, teasing her, attempting to make her give way. She supposed she might have to in the end, because she did want to marry him, even if he was the most trying wretch! Not because it would cause too much trouble to cancel the wedding at the last moment, but because she loved him. She loved him so much she could not imagine her life without him.

The sun was warm on her head as she walked. She looked about her, remembering all the times when, as a child, she had played in these fields and ridden the bridle paths on her pony. Soon her family home would be sold, Jack would go back to France—and if she came here again it would be to visit Harry and Sarah. There was a tinge of sadness in the realisation, but the world moved on and she must move with it.

Entering the woods near Longbourne, Cassie knew a moment of disquiet, but refused to let herself be afraid. If she once gave way to fear, she would never be able to walk alone again. Besides, the poacher she had disturbed would not dare to come here again. She felt a brief moment of pity for him. He must be in terror of his life. If Vincent had threatened to kill Major Saunders just for trying to kiss her, she did not dare begin to imagine what he might have done to the poacher who had knocked her senseless!

She smiled to herself as she recalled the incident with Major Saunders the previous evening. When one stood back and looked at it from a distance, it was so ridiculous!

After she had been walking for some minutes, she heard a cracking sound just ahead of her, as though someone had trodden on a stick. She took a deep breath, but would not let herself call out to ask who it was. Instead, she bent and picked up a fallen branch herself, preparing to defend herself if necessary. Then, as she came into a clearing, she saw Vincent sitting on the trunk of a felled tree and knew that he was waiting for her. She dropped the branch and went forward, her heart beginning to leap like giddy lambs in spring. He looked up and smiled as she approached.

'Hello, Cassie. Have you a few moments to spare?'

'Yes, of course,' she said. 'So you did not go to Carlton House after all?'

'Did you really think I had?'

'Only for a few seconds.' She shook her head at him. 'Really, Vinnie! Your poor mama seemed to imagine you were about to throw yourself in the river or sink into a decline.'

'But you did not believe her?' Vincent laughed as he saw the expression in her eyes. 'No, I thought not. Serves me right for sending you such a ridiculous message, does it not?'

'It was very foolish of you,' Cassie said in a scolding tone. She held her smile inside her. He must not be forgiven all at once. It would not be good for him to imagine he could always have his own way. 'Did you think I would not know it for a Banbury tale?'

'If I did, I should have known better, but I must confess it was done in a puckish mood.' He made room for her to sit on the log beside him, his eyes quizzing her as she sat down. 'I fear I do have a rather odd sense of humour, my love. In fact, we have both been a pair of fools, wouldn't you say?'

'I think we might have been more open with each other,' she said, fixing him with a look that made him wince. 'Why did you not tell me about the promise you made to Jack? It would have cleared the air and I would have understood, had you explained. And why did you break your own straw?'

'Did Saunders tell you that last night?' She nodded and he sighed. 'I thought at the time he had seen me, but he said nothing then. I did not tell you what had taken place, because I knew you would be angry. You were so very annoyed with poor Kendal, who was only doing what he considered the decent thing. He may be a pompous bore, my love, but he means well. He had no idea you had been left a fortune by your mother's aunt.'

'Yes, I know,' she said on a sigh. 'I have realised I misjudged him, and I have apologised.'

Vincent nodded, his eyes warm with approval. 'I was sure you would when you were ready. Imagine the quandary I found myself in, Cassie. You had opened your heart to me over this matter, and I could not but take notice. You would have been furious had you discovered that stupid promise.'

'Yes, I suppose so—but you have not told me why you broke your straw.'

'I wanted to make sure I was the one to ask,

because I felt I owed it to Jack. He was in a terrible state that night, and would never have spoken the way he did had he been able to think clearly.'

'But why did you feel you owed him something? He had no right to ask such a thing of you—of anyone.'

'I owed it to him because I felt responsible for his death. I forced him to come with me that day, Cassie. We rode into an ambush and when he fell I believed he could not have survived. I rode on and left him lying there. For months after that I was torn by guilt and indecision. I felt it was my duty to ask you to be my wife, but I was sure you would hate me for being the cause of your brother's death. And if I did not tell you the truth, it would always be between us…it was my fault, Cassie. All he has suffered was because of me.'

'No, no, that is not true. Jack explained it all to me. He told me that you had no choice, that in your place he must have done the same and ridden on.'

Vincent looked grave. 'It haunted me. I blamed myself a thousand times for taking him with me on that mission.'

'So you waited for months to come to me, because your conscience was troubled…' Cassie turned her clear gaze on him. 'What made you decide to ask me at last?'

'My life was empty,' Vincent said. 'I missed Jack terribly. I was haunted by guilt—and Mama told me

I ought to marry. It was in my mind that I might as well make a marriage of convenience.'

'Yes, I do see. I imagined it must have been something of the sort. You needed a wife and you could honour your promise at the same time. It must have seemed a good compromise. You thought I would be grateful for the offer. After all, I am not pretty and you believed me to be penniless.'

Her face was pale, her gaze averted. When he took her hand in his it trembled and when she turned to look at him, her eyes had the look of a wounded doe.

'Do not look like that, my darling,' he said softly. 'Please, I beg you. You know that is not how I feel now, do you not? Surely you must know, Cassie!'

Her cheeks washed with deep rose as she saw the intent look he gave her, a look so terrifying, so full of promise, that her heart almost stopped beating. 'I…I was not sure. It has sometimes seemed to me that you felt more than mere liking, but then—'

'A great deal more,' Vincent replied, his voice husky with passion. 'Indeed, I have been at pains to disguise my feelings for you for fear of scaring you off, my love. You told me you wanted only a comfortable arrangement. You did not wish for love…' There was a sparkle of wickedness in his eyes now. 'I remember perfectly that you made your conditions for marriage very plain to me.'

'Yes, I know I did.' Cassie hung her head. 'Was

that not very foolish of me? Jack and I had been so very close, you see. We shared our thoughts and our jokes, sometimes without even a word being spoken. I believed I could never be as close again to anyone else. Indeed, I may have been a little afraid to love, lest I somehow lost that person and was hurt again. All I wanted was a complaisant husband and a position in society. Some people were very odious after my father shot himself, you know.'

Vincent caught her hand, holding it tightly in his own. 'Well, you have your place in society for what it is worth, my dearest.' He smiled at her, a twinkle in his eyes. 'But I believe you discovered last evening that I have a very serious fault. I cannot contemplate another man making advances to my wife with any degree of complacency. I think I might well have shot to injure or kill had Mama's timely intervention not given me time for reflection.'

'I must say, I thought she acted her part very well and deserves some credit,' Cassie murmured, a gurgle of laughter escaping her. 'She must have learned how to faint at will long ago.'

'You mean she is a shameless blackmailer who will use all her feminine arts to get her own way?' Vincent smiled ruefully. 'Of course I have always known it. Mama does not like scenes or loud voices. She uses her vulnerability to get her own way. She is not brave enough to stand and fight as you do, my love.'

'But her way has its uses,' Cassie said, 'if it enabled you to go off and settle your own affairs in your own time?'

'Saunders fired in the air, as I did.' Vincent looked at her. 'I could not back down, Cassie. I had to go through the motions for the sake of honour.'

'Yes. Lady Longbourne said it would be that way.' Cassie gave him a wicked look. 'She told me that your father and Sir Bertram once fought a duel over her—and that it ended with them going off to get drunk together.'

'No? Did it?' Vincent laughed. 'I had no idea—though I knew she was in love with Bertie even before my father died. He was riding home after an evening spent in gaming and hard drinking, you know—and fell from his horse. He died almost instantly. Mama waited the full six months before marrying again, and I do not believe they became lovers until after the wedding. Which showed quite remarkable restraint on his part, don't you think?'

'I think it must have been one of those very special relationships,' Cassie said, gazing up at him thoughtfully. 'That is why she will not marry again. You must not hope for it, Vinnie.'

'I shall not again,' he replied. 'It was only because she seemed to have no purpose in life. I hated to see her so unhappy—but she is so much better now. She has become so fond of you.'

'As she will be of Sarah,' Cassie said. 'And her grandchildren, Vinnie. I am sure she will be devoted to them, and of course we must all see that she is not on her own for long.'

'Her grandchildren?' Vincent's brows rose quizzically. 'Am I to take it that you will marry me?'

'I might,' said Cassie, her eyes bright with challenge. 'If you can convince me that it would be in my interests to do so.'

Vincent was amused at the mischief he sensed going on in her head. 'And how am I to do that, Cassie?'

'Well…' she replied, appearing to consider. 'You might start by kissing me the way you did in your study. And you might continue by telling me why you want to marry me.'

'As if you did not know the answer,' Vincent said, reaching out for her. 'For once in his life, Septimus was perfectly right—you are a wicked jade!'

'You still have not told me,' Cassie cried, jumping to her feet as he tried to put his arms about her. 'Time is running out, Vinnie. You must soon make up your mind.'

She threw a teasing look at him and started running. Vincent did not hesitate this time, but pounded after her, catching her before she had gone more than a few yards. He grabbed hold of her, swinging her round to face him, then he bent his head to kiss her lips.

It was such a long, tender, passionate kiss that it had her near swooning in his arms. She swayed and sighed when he released her at last, then smiled up at him confidently before nestling her head against his shoulder.

Vincent kissed the top of her head. 'You smell of flowers,' he murmured huskily. 'Do you know you have bewitched me, Cassie? I have been able to think of nothing but you for weeks.'

She looked up, pulling a face at him. 'And I have been breaking my heart for you.'

'No? Have you?' He touched her cheek, running one finger down it and over her chin, to the little hollow at the base of her throat. His face held a kind of wonder that made her want to hold him close for evermore. 'You gave no sign of it, Cassie. I was not sure you cared particularly for me at all. Did you have no idea that I adored you?'

'There was one moment when I thought you must love me,' she said frowning. 'Why were you in such torment when you proposed to me, Vinnie?'

'It was my idiot half-brother.' He explained what had happened and how he had felt about the resulting gossip. 'I was torn in two, Cassie. I thought you might hate me for ruining your chances of being a success if I let you make your début with such rumours flying around. For had you not been wearing my ring, they would have thought there was something smoky. I cursed Harry a thousand times, let me tell you. I wanted to be open with you, and yet I was afraid to tell you the truth.'

'Which was?' Her eyes gazed into his.

'That I was falling desperately in love with you, of course. But I would have preferred to wait, to give you a chance to know me. I did not know how to be with you, Cassie. I had never felt so—so lost and vulnerable. And I was terrified of losing you if you heard the story of the straws from one of Jack's friends.'

'You need not have been afraid of losing me.' She reached up to touch her lips to his. 'And as for that nonsense last night—you must have known why I wanted to stop you fighting?'

'Because you thought one of us might be killed?'

'It was mostly you, Vinnie. I knew Jack was in no danger. You would never have given way to him. I knew you would fight the duel yourself. And I did not want you to die.' She lifted her head, eyes flashing. 'I dare say you had not thought—but it would have quite ruined our wedding, you know.'

'Oh, Cassie! You little witch!' Her future husband was entranced. 'Shall I ever have best of you? Shall I ever teach you to show your husband the proper respect?'

'You may try,' she replied, demure now. 'But I am not perfectly certain you will succeed.'

'Nor am I,' said Vincent, a rueful look in his eyes.

'But if we can meet halfway, as we have today, I confess that would please me best of all.'

'Oh, yes,' Cassie agreed. 'I believe there may be hope for that, my dearest Vinnie.'

He held his hand out to her. 'Should we go home now? I fear Mama may have the hysterics if we do not reassure her that she need not throw away all the wedding food.'

'Oh, I do not imagine she doubted it for a moment,' Cassie murmured. 'She is much wiser than you may imagine...'

Chapter Thirteen

'You look so beautiful, my dear.' Lady Longbourne dabbed at her eyes with her lace kerchief, and for once the tears were quite real. 'I do not recall who once said to me that you were a plain gel, but whoever it was, they were very wrong.'

Cassie smiled and shook her head. 'It is the dress, Mama, and the diamonds Vincent sent me. I am still plain little Cassandra Thornton, who used to live down the road.'

'Well, you were a little plain as a girl,' her ladyship admitted judiciously. 'But you certainly aren't now. There's a glow about you. I am sure Carlton may think himself fortunate to have such a lovely bride.'

'Perhaps he does,' Cassie countered. 'But there is no accounting for the thoughts of gentlemen who are in love with one. I dare say he will recover soon enough.'

'Bertie never did,' said her ladyship with a sigh. 'He kissed my hand and told me I had given him perfect happiness only a few moments before he slipped away from me. Do not believe those who would tell you romance does not last, my dear. It is very much up to you as a woman to keep it alive.'

'You are very wise,' said Cassie and kissed her cheek. 'I shall think myself very fortunate if I inspire such devotion in my husband as you did in yours.'

Lady Longbourne patted her hand. 'I believe you already do,' she said in a choking voice.

Cassie glanced at herself in the mirror. She *was* looking quite handsome in her splendid gown of cream satin and lace, and the pretty headdress of silk flowers into which she had woven one of the Carlton heirlooms. She hoped Vinnie would approve of the use she had made of his grandmother's diamonds, but she wanted to wear the simple necklet he had given her on the day they became engaged.

She was still unable to imagine why Vinnie loved her, but she could not doubt that he did. The kisses he had given her in the woods, before they had walked hand in hand back to the house, had left her in no doubt of his feelings.

'If I were not a gentleman,' he had whispered hoarsely against her ear, 'I should make love to you now. I do want you so desperately, Cassie, and I am not as patient as Sir Bertram.'

'Are you not, my dearest?' She had smiled up at him and touched his face, a hint of mischief in her own. 'This honour thing can be rather a nuisance at times, don't you think? Tell me, Vinnie, why do gentlemen set such store by it?'

'Careful, minx! You are pushing me to the limits.'

'Perhaps that is what I wish to do—you see, I am not a gentleman.'

Cassie sighed as she recalled his very satisfactory response to her teasing. She turned as Lady Longbourne fussed over the last details of her dress, and then she sneezed three times in a row.

'Cassie!' Lady Longbourne looked at her in dismay. 'I hope you are not about to go down with a cold, my dear?'

'No, of course not,' Cassie said, sounding a bit nasal. 'Poor Janet warned me I would catch hers, but I never take chills. I have not had a cold in years.'

'Do not tempt fate, dearest,' Lady Longbourne begged her, looking faintly anxious as Cassie sneezed again. 'You do look a little flushed, now I come to think of it. I thought it was merely excitement, but after this I wonder.'

'You must not worry.' Cassie studied herself in the mirror. She *did* indeed have a high colour and she *was* feeling a little warm. 'No, no, I am sure it is just excitement. I shall be fine…'

The church was overflowing with friends of the bride and groom. Cassie walked to take her place beside Vincent, supported by her brother's arm. Jack's appearance caused some comment, as was to be expected, but most people had by now heard the news and thought his gaunt looks explained the reason for his having been reported dead. He had clearly suffered, and they were all genuinely glad to see him home.

Everyone thought Cassie looked very well, especially for a girl who had always been thought a little plain. One or two did remark on her high colour, which was really not like her at all.

Cassie smiled as Vincent turned to look at her, a smile of welcome in his eyes. She managed an answering smile for him but was beginning to feel really rather odd: a little light-headed and not quite well. Lady Longbourne had insisted on giving her a little brandy with sugar and hot water before they left the house. She wondered if perhaps the unaccustomed glass of strong spirits might have gone to her head, and hoped she would not say anything foolish when it came time for her to make her vows.

She did manage to say the right words, however, and to walk proudly from the church as Vincent's wife. Her hand trembled on his arm as they were showered with rose petals, but she only smiled when he looked at her inquiringly. It would have been so missish of her to let anyone guess that she had started to feel quite ill. But she did wish the bells were not quite so loud. Her head was aching terribly and she felt shivery.

Cassie was made of sterner stuff than to give in to a mere chill. As soon as they were back at Longbourne, she slipped upstairs to tidy herself, patting her face with cool water because it felt so hot. She asked Janet, who was now on her feet again, to make her a glass of brandy and sugar water.

'You've caught my cold,' Janet said, looking at her in dismay. 'I knew you would. I was afraid of it from the start. And it has come out on your wedding day!'

'Well, it cannot be helped,' Cassie said with a little shrug. 'At least it's only the fever so far. I have not got a red nose, so I must be grateful for that.'

Janet was helpless to prevent her going down to join her guests at the reception. It would have ruined everything had she retired to bed, but it was obvious that she was far from well.

The brandy helped, though it had the effect of making Cassie feel even more light-headed than before. However, she managed to keep smiling as she stood with Vincent to receive the congratulations of her friends.

'You look a bit flushed,' Jack remarked to her later as he kissed her cheek. 'You feel hot. What's wrong, Cassie? Are you ill?'

'It is just a bit of a cold,' she said in a low whisper. 'I shall be perfectly all right when we are all sitting down.'

She did indeed feel better when she was seated, though she could not bear to eat anything. The toasts and speeches seemed to go on and on for ever, and she began to wonder if it would ever be over. From time to time she sipped her wine, which seemed to help. Everything was muted, somehow distant, as if everything was far away. Her head ached, her throat was sore, but it did not feel as if it was happening to her. She was floating away towards the ceiling.

'What's wrong, Cassie?' Vincent asked, looking at her in concern. 'Are you ill? You look very flushed.'

'No, no,' she assured him. 'I am perfectly well.'

She smiled at him reassuringly. She even managed to cut the cake, her hand trembling beneath his on the knife handle, but it was when the music struck up and everyone called for the bride and groom to dance that she finally came unstuck.

She rose to her feet willingly enough, but when she tried to move she felt her legs had turned to jelly and she stumbled against Vincent. He held her, steadying her, a look of suspicion in his eyes as he caught a faint whiff of brandy.

'Have you been drinking spirits, Cassie?'

'Janet made a toddy for me…only a little brandy

with hot water and sugar.' She gazed up at him a little unsteadily. 'Are we going to dance?'

'If you are sure you can manage it?'

'Of course I can.' She gave him an indignant look. 'Do you think I am insh...inshtoxicated?'

'Not at all, my love,' lied Vincent valiantly. 'I am merely intrigued to know why...'

At that moment Cassie sneezed violently and then sat down on her chair with a bump. 'Do you know, I think I shall not dance,' she said, giving him a rather owlish stare. 'My legs feel all at sea.'

'To say nothing of a slight dizziness, I suppose?'

Cassie was now looking decidedly feverish. 'My head aches,' she said. 'I am very sorry, Vincent, but I think, I really think that...' She gave a little sigh and would have fallen from her chair had he not been there to support her.

Lady Longbourne came hurrying up to them at that moment. 'Oh dear, I was afraid of this,' she said, looking rueful. 'She has a nasty cold. It started this morning and I gave her a glass of brandy. Quite a strong one.'

'And Janet gave her another,' Vincent said, a wry smile on his lips. 'She has eaten nothing, but she did drink some wine.'

'Oh, how unfortunate,' said Lady Longbourne. 'It seems the fever has quite overcome her, poor love. I suggest you carry her upstairs, Carlton. I believe it may be best if you delay your journey until tomorrow or even the day after. You must see that Cassie really is not fit to go anywhere but her bed?'

Cassie opened her eyes as Vincent bent to lift her in his arms. She smiled up at him enchantingly. 'Take me to bed, Vinnie,' she said. 'I am so very tired.'

'You are ill, my love,' he said as his arms went beneath her knees, and he caught her up. 'You foolish girl. Why did you not tell me how you felt before this?'

'Wanshted to marry you.' She gave him a dreamy look as her arms curled about his neck. 'Didshn't want to postpone the wedding for a silly cold.'

Vincent hid his amusement as he glanced at his mother. 'You will make our apologies, Mama. Please ask everyone to dance and amuse themselves. I shall of course return after I have seen Cassie settled, to thank them for coming.'

'Of course. Poor Cassie…'

Vincent strode from the dining room, carrying his bride and bravely ignoring the startled looks from his guests. He knew he could trust his mother to explain away Cassie's rather curious behaviour. For himself he cared little what others might think, but he suspected that his young wife might feel very embarrassed when she remembered her wedding reception.

She was half asleep when he laid her very gently on her bed. Janet was waiting to attend her, and looked apologetically at Vincent as she realised what was wrong with her young mistress.

'I think this is partly my fault, sir. I made her a hot toddy.'

'Yes, she did mention it.'

'She asked me to make it strong so that she could get through the reception without feeling the effects of the cold, sir. I think I must have given her too much brandy.'

'Mama also gave her a strong brandy before she left for church—and though she ate nothing downstairs, I know she drank at least a glass of wine.'

'Oh, dear, how unfortunate.' Janet smiled as she saw that his lordship had a wry amusement in his eyes. 'Miss Cassie—or her ladyship, as I should say!—has hardly ever been ill, sir. I warned her not to come near me when I first took the cold, but she would—and now look what's happened.'

'We must hope it is not the influenza.'

'Oh, no, sir, I do not think it. I was over my cold in three days. I dare say her ladyship will be the same.'

Cassie gave a little moan and opened her eyes. She smiled up at Vincent invitingly.

'Are you going to kiss me?'

Vincent chuckled and sat down on the edge of the bed. He bent over her, kissing her very gently on the mouth.

'I dare say you are hoping to give me your cold,

you little wretch, but I shall brave it.' He stroked her forehead, which was very hot. 'You must rest now, my dearest love. Janet is going to give you a nice hot drink of lemon barley, and then you must sleep for a while.'

She caught his hand. 'Do not leave me, Vinnie. I want you to stay here and cuddle me. I like being kissed. It is excessively nice.'

'Yes, so I believe.' He kissed her again, very softly on the mouth. 'I should like nothing more than to stay with you, my love, but I think you should go to sleep now. And I must not neglect our guests.'

Cassie murmured something and closed her eyes. Her head ached, but it was so comfortable in her bed and she seemed to be drifting away on a fluffy white cloud.

'You leave her to me, sir,' Janet said. 'She will sleep it off now, I think—and knowing her, she'll be right as rain in the morning.'

'Well, we must hope she is better.'

Vincent walked to the door, then glanced back at his bride who was snuggling down like a sleepy kitten in the covers. He smiled ruefully to himself as he left her there. It was not going to be quite the wedding night he had anticipated, but Cassie's rather delightful behaviour had encouraged him to think that she was well worth the delay.

* * *

Cassie awoke the next morning feeling wretched. Every bone in her body ached and she had a dreadful suspicion that everything was not as it ought to have been. She sat up, moaning as the room seemed to spin around her and she realised she was in the bedroom she had been using this past week or so at Longbourne.

Why was she still here? What had happened? Oh, no! She rather thought she must have fainted at the wedding reception. How very lowering!

She saw a jug of barley water on the table beside her bed, reached for it, poured a little into a glass and took a swallow. Her throat felt better. So why did her head still feel as if it had a hundred and one drums banging inside it?

She was just thinking about getting up, when the door opened and Janet came in, carrying a tray.

'I thought you would be awake, your ladyship,' Janet said, giving her an intent look. 'I have brought you a little thin gruel and something to ease your head.'

'Gruel?' Cassie pulled a face at her. 'Must I, Janet? Could I not have rolls and honey?'

'Do you feel up to them?' Janet stared at her uncertainly. 'I thought you might still have a sore throat?'

'It feels much better,' Cassie said. 'But I do ache all over. I suppose it must have been the fever. I felt so strange yesterday. As if nothing was quite real.'

'Yes, I expect you did,' Janet said, not quite meeting her eyes. 'I dare say it was the fever—though the brandy and wine may have played its part.'

'Oh, dear,' said Cassie, looking conscious. 'Do you suppose I was a little intoxicated, Janet?'

Mindful of his lordship's instructions when he had looked at his bride earlier that morning, Janet hesitated.

'No, of course you were not intoxicated,' Lady Longbourne said as she breezed in, wearing a very fetching pale-apricot dressing robe and a lace cap. 'You had a nasty fever, and you may be sure I told everyone how brave you were to go through with the wedding at all.'

'I did feel quite ill,' Cassie replied, a faint blush in her cheeks as she began to remember certain things. 'But—but it did not seem to be happening to me at all. I do hope I did not do anything foolish during the reception?'

'Certainly not. I am always the same when I have a cold,' Lady Longbourne assured her. 'Drink the tisane Janet brought for you, my love. I believe you may find it will make you feel much better.'

'Thank you.' Cassie picked up the glass and took a tentative sip. It tasted unspeakably awful, but she swallowed it down without a word of complaint. 'Perhaps if I feel better, I shall get up later.'

'I should stay in bed today, if I were you,' her

ladyship advised. 'People have been asking about you already. There are several bunches of flowers for you and concerned messages. I shall send them all up to you directly.'

'You are so kind. Everyone is.'

Lady Longbourne smiled and went away.

Cassie tasted the gruel and pulled a face. 'Please take it away, Janet. I would much prefer a pot of hot chocolate and some rolls.'

'As you wish, your ladyship.'

'Please,' Cassie begged, horrified. 'Do you think you could call me Miss Cassie as you always did— at least in private?'

'Yes, miss.' Janet smiled at her in approval. 'I should think I could…in private, mind. You must remember your dignity in front of the other maids. And there must certainly be no more escapades! His lordship will expect you to behave like a lady now that you are his wife.'

'Yes, Janet. I know I have to behave properly in future. Please do not scold me…' Cassie closed her eyes as the hammers began again. 'Forget about breakfast, if you please, I think perhaps I shall just have a little sleep…'

When she opened her eyes again, it was to find Jack standing at the foot of her bed. He was holding a wicker basket, which he placed into her hands as she yawned and sat up, smiling at him sleepily.

'Lady Longbourne thought I ought not to come up to your bedroom, but Vinnie said it was all right, so here I am. I leave for France later today, Cassie, and I wanted to make sure you were all right before I go.' He looked at her anxiously. 'You are, aren't you?'

'Yes, of course. I am glad you came, Jack. I should have hated it if you hadn't. What have you brought me?' A mewing sound came from inside and she opened the top to see a little ball of white fluff. 'Oh, a kitten! How lovely. You spoil me, Jack. That beautiful silver necklace you gave me as a wedding present, which I know belonged to Grandmother and is something I have always loved—and now this.'

'You deserve far more,' Jack said, bending to kiss her cheek. 'I am so fond of you, dear Cassie. It was a rotten shame your being ill for the wedding. I cannot say I blame you for getting a little squiffy. I would have done the same in your shoes.'

'Oh, no, was I?' Cassie stared in dismay. 'What must people have thought?'

'No need to worry. Lady Longbourne convinced everyone you had a virulent fever which had laid you low, but Vinnie told me you had been knocking back the brandy. I believe he secretly found it all rather amusing.'

'Did he, indeed?' Cassie scowled. 'Well, you may both think it funny, but I was feeling very ill.'

'Of course you were, and it is not a bit funny,' her brother said, but could not prevent a chuckle escaping. 'No, no, I am sorry, love. I know you were feeling under the hammer. Do not poker up. It may be ages before I see you again, and I do not want to quarrel with you.'

'It will not be so very long,' Cassie said, her outrage fading as swiftly as it had flared. 'Because I mean to ask Vincent to bring me to visit you and Louise when we are on our honeymoon.'

'That *is* good news.' Jack looked pleased as he bent to kiss her cheek. 'I hope you will love Louise as much as I do—and now I ought to be off.'

She caught his hand. 'Take care, Jack—and whatever happens in the future, always remember that I love you.'

'I love you, too, Cassie.' He smiled, let go her hand and went out of the door.

Left to herself once more, Cassie decided that she really was feeling much better. Her headache had gone, and her throat was not at all sore, though she did still have the sniffles and was obliged to blow her nose once or twice. However, that was nothing to make a fuss about, and certainly would not oblige her to stay in bed.

She decided to get up, dressing herself in a plain gown that she had owned for some time which was easy to fasten by herself. On no account was she going to send for Janet, who would be sure to scold her and try to make her stay in bed.

She brushed her long, glossy hair, leaving it hanging loose on her shoulders, because she could not be bothered with putting it up in its usual style. A glance in her mirror told her that she did not look exactly elegant. Indeed, some of her London friends would think her positively dowdy, but she wanted to escape before anyone could tell her she ought to go back to bed.

Almost everyone had been in to visit her except Vincent. Cassie was frowning as she went downstairs, clutching the kitten her brother had given her. Why hadn't her husband visited her? She knew he had been in earlier, when she was asleep, but not since she had first woken. Was he cross with her for embarrassing him at the reception?

Cassie could not perfectly remember what had happened, but she seemed to recall Vincent carrying her upstairs. Had she really clung to him and asked him to kiss her? Oh, how shameless of her! What must he have thought?

She slipped out of a side entrance, hoping to avoid being seen, and made her way slowly to a small, walled garden she knew was hardly ever used. It was warm and sheltered, and on that summer afternoon, very peaceful. Just the place to be alone with her thoughts.

Cassie found a dry patch of grass beneath the apple tree, spread her shawl on the ground and sat down. She stroked the kitten on her lap, talking to it as she tried to think of a name for her new pet.

'Shall I call you Fluffs or Snowy?' she asked, holding the kitten and kissing it on top of its head. 'Or are they both too ordinary? I really ought to think of something better...' She yawned. 'Pray forgive me, Fluffs, I do not know what has happened to my manners.'

Setting the kitten down on the grass beside her, Cassie started to pick daisies and make them into chains. She hung them round her neck, then, beginning to feel sleepy, lay back on the grass and closed her eyes. It was so warm and tranquil here in this garden... When she opened her eyes again some twenty minutes or so later, it was to find Vincent sitting opposite her.

He smiled as she yawned, stretched and sat up. 'You looked so peaceful. I was reluctant to wake you—and the ground is very dry so I did not think you would take harm.'

'Have you been there long?' Cassie glanced at him a little shyly. He looked so handsome, dressed casually in just a pair of pale cream breeches, top boots and a white shirt. She hoped he could not read her mind, or he would know how very much she wanted to put her arms around him.

'A few minutes. Janet told me you had gone out, so I came in search of you. I did not think you would have gone far, and a gardener happened to see you come here.' His eyes went over her, bringing a flush to her cheeks. 'Is your cold better today?'

'Yes, much better,' she replied. 'It was so foolish of me to collapse like that yesterday. I never take colds as a rule.'

'Are you sure you should be sitting out here? Would you not have done better to stay in bed for another day?'

'I hate lying in bed for no good reason. Besides, it is so warm I am sure I shall not make my cold worse. I was playing with Fluffs...' She looked about her, frowning. 'Oh, no! She has gone. I should have watched her. She does not know her home yet. I am afraid she will be lost.'

'Fluffs?' Vincent raised his brows.

'A kitten. Jack gave her to me. She is an adorable ball of white fluff so—' She stopped speaking as they both heard the pitiful mewing. Cassie looked up at the branches of the apple tree and gasped. 'Oh, no! You foolish kitty. How did you get up there?'

She jumped to her feet as if about to climb after the kitten, but Vincent caught her arm, firmly restraining her. 'No, Cassie. You must wait here. Leave this to me. I do not want to have to rescue you and that ridiculous animal.'

'There is no need to be cross, Vinnie. I wasn't going to climb the tree. I am not a child anymore. Besides, Janet has already told me I have to learn to behave as a lady. There are to be no more escapades, no more scrapes.'

His brows rose in disbelief. 'I shall believe that when I see it!'

She laughed as he began to look for a foothold, his expression somewhere between resignation and doom.

'Do be careful, Vinnie,' she urged. 'Some of those branches might not bear your weight. Perhaps we should send for one of the gardeners to bring a ladder?'

'I am not yet too old to climb a tree!'

Oh, dear! thought Cassie. He was cross! She refrained from answering, watching anxiously as he began to climb very slowly and carefully. Several small twigs and leaves came fluttering down to shower over her. The apple tree was old and in desperate need of pruning. She held her breath as Vincent inched his way towards the kitten, who was crouching in a fork between two branches and watching his advance nervously.

'Here, kitty,' Vincent said, making a coaxing noise that caused Cassie to smile to herself. 'Kitty… kitty…' He was just below the kitten and reached out to try and grab it. The startled creature lashed out with its claws and scratched his hand, making

Vincent swear and almost lose his balance. 'Wretched creature!'

The kitten arched its back, hissing angrily. Vincent made another grab, but it leapt at him, landing on his head so that he swore again and jerked involuntarily. The kitten then made a death-defying leap onto Cassie's chest as she stood beneath the tree looking up. Its claws went through the thin material of her gown and she gave a little shriek. The kitten sprang to the ground and ran off into the bushes. Vincent glanced down at her, lost his balance and caught at a branch which was not strong enough to hold his weight. There was an ominous cracking sound, a rather rude oath from Vincent, and then he came sliding and slithering down the tree to land on the ground with a bump. He lay on his back, eyes closed and very still.

'Vinnie!' Cassie cried. 'Oh, Vinnie, my dearest love!' She rushed to his side, kneeling down and bending over him in acute distress. 'Vinnie, speak to me! Are you hurt, my love? Oh, please do not be hurt. I cannot bear it if you die. Please do not leave me.'

She was running her hands over his face, her own pale with fright, when he suddenly reached out and pulled her down on top of him. In another moment he had rolled her over so that she was beneath him on the ground. She stared up at him, her fear draining away as she saw the wicked intent in his eyes.

'Oh, you wretch,' she whispered, suddenly breathless. 'You scared me. I thought you badly hurt.'

'I shall no doubt have bruises all over,' Vincent retorted drily. 'I shall look to you to tend them for me, my sweet.'

'Would you like me to rub liniment in for you?'

Cassie's tone was deceptively earnest and earned her a scowl from her husband. 'I know I am ten years older than you—but do you think me so decrepit?'

Her suppressed giggles made his eyes smoulder. 'You are a minx and a jade, Lady Carlton. You need to learn respect for your husband. I believe I shall have to discipline you.'

His mouth gently took possession of hers, but the kiss quickly deepened, their bodies straining against each other's with such urgency that both were shaken. Vincent released her ruefully, touching her face with the tips of his fingers.

'I do not believe this is quite the place or the time, my love. I was sent to find you because nuncheon is served.'

'We must not delay, then,' Cassie said, eyes bright with mischief. 'How very shocking it would be if I were to miss nuncheon. I do not know how I should ever face anyone again.'

'We could always sneak up to your room and pretend I could not find you.'

'Yes.' Cassie gurgled with laughter. 'I suppose we could.'

They walked hand in hand towards the house. But as they approached the door, Sir Septimus came out, carrying his wife's dog, which he dropped none too gently on the lawn.

'Wretched animal,' he said on seeing them. 'All such creatures ought to be drowned at birth, if you ask me.'

'Uncle, I have never agreed with you more in my life,' Vincent said. 'Especially kittens. Fluffy white ones.'

'Oh, Vinnie!' Cassie cried. 'We forgot Fluffs.'

'We shall send a footman to look for her, Cassie. And if one is not sufficient, we shall send more.'

'Yes, Vincent. Just as you say.'

'And how are you this morning, Lady Carlton?' asked Septimus. 'I must tell you, you had us all worried yesterday—but you seem to have made a remarkable recovery.'

'Oh, I am much better now,' said Cassie and promptly sneezed. 'Colds usually do not affect me at all. I cannot think what made me so unwell yesterday.'

'Nor can I,' murmured Vincent and gave her such a look that she blushed. 'It was quite unaccountable.'

Septimus looked at him, eyes narrowed as he

caught their bantering mood. 'Humph!' he said. 'Carlton, I must tell you that you have torn your breeches. What on earth have you been doing?'

'Climbing trees,' replied Vincent. 'Excuse me, Uncle. I believe we must go and change before we join you all for nuncheon.'

His hand closed over Cassie's arm, and he propelled her into the house and towards the stairs. As they reached the top of them, however, they were met by Harry.

'Glad to see you up and about, Lady Carlton,' he said. 'Vinnie, may I please have a word?'

'Later, Harry. I must change my clothes.'

'Oh…sorry.' Harry frowned. 'You've torn your breeches, Vinnie, did you know?'

'Climbing trees,' Cassie murmured, eyes brimming with laughter. 'It is a sad fault in a man of his advanced years—but I hope to cure him of it in time.'

'Jade!' Vincent's grip tightened on her arm. 'Excuse us, Harry.'

He steered Cassie past his astonished brother and into her bedroom, kicking the door shut behind them. Then he reached out for her, pulling her fiercely into his arms.

'Do you know how very much I—?'

The door opened again. 'Cassie…' began Lady Longbourne, then stopped, a faint colour in her cheeks. 'Do forgive me, Carlton. I did not realise you were here. I came to see if Cassie had returned and would be coming down for nuncheon.'

'I am here because I wish to be with my wife, Mama, and because I need to change my breeches—and, before you tell me, I *know* they are torn.'

'Really, Vincent! What have you been doing?'

'I am tempted to tell you,' Vincent replied, his patience quite at an end. 'Except I have not been doing anything, because there are too many interested persons in this house. In answer to your question, no, Cassie will not be coming down to eat. As soon as we have both changed, we shall leave for Carlton House. A picnic basket may be prepared for us, and if we feel hungry we shall eat when and as we choose—but alone. Certainly alone.'

'Well, there is not the least need to lose your temper, Carlton,' his offended mama said and frowned at him.

'I am not losing my temper,' said he, but was. 'I merely wish to be alone with my *wife* for a few minutes. I do not think that too much to ask, do you?'

'Dearest Vinnie.' Cassie touched his hand, making him look at her. 'I think you are a little cross, my love, and you know there is no reason for you to be. We have the rest of our lives together. And as it happens, I am very hungry.'

'Are you, my darling?' Vinnie looked down at her, his impatience melting away as he realised she was right. She was his now and he did not have to grab at his happiness. 'Very well. We shall be down in ten minutes, Mama.' He smiled at her sweetly. 'And please shut the door behind you as you leave…'

Chapter Fourteen

Changed into the breeches he had worn for his wedding, Vincent did full justice to the cold meats, bread and raised pies set out for their meal. He noticed that Cassie ate only sparingly of some bread and butter and a little chicken. Indeed, she did not seem particularly hungry at all. His eyes gleamed. Later, when they were alone, he would challenge her on this point.

However, nuncheon over, the new Lady Carlton seemed very willing to set out on the journey to her future home. She kissed all her friends, and went out into the courtyard where the carriages were drawn up ready, horses champing at the bit, grooms, and footmen everywhere.

Lady Longbourne was tearful. She clung to Cassie affectionately for some seconds.

'Enjoy yourself, my love. I would not for the world have you come home before you are ready—but I shall look forward to a long visit when you are settled.'

'Do not forget you have Harry's wedding to plan, Mama,' said Cassie, kissing her. 'Besides, I shall write and tell you of all the places we visit—and I shall collect lots of interesting things to show you on my return. And you must come to us whenever you wish, of course.'

'You are such a sweet, generous gel. Carlton is fortunate to have found you, my dear.' Lady Longbourne let her go at last and blew her nose.

'Goodbye, Lady Carlton,' Sir Septimus said when it was his turn to take his leave of her. He kissed her hand. 'I dare say you know how to keep this young cockerel you've married in hand. But if he gives you any trouble, send for me. I shall engage to set him right.'

'I shall most certainly,' said Cassie, and impulsively kissed his cheek. 'And of course you and your family will naturally always be welcome to visit.'

Sir Septimus glowed and insisted on handing her into the waiting carriage himself. Vincent watched with amused indulgence, then climbed in after her and signalled to a groom, who closed the door.

'Are you not riding today?' she asked, deceptively innocent.

'No, I am not,' replied her husband. 'At least I shall have you to myself all the way to Hamilton.'

'Hamilton? Your estate in Surrey? I thought we were to go to Carlton House?'

'That was Mama's plan,' said Vincent, a little smile about his mouth. 'But I have decided that Carlton is too close to Longbourne. It would not surprise me if my dear mother does not decide to pay a visit there within a few days…'

'Vincent!' Cassie cried, quite shocked. 'How can you think she would do such a thing?'

'I know my family,' he replied wryly. 'And now that you have assured Septimus he will be welcome at any time, I dare say we shall never be rid of him.'

She looked at him doubtfully. 'Do you not like to see your family, dearest?'

'Naturally. But not all the time—and not while we are on our honeymoon. It is the strangest thing, I dare say, but I have a fancy to spend a little time alone with you, Cassie.'

She laughed as he gave her a smouldering glance. 'Well, at least we are alone now. And I can get rid of this…' She began to undo the ribbons of a very pretty straw bonnet. She took it off and laid it on the seat opposite then sighed. 'There…that is very much better. Do you not think so, Vinnie?'

His eyebrows rose. 'I thought it suited you well, my love—did you not care for it?'

'It looked well enough—indeed, it is one of my favourites,' she replied a sparkle in her wicked eyes. 'But now you will be able to kiss me so much more easily—will you not?'

'Ah, yes, I perceive now that it is a very good idea,' he murmured with satisfaction. 'I had not thought of that, but it was a good notion of yours, my love.'

And with that, he took her in his arms and began to kiss her in a way that was most agreeable to them both.

Hamilton Manor was indeed much larger than Carlton House, as Vincent had once told her. It was considerably older, of course, and built of mellowed red bricks with three wings at the back, which made it look rather like a capital E, a style much favoured at the time it was built in the age of the great Elizabeth. However, despite its age, it had been kept up and inside many modern improvements had been made to make it more comfortable.

'Oh, how lovely,' Cassie murmured her appreciation when she was helped out of the carriage late that evening. Although it was too dark to get more than an impression of the outside of the house, the courtyard gardens were filled with the perfume of roses and honeysuckle. 'It smells so gorgeous. I think this garden must be absolutely lovely when one can see it properly.'

'I am sorry to arrive so late at night,' Vincent apologised, for it was close to the witching hour. 'But I thought you would rather sleep in your own home than an inn tonight.'

'Yes, oh, yes, I should,' Cassie agreed and valiantly tried to smother her yawns. 'I am excessively glad to be here, Vinnie. And I shall see the gardens in the morning.'

She was escorted into the house, where a few of the servants who had been ordered to wait on their master's arrival had hastily gathered in the large entrance hall.

'Forgive me for giving you so little notice,' Vincent said to his butler. 'It was a last-minute change of plans. I trust our rooms are ready, Morton?'

'Oh, yes, sir,' the butler replied. 'Your instructions were that we might expect you at any time. We have been in readiness since yesterday, my lord. A cold supper is laid in the morning room, should you wish for it.'

'Thank you. I knew I might rely on you. If Mrs Morton would show her ladyship upstairs, please? My wife is a little tired from the journey. You may send a tray up to her rooms in ten minutes. Only the porter need remain on duty after that. Her ladyship's maid will unpack the small trunk. Everything else can wait until the morning.'

'Yes, sir. Thank you, sir.'

Cassie had been briefly introduced to the more important members of her household. She was too tired to remember their names, but Janet would remind her in the morning. She followed Mrs Morton up the main staircase and along the landing to a suite of rooms in the west wing. As she was shown into the first rather pleasant sitting room, which was furnished in shades of blue and cream, she was relieved to see her faithful Janet was already in her bedchamber, waiting for her, her night things unpacked and ready.

As she walked into the bedroom itself, Cassie looked about her with a feeling of pleasure. The walls were covered with a green silk paper which had a repeat pattern of self-coloured daisies running through. The bed hangings, covers and upholstery were all of a lighter shade of green with borders of exquisite embroidery which was made to look like looped daisy chains.

'It is just like a summer meadow,' she said. 'Even on wet days when I cannot go out, I shall feel as if I am outside.'

Mrs Morton nodded, smiled and went away, leaving her new mistress to the ministrations of the faithful Janet.

Standing still as Janet helped her out of her travelling gown, she sighed with relief. Warm water had been carried up and Cassie went behind a magnificent painted screen to wash and pull on the soft, filmy nightgown Janet had spread ready for her. She was then helped into a very elegant satin dressing gown.

She sat down on the stool in front of her dressing

table, glancing at the pretty silver-gilt brushes and trinkets set out there.

'I have not seen these before—oh, they have my initials on them. Carlton must have had them engraved for me.'

'You will find a rather special desk in your private sitting room,' Janet told her, looking rather like the cat who has just found the cream. As Lady Carlton's personal maid, her own position had suddenly shot up several notches, and she was feeling very pleased with what she had found here: it seemed she, too, was to have her own sitting room! 'All the trays and pens have your initials, Miss Cassie. His lordship has been to a great deal of trouble to make things nice for you.'

'Yes, he has, hasn't he?' Cassie smiled at her maid in the mirror. 'I believe we shall be very happy here, Janet.'

'Yes, Miss Cassie. I am sure we shall.' Janet finished brushing her hair and laid the brush down with a smirk of satisfaction. 'Is there anything else I can do for you, miss?'

'No, thank you, Janet.' Cassie stood up and kissed her cheek. 'You may go to bed now. I shall not need you again tonight, and I am very sure you must be quite exhausted.'

'Goodnight then, milady. I hope you will be very happy.'

Cassie smiled but made no reply as Janet left through the sitting room. She heard her pause to direct the butler where to set the tray he had just brought up for his master and mistress's supper, then the door closed behind them both and all was quiet.

Cassie removed the silver top from a pretty blue glass perfume flask and tested a little of the scent on her fingertip. It smelled nice so she applied some behind her ears and to her wrists. Then she heard the door of the dressing room open and Vincent walked in. He had changed into a long, dark blue dressing robe, and she noticed his feet were bare, which made her very aware of the change in her situation.

He smiled at her as she stood up, sending delightful little shivers down her spine. 'I love your hair like that, Cassie, loose on your shoulders. You look lovely.'

She blushed, her gaze dropping as she saw the flame of desire in his eyes. 'Oh, Vinnie. I am not pretty. You know I'm not.'

'Pretty?' His eyebrows rose as he moved towards her. 'No, you are not pretty, Cassie—you are beautiful.'

She gazed up at him, eyes wide, mouth soft and inviting. 'I think you must be seeing through the eyes of love, Vinnie.'

He took her by the hand and led her to a long mirror set in the corner of the room, then turned her to face it. His arms went round her from behind, his lips against the softness of her hair.

'To me you are the most beautiful woman in the world,' he murmured huskily, and she felt a tremor run through him. 'Look into your eyes as I do, Cassie. You have a beautiful soul. Your beauty is not just skin deep, it comes from within—it is the kind of beauty that the years cannot take from you.'

At that particular moment Cassie's eyes were dark and glowing with the love she felt for him. And, knowing herself truly loved, she *was* beautiful.

'It is the candlelight playing tricks,' she said, laughing and turning within the circle of his arms to slide her own arms up about his neck. Her perfume and the softness of her flesh had an intoxicating effect on him, and Vincent moaned with longing deep in his throat. 'Kiss me, Vinnie,' she whispered huskily. 'Make me yours, my darling. I do so very much want to be all yours.'

'You are not too tired?'

'No,' she said, and in that moment the tiredness fled, leaving her eager and willing as he caught her up and carried her to the bed. 'No, I am not tired at all.'

Vincent's loving was beyond all that she had imagined or ever hoped for. His kisses roused her to a quivering ecstasy so that when his mouth moved ever lower, seeking out the secret, tender places of her body, she melted with pleasure.

'Oh, Vinnie…I do love you so.'

'And I adore you, my lovely wife.'

Now she was ready for him, moist and trembling with the passion his tender caresses had aroused in her, and though his entry caused her some initial pain, she was soon swept away on a rising tide of desire and sweet pleasure that lifted them both to joy such as neither had ever known. For only when passion is mixed liberally with love can the meeting of flesh with flesh be so complete, so right, so true, so all consuming that two people become one indivisible being.

Later, when they lay still and content, wrapped together in the warmth of perfect understanding and love, Vincent began to talk…to tell her of the things which had for so long lain hidden in his heart.

'Somehow I never forgot the girl who made me climb a tree twice for her,' he whispered softly against Cassie's ear. 'When I went to London, I was young and, like many men, sure of my own pride and manhood. There were women…' His arms tightened about her as he felt her stiffen. 'But the pleasure I found in their arms was fleeting. And I soon tired of them. I had friends. Jack was my closest, always. He invited me to stay at his home many times, but I was always too busy to come, or so I told myself. Then the war came. We both joined up as officers on Wellington's staff—and one night, Jack asked me if I would marry you should he die.'

Vincent kissed the nape of Cassie's neck. She snuggled back into the curve of his body, the warmth of him making her feel safe and content.

'I refused. I did not believe I could make you happy by offering such a marriage, and I was so restless within myself that I hardly knew what I wanted. My friends thought I was very brave because I risked death without a thought, but I had no fear of dying.'

'But if you refused Jack…' Cassie turned her head to look at him. 'I don't understand?'

'I refused the first time when he asked only me, but then, after your father died, he asked five of us at the same time. I had no choice but to promise when the others agreed. So I made sure I drew the short straw. If anyone was going to offer you a marriage of convenience, it was going to be me.'

'Why?'

'Because I had never forgotten your spirit. I still thought of you as a child who refused to give in. I believed some of the others who had given their promise to Jack might attempt to crush that spirit— and I was not prepared to risk that.'

'And yet you did not come?'

'I had everything prepared,' Vincent said. 'Yet still held back. I think perhaps I was afraid. Some years had passed since we had met. I thought you might have grown up into a very proper young lady, and I did not want you to have changed. I wanted you still to be the girl who had made me take her kitten first.'

Cassie turned on her side so that she could look at him. 'But I was such a plain, naughty child, Vinnie. I was so stubborn—and you ripped your breeches coming back for me. When you went off at once, I thought you must be cross.'

'Embarrassed,' he confessed with a laugh. 'I rather think there was more of me on view than was decent.'

'Yes, there was,' she said, and laughed. 'But you forget. Jack often swam naked in the river when we were children. I was quite used to a gentleman's anatomy.'

'Wicked jade! If it didn't spare your feelings, it did mine.'

'Oh, Vinnie! You were my white knight, but instead of carrying me away on your charger you went off as if the devil himself were after you.'

Vinnie kissed her at the base of her throat, just at the pulse spot. 'No wonder I adore you,' he murmured huskily. 'I have never met anyone like you. Something about you touched me even then.' He ran his fingers down the ridges of her spine, making her gasp as desire shot through her like hot threads and she arched against him. 'I cannot say that I loved you that day. It was not love then—just a fleeting thought that we might be kindred spirits.'

'You mean because I was always getting into scrapes—as you did when you hung a pair of corsets on the church spire at Carlton?'

'Who told you that?' Vincent stared at her in surprise. 'Was it Harry?'

'No. Miss Simpson. She told me a lot of interesting stories that night, Vinnie—and many of them were about you.'

Vincent chuckled, much amused. 'I see I must pay more attention to that lady in future. I have underestimated her.'

'You went to hide yourself in your billiard room, I expect?' She touched his cheek. 'At first I wished I might come with you, but afterwards I was quite glad I stayed.'

'What else did you learn from her?'

Cassie nestled closer, pressing her lips against his naked shoulder. 'Reading between the lines of what I heard and what I had myself observed, I came to think that perhaps you might sometimes have been lonely.'

Vincent smiled and cupped his hands over her buttocks, pressing her closer to him so that she could feel the pulsing heat of his manhood and know that he wanted her again.

'How strange that you should see it. I do not blame Mama for preferring Harry to me. He is always so easygoing, as you know—and she loved his father very much. I fear there were times when she came close to hating mine. And perhaps he deserved it. He was a violent man, and not kind to his family.'

'Vinnie, dearest…'

'She loved me as much as she could,' he went on, 'but I reminded her of things that hurt her. There was always an emptiness inside me, but I do not believe it was Mama's fault. I think I should still have had it had I been her favourite son. I have always known that I was searching for something— someone.' His arms tightened about her, his mouth against her hair. 'And now I have found my special person. The one woman who can make me whole.'

'Oh, Vinnie…' Cassie began to weep, her tears making his shoulder damp. 'Do not set me on a pedestal, my love. I am not sure I can measure up to the image you have of me.'

She got no further. His mouth was on hers, tongue teasing, probing as it sought entry. And then he rolled her on to her back, taking her with such a hungry yearning that Cassie moaned with pleasure as everything else was swept from her mind, and she knew that she was indeed a part of him. She would never need to feel jealous of La Valentina again, for she knew Vincent was hers and hers alone.

And she knew that she too had found a safe haven for all the love and sweet passion she had held inside her for so long.

* * *

Cassie woke to find the bed empty. It felt cold and for a moment she wondered where Vincent had gone. To his own room perhaps? She got out of bed, pulled on her wrap and went through the connecting door to investigate. His bed had not been touched, the covers still turned down as they had been the previous night, and his room was empty. However, she saw his dressing robe thrown carelessly over a chair and guessed that he had dressed and gone out. Perhaps for an early morning ride.

She wished that he had waited so that she might have gone with him. She would ask him to do so another day.

Returning to her own bedchamber, Cassie wandered over to the window and gazed out. It was so beautiful! She had not dreamed of such a lovely view.

The park led to a lake, which glistened in the morning sun, and beyond that were gentle hills that seemed to stretch away into the distance and out of sight. Then something caught her eye and she drew a sharp breath of delight, for there, wandering at will—and only a short distance from the house—was a herd of deer presided over by a magnificent stag. There were at least fifteen and she saw two fawns keeping close to their mothers. They seemed to be grazing on food which had been specially put out for them, and were obviously quite tame.

Hearing a slight noise behind her, Cassie turned and saw her husband had entered the room. He was dressed for riding and had obviously been out, for his face had the glow of exercise and fresh air about it.

'Do come and look,' she said, holding out her hand to him. 'The deer are almost up to the house.'

'It was Grandmother Hamilton who started to feed them near the house,' he said, smiling at her pleasure. 'Grandfather grumbled when they sometimes broke into the kitchen gardens and trampled on the vegetables, but she loved to see them so he kept up the feeding even after she died—in her memory. I went out this morning early to make sure the food was there. I wanted you to see them when you woke up.'

'Oh, Vinnie, how thoughtful you are,' she said, gazing up mistily at him. 'You knew how much that would please me. It is a wonderful surprise.'

'I always want to please you,' he said, kissing her hand. 'Now, hurry and get dressed, my love. It is a little cooler than of late, but a lovely morning. And I want to show you my best surprise.'

'Now what have you been up to?' she asked, eyes sparkling.

'You will find out when you come down.'

He went away again. Cassie rang for Janet, and it was not quite five-and-twenty minutes later when she went down to find her husband impatiently pacing the hall and waiting for her. He looked up, a look of such delight coming into his eyes as he saw her that her heart filled with love for him. He held out his hand, and she ran gladly down the last few steps to meet him.

He was so impatient!

'What is it, Vinnie?'

'Come outside and I shall show you.'

She let him lead her outside, and then she gave a cry of pleasure as she saw the light curricle and a pair of beautifully matched grey horses standing in the courtyard, their manes and tails shining like pure silk in the sunlight.

'Are they for me, Vinnie?' She looked at him in dawning wonder. 'Oh, you knew it was what I wanted—something I could drive myself. And the horses! They are such thoroughbreds!'

'Nothing but the best for you, my love,' Vincent said, a glint of satisfaction in his eyes as she went over to pat and fondle the horses. 'It took me quite a time to find the right pair. And I had the curricle made specially light so that it will be easy for you to handle. Once I have taught you how to drive it, you will become known for your style.'

'I shall be like Letty Lade!' Cassie cried, laughing. 'Or perhaps not quite…'

'You will be known as the dashing Lady Carlton,' Vincent told her, a wicked gleam in his eyes. 'But

I warn you, I shall be a hard taskmaster, Cassie. You will not be allowed to drive in town until I am satisfied you can do it with style and safety.'

'No, of course not,' she said. 'When can I have my first lesson, Vinnie? Can we go now? Oh, please, do say yes. I cannot wait to try my skill.'

'I do not see why not,' he said and smiled. Then he gave her his hand and helped her up on to the box. It was as he was showing her how to hold the reins lightly in one hand that they saw a horseman ride into the courtyard. Vincent frowned. 'Good grief! I think that is Harry…what in the name of blazes is he doing here?'

Harry came riding up to them. 'Thank goodness I caught you,' he said. 'I came on ahead to warn you, Vinnie. Mama had a terrible quarrel with Septimus yesterday, just after you left. She set out not two hours later for Hamilton. I persuaded her to stay at an inn last night, and came to warn you—she will be here within the hour.'

'Of all the…' Vincent swore furiously. 'Could you not find some way to prevent her, Harry?'

'She would not have it that you were here,' Harry said, looking apologetic. 'I told her I thought you had changed your plans, but she knew best. She was certain you were at Carlton, and said she would not dream of intruding on you there, and that she was certain you would not mind her coming here, because she refused to stay another moment in Septimus's company. And he would not budge, you know how thick-skinned he is, Vinnie.'

'Well, you can just ride back and tell Mama that we *are* here, and she can turn round and—'

Cassie laid a gentle hand on his arm. 'Do not be so unkind, Vinnie darling,' she said. 'Your mother is very welcome to stay for a few days if she wishes—besides, we shall be going to France very soon, to visit Louise and Jack.'

'Are we never to be alone together?' Vincent glowered down at her. 'Damn it, I want you to myself, Cassie.'

Cassie leaned towards him and whispered in his ear. Harry could not hear what was said, but whatever it was, a change came over Vincent's face and he was smiling again.

'No, you are very right,' he said and laughed huskily. 'She cannot follow us there, can she?'

Cassie blushed as she looked at Harry. 'Would you go on up to the house and let Mrs Morton know Lady Longbourne is expected, please, Harry? And pray tell Mama that we are very sorry but we shall not be able to welcome her personally as we are going for a drive—a rather long drive, as it happens, that may keep us away most of the day. However, she is to make herself quite at home, and we shall all dine together this evening.'

She turned to smile up into the frustrated eyes of her husband.

'And now, Vinnie—perhaps you would like to drive for a while? Just to show me how it is done?'

'Make a quick getaway, you mean?'

'Exactly so, my dearest.'

Vincent laughed and whipped up his horses, leaving a cloud of dust behind as he drove them out of the courtyard, through the park and away over the gentle hills.

Harry stood watching for a moment, then smiled to himself as he turned his horse. There was no doubt that Cassie was up to every trick in the book, and he rather thought he might need a few of them himself in the future…

* * * * *

millsandboon.co.uk Community

Join Us!

The Community is the perfect place to meet and chat to kindred spirits who love books and reading as much as you do, but it's also the place to:

- **Get the inside scoop from authors about their latest books**
- **Learn how to write a romance book with advice from our editors**
- **Help us to continue publishing the best in women's fiction**
- **Share your thoughts on the books we publish**
- **Befriend other users**

Forums: Interact with each other as well as authors, editors and a whole host of other users worldwide.

Blogs: Every registered community member has their own blog to tell the world what they're up to and what's on their mind.

Book Challenge: We're aiming to read 5,000 books and have joined forces with The Reading Agency in our inaugural Book Challenge.

Profile Page: Showcase yourself and keep a record of your recent community activity.

Social Networking: We've added buttons at the end of every post to share via digg, Facebook, Google, Yahoo, technorati and de.licio.us.

www.millsandboon.co.uk